THE MAN FROM THE OCEAN

BRIDGET SHEPPARD

ISBN: 979-8-218-72868-7
ebook ISBN: 979-8-218-72869-4

Editing: Mary Pat Smith
Cover Design: Julia Park
Interior Formatting: Caerus Kourt

ALSO BY

BRIDGET SHEPPARD

THE CHAOS SERIES

Light in the Chaos
The Chaos of Time

FOR ALL THE AMAZING TEACHERS IN MY LIFE—
THOSE WHO INSPIRED ME
AND THOSE WHO INSPIRE MY CHILDREN.
WHERE WOULD WE BE WITHOUT YOU?

CHAPTER 1

THEY WERE LIKE wisps of a dream you can't quite catch once awake. Little flicks of light or movement at the corners of her vision. As the shapes grew over time, they reminded her of wobbly, otherworldly beings seen from underwater with chlorine-filled eyes. Then she'd take a breath and they would disappear.

If anyone had asked Olivia what her current life status was, she'd say dead-tired. Her job as a contracts manager smothered her with stress when she was doing it, and played a haunting part in her dreams when she wasn't. She didn't need the addition of some strange vision problem that couldn't even commit to a full-time relationship.

October was moving along like it always did, still too hot in Northern California and most stores already teeming with Christmas decorations. That Wednesday morning was typical, except the clouds over her portion of the state had decided to rain. She'd also made the grave mistake of waiting a few extra minutes before leaving her house. She knew better, but she'd needed those last sips of coffee from her first cup.

The drab tan 1980's office building now looming before her had a miniscule parking lot. It didn't make sense that any engineer in his (could *not* have been a her) right mind believed that pitiful lot would have been enough for a three-story commercial building.

Olivia heaved a sigh as she drove through the two rows of parked cars. She wasn't late, but everyone who worked in the building knew better than to be anything but early if they wanted a spot in the lot. Of course, available street parking spread out over several surrounding blocks, but the rain was coming down in sheets. Thinking back, the weather should have been her first clue that something was wrong.

As she turned her secondhand sedan back onto the first row for one last look, a beam of sunshine glinted off a group of cars to her right. An unnerving feeling made its way down her spine. There was no sunshine; the sky was covered in merciless clouds.

What was that? Panic knocked at the edges of her mind.

Time seemed to slow. The black, silver, white, and blue of the vehicles around her blended together. Olivia's eyes snapped closed as she attempted to slow her racing heart. A headache was building near the back of her skull. Allowing her eyes to drift open, she took in the scene around her with horror. The driverless vehicles seemed to have moved of their own accord, now nearly on top of her own. And they were all red. Every—single—one. The color oozed and flowed, rising, threatening to consume her.

"What the hell?" she screamed and scrambled for her seatbelt, but her slick hands couldn't seem to find the buckle.

Blink. Everything was normal. Pouring rain, no sun, different-colored cars parked in their spots. Olivia startled in her seat at the honk from a grotesquely large truck. She was stopped in the middle of the lane, a line of vehicles building behind her.

Just breathe, she commanded as her headache drifted away. Had she had a headache?

Another honk forced her to put her foot on the gas and make her way out of the lot, an electric feeling buzzing through her veins.

During the walk back to her building, the rain lightened and she heard seagulls calling from overhead. The sound made her smile as she thought of the ocean. Living near the vast yet comforting sea was the dream.

Olivia stopped walking—closed her eyes. The ocean breeze and salty water enveloped her like a blanket. The sun reflected off the sand, highlighting the tiny stones washed in with the tide. Joyful laughter echoed from somewhere nearby, and a familiar voice called from behind her.

Then the scene abruptly melted away. Her office's front door greeted her with its usual stoic sadness.

How did I get here?

But instead of fear at the thought, Olivia felt only frustration. She didn't have time for daydreams that stole her from reality.

Work-induced exhaustion and stress. That's all this weird morning was. Much of the time, she felt like she was hosting some sort of low-budget educational show for her clients, but they'd only ever learned the meaning of words like "rant" and "argue." On top of that, the new coworker creeped her out: staring at her whenever they weren't separated by a cubicle wall, but saying very little when she acknowledged him.

Her world seemed to right itself as she hung up her rain jacket, settled into her desk chair, switched on her computer, and took a large sip of the coffee she'd brought from home. Olivia had tied up the brown waves of her hair before she'd left her house, but a few rain-soaked tendrils still had to be brushed from her face.

Her deep breaths coincided with the noise swirling through the cubicle-crowded room as the office came to life.

Olivia gave a reflexive cringe as she noticed the blinking voicemail light on her phone and stood to reach for a file in the cabinet over her computer. There was no time to cry out as a blinding flash of light and wave of deep fatigue folded over her.

Blink. The new coworker's face was directly in front of hers, or rather, over hers. Several of her colleagues, including her manager, were in her periphery, their faces looking down at her with a variety of strange expressions.

Am I on the floor?

"Did I pass out?" Her voice shook. Embarrassed heat assaulted her cheeks. She closed her eyes to fight off the sudden urge to cry.

"You did, Olivia! Don't move!" Her colleague Courtney screeched, pushing her hand forward. "We called an ambulance!"

"No, that's not necessary," Olivia stuttered. "I'm fine." She tried to get up but winced as she noticed the pain in her head: an ache from deep in the back of her brain.

The new guy backed up, but not enough for her to sit fully upright. He said nothing.

He's not going to let me get up! She inhaled deeply. *No, that's ridiculous; he'll move.*

"I think I just need to go home and get some rest." Olivia tested her theory, and the guy did in fact push himself away as she cautiously stood. The awkward group backed out of her cubicle.

Then she heard voices down the hall. A minute later, two EMTs strolled through the growing crowd of her coworkers. If an actual hole in the floor could have swallowed her, that would have been perfect.

"Oh, I'm fine. I'm sorry for wasting your time," she said, noting the frantic tone in her own voice.

"I think you should go to the hospital to get checked out. You hit your head." Her manager frowned, more serious than she'd ever seen him.

It was only then that Olivia realized there was blood running into her right eye from a gash above her eyebrow.

"Okay," seemed to be all she could manage and wondered if she was in shock. Fumbling for her jacket, purse, and travel mug, she stumbled from the office, the two EMTs offering support. Climbing into the back of the ambulance felt like pushing herself through churning water, her legs barely allowing the movement.

What a nightmare.

The female EMT in the back of the ambulance was all business, refusing to crack a smile when Olivia tried to joke about fainting. She took Olivia's blood pressure and noted it was a little high. While attending to the cut on Olivia's forehead, which would need stitches, the woman asked a myriad of questions. And although Olivia mentioned the headache and how tired she was, there wasn't anything else obviously wrong.

At the hospital, Olivia's blood pressure had returned to normal, which shocked her because she still felt like her heart was racing. The nurse and emergency room physician both asked if she could be pregnant. A snort of laughter erupted from her, which she immediately tried to hide with a cough. She hadn't had sex in a long time. The nurse and doctor stared back at her, the nurse with a frown, the doctor with a raised eyebrow.

"Oh, no, sorry." Olivia tried to regain her composure. "I'm definitely not."

The doctor stitched the gash above her eye, confirming that she had somehow avoided a concussion. After a scan and tests, she recounted her experience for what felt like the millionth time. This time the resident and attending physicians, as well as a medical student, and two nurses were crowded into her small exam room. "They were just these quick flashes of light, and the headache came on fast, at the back of my skull."

She kept the part about cars turning red to herself. She was embarrassed enough as it was.

"Your CT scan and bloodwork look normal," her original physician stated, staring at his computer screen. "You have no history of fainting or neurological conditions?" he asked for what felt like the billionth time.

"No, I hardly even get headaches."

He sighed and leaned back in his rolling desk chair, his eyes flicking to each of his colleagues in turn. "Could be stress, diet, exhaustion, which you suggested are current things you're dealing with. Monitor how you're feeling, try to get some more exercise and sleep, and come back if you faint again or have additional symptoms. Follow up with your primary physician as soon as possible. I'll sign a note for work if you need one. It wouldn't be a bad idea to take some time off." His eyes met hers with a meaningful expression.

The medical staff filed out of the room, both doctors shaking her hand before they left. One nurse returned to provide Olivia with a copy of her discharge paperwork, including a note from the doctor excusing her from work for a week.

A week! There's no way. Olivia's head buzzed as she walked out of the hospital into the still-cloudy day.

She stopped so suddenly that a couple behind her yelped in surprise as they came within inches of colliding with her back. They sent her frowns as they maneuvered by, but she barely registered them. How was she going to get back to her car? She had no intention of calling any of her coworkers.

Thumbing through the apps on her phone, she ordered an Uber to take her to her car, which was waiting on the street near her office.

Olivia stared at it for a few seconds before climbing in. There was a fine layer of sand covering the vehicle from front to back, as if it'd been sitting near a windy beach for days. Blink. The sand was gone.

God, what is wrong with me? Sleep. I just need sleep.

It felt downright wrong to be arriving back at her suburban house before five-thirty, which was the earliest traffic ever allowed her to return home on a work day. She lay down in her bed but was startled awake from a dream, broken images of waves still rolling through her brain.

The same thoughts barraged her repeatedly. Could it be something severe they somehow didn't find at the hospital? She should call her doctor's office now and make an appointment. But the CT scan hadn't shown anything, so it wouldn't hurt to wait until tomorrow.

After some restless pacing, she sat down, drumming her fingers on one of the worn arms of the hand-me-down couch she'd acquired in college. She resisted the urge to google her symptoms, but just barely. After making and only eating half a sandwich, Olivia lay down on her couch and flipped through the channels of mindless afternoon television.

I could never make it through a week of this. How could anyone make it through a week of this?

Then, quite suddenly, she found herself in the middle of a dream. She stood on rocky sand, staring out at the troubled ocean. The sky was full of gray clouds and fog hung all around her. She was dressed in warm clothes, a soft beanie covering her damp hair, several strands of which had escaped and were dancing around her face. But she was happy. She felt at home.

Olivia heard that same voice behind her—the one she'd heard in her earlier daydream. It called out to her in the middle of a rumbling laugh, but no, the laugh was actually a scream. The voice was screaming for her, and whoever owned it sounded as if they could barely breathe. Olivia turned toward the sound, toward the sea, trying to call back, to offer some kind of solace. She was happy, so why did they sound so afraid—so sad?

No, she wasn't happy. She was terrified and confused, chest aching from the pain in her heart. What was happening to her? Olivia squinted at the ocean through the fog. But it was a river now, rapids flowing wildly past. And on the bank, there was a pool of blood, growing ever larger. A garbled scream ripped from her throat.

Olivia's eyes snapped open as she jolted awake. It was dark outside now; thunder growled in the distance and rain pelted the roof. Her shirt was soaked with sweat.

"What was that? What's wrong with me?" She forced deep breaths into her lungs and stood up slowly, fighting against the lightheadedness brought on by panic.

She stalked the rooms of her house, switching on as many lights as possible while her body shook. It wasn't cold, but she pulled a warm cardigan out of her closet anyway and shoved it on, then padded into the kitchen, trying to ignore the images from her dream that continued to flash through her mind.

Should I call someone? Should I go back to the hospital?

Olivia immediately rejected that idea. They hadn't found any-thing, and, overall, she felt fine. She picked up her cell phone and stared at it for several moments. Only a couple of numbers in her contact list were people she'd really call friends, because trust had never been something that came easily to her. Olivia's closest friend, Stefanie, had kids. Olivia didn't want to intrude on their sleep or routine.

Then she saw her mother's number. She'd only had her mother after her dad left. These days, Olivia and her mother had what might be called a strained relationship at best. They still got together on holidays and spent time together on a few other random days of the year, but they didn't depend on each other. Their communication style was mostly question-and-answer as needed.

Olivia had been six when her dad left, so she didn't remember much of their time as a family of three, but she did remember the feeling of anger that flowed from and around her parents before they split up. When she worked hard to remember, Olivia thought she could almost pull the smallest happy memories from her mind of the days before the hatred between her parents began, but maybe that was wishful thinking. Maybe they'd never been happy.

She came out of her daydream and put her phone on the charger in the kitchen, deciding against calling anyone. Instead, she pulled up her favorite Jackson Browne album and blasted it through her Bluetooth speakers. Music always helped. She threw on an old baggy shirt and sweatpants and lay back down on her couch. This was just a nonsensical day.

If I can just get to tomorrow, everything will be fine.

CHAPTER 2

IN THIS DREAM, there was a river. She knew it was a dream, but her mind was heavy and holding her hostage, even as she tried to fight herself awake.

Olivia tried to turn away from the water but couldn't. It was so cold; she wrapped her arms around herself, trying to keep her body from shaking. In real life, she lived a little less than a mile from a large river that ran through her portion of California. It was a small hike down into the canyon where the water wound its way through tree-lined slopes of dirt, rock, and the underbrush that was home to many types of wildlife. At this time of night, it would be pitch black in the canyon, except for any light that came from the moon and stars.

She attempted to force her gaze onto her dreamworld surroundings, but still couldn't seem to pull her attention from that swirling water. The darkness felt like a weighted blanket folding around her. Olivia tried to move but the river held her in place, its iciness seeping into the bones of her legs, then into her torso and arms. Wait. She felt the water. She *felt* it. She thrashed, begging her brain to let her wake up. The river rose quickly—so fast that in the span of a few breaths, it was just under her chin. She was going to drown if she couldn't get out.

Once again, her eyes shot open, and she let out a startled gasp. All around her was darkness, although she could see a crescent of moon and some stars in between the separating clouds. Realization seeped into her brain. She was outside. She was in the canyon. She was cold and wet. She was standing in the water, and it was up to her waist. Not in a dream—in reality. Olivia cried out, trying to rush back out of the water, stumbling before she caught herself. The river felt like it was trying to keep her. She sat down hard on the shore when she reached it, trying to slow her heart and her breathing.

How did I get here?

Looking down at her body, she noticed she had her tennis shoes on and was in the same clothes. Goosebumps covered her bare arms. She checked her pockets—no phone. Her watch was wet but seemed to be working. It was almost one o'clock in the morning.

"Please don't say I drove," she murmured to herself as she made her way up a familiar path. She'd hiked down to the river so many times, she knew her way, even in the black of night. Not that that meant she got out unscathed. She stumbled more than once and cursed the branches that scratched her skin.

Olivia was shaking like she might break apart by the time she made it to the small parking area at the top of the path. Her car wasn't there. In fact, the lot was empty—the gate used to keep drivers out after sunset was closed. She climbed around it, turning to take one last, quick look toward the path. Her mind was in a frenzy, unable to settle on any one coherent thought.

There was a slight breeze following the previous day's rain. She'd never felt as cold as she did on the walk home. But it wasn't just a physical cold; her very soul felt frozen and on the brink of splintering apart. By the time she stepped inside her unlocked front door, her teeth were chattering so hard her jaw hurt. A random mix of Jackson Browne and similar artists was now playing, the album she'd originally turned on long-since over. She turned off the music and dragged herself to the bathroom to start a hot shower.

As Olivia stepped into the almost unbearable water, her thoughts swirled like the steam spilling from her shower and fogging up her bathroom mirror. *How long was I in the river? How did I get all the way down there without waking up? How did I make it so far into the water, believing it was just a dream?*

A dream that held her captive.

While the scalding water poured over her, Olivia tried to soothe her anxious mind. She wasn't crazy. It felt like there was a glitch in her brain. Or maybe she had some kind of rare virus. She didn't seem to have any symptoms of a traditional sickness, but clearly, she wasn't well.

She didn't want to go back to the hospital. But it was wasn't just that. She also felt this nagging thing inside her—a vague idea of something developing in her mind. What was it? It sat there on the periphery of the thoughts she was able to grasp.

1 0 1 0 1 1 0 1 0

Olivia called out sick from work, which was something she never did, so guilt was eating her insides. But she wouldn't be able to concentrate on her unruly clients. What if something happened again? That strange feeling seemed to be growing in the back of her mind, but she still didn't understand what it was.

She took a couple of deep breaths before hesitantly selecting the number in her phone. It rang four times, each one filling her with more dread. Just as she was about to hang up, the voice that inspired immeasurable anxiety and insecurity within her came on the line.

"Hello?"

"Hi, Mom."

Silence for a few moments, as if her mother wasn't sure if it was really Olivia or someone playing a joke. "Oh, hi, Olivia. How are you?" Bethany Lawrence, who always went by Beth, responded.

It'd probably been two months since they'd talked. Over the years, it had grown increasingly harder for Olivia and her mother to hold an actual conversation. To Olivia, it often felt like she was a reminder of the angry life her mother had lived before the divorce—one that Beth couldn't shake.

Still, after hours of contemplation, the call felt like the right thing to do.

"I'm okay. I've been," but there was no way she was giving Beth the details of what had happened to her, "feeling really tired. Did I ever sleepwalk when I was little? I've been having bad dreams, and I got out of bed and walked around during the last one."

This time the pause before her mother's response was almost imperceptible, but Olivia caught it.

"No, you never had issues with anything like that." Beth's tone was casual, but there was something there that Olivia knew wasn't quite right.

"Did anything scary ever happen to me near a river? Or a creek maybe? At first, I was dreaming about an ocean, but then it turned into a river, and the feelings of terror and confusion I was having seemed so real."

"Olivia, I can't interpret your dreams." Her mother sighed, but Olivia was sure she heard a slight shake in the woman's voice. "Maybe you should talk to a therapist if you're concerned?"

This was a mistake. But interesting how she didn't answer the question.

"Yeah, maybe. How—How are you doing? Do you and Will have any plans for Thanksgiving?"

Thanksgiving was more than a month away, but that was how hard it was to think of anything else to talk to her mother about.

Will was her mother's husband of ten years. Beth had had a string of weird relationships after the divorce, like she was trying to firmly break away from her past. The men always ended up leaving for various reasons. But Will had been different from the beginning. Maybe the fact that Olivia was grown and well out of the house had helped. Will, who had no kids of his own, was kind to Olivia, but neither of them had tried to develop any type of real relationship.

"I think we'll just be having it at our house. Will's sister and mother will be coming over like last year. You can join us if you want to."

The idea of a small gathering was no surprise to Olivia. Beth didn't have any relatives close by and only a few friends she saw infrequently. It had always seemed to Olivia like her mother appreciated isolation over nurturing the relationships in her life. She and Will rarely went out, and they seemed fine with that. But Olivia feared her mother's isolation had drifted into her own life and resulted in a second generation's lack of significant relationships.

Olivia had once found old photographs taken pre-divorce, before she was born or when her mother was pregnant. From those photos, it looked like her parents had hosted huge Thanksgiving and Christmas gatherings, but Olivia didn't recognize many of the people smiling at the camera.

"Yeah, sure. That sounds nice." Olivia twirled a loose thread from her shirt around her finger, tugging it from its seam.

Her mind wandered momentarily. Maybe she should finally take Stefanie up on her annual offer to come to her house for Thanksgiving. She wouldn't tell her mom for now, but truthfully, she would have rather been alone this year than spend another awkward holiday with Beth and Will.

"Great. You can bring the pumpkin pie. Well, I've got to go. I'll update you on the Thanksgiving plan when it gets closer," Beth said, her tone firm in its finality.

"Okay."

The phone call ended. No "It was nice to talk to you" or "I love you." That was never the way their conversations ended.

Olivia breathed a sigh of relief and put her phone back on the counter. She'd known she wouldn't get any information or comfort; she never should have called. She rubbed her tired eyes, a gasp escaping her as the flickering lights returned to her vision.

A sudden headache pounded in her brain; her vision blurred. She stumbled to the sink, trying to remember where she'd left the Tylenol bottle. The giant scarlet oak tree in her backyard caught her attention through her kitchen window. She whimpered in fear as her eyesight cleared, her brain slowly registering that not only were the tree's leaves bright red in all their autumn glory, but the *entire* tree was a deep, blood red. The thick crimson color was spreading from the tree and soaking into everything else. It oozed and rose all around her, much like it had when she'd been in her car the morning before, converting every object in her vicinity into that one horrifying color.

Olivia sank to the floor shaking as the universe seemed to tilt. She shook her head, trying to take normal breaths. Her brain was hammering against her skull, and her vision narrowed to a tunnel. She opened her mouth to scream, but no sound came out. Then everything went black.

CHAPTER 3

THIS TIME IT was pictures flashing through her mind, a slide-show of famous places all in one famous city. Had she seen these places before? She wasn't sure, but she knew them immediately: the Golden Gate Bridge, Golden Gate Park, the Museum of Modern Art, Coit Tower. San Francisco. Then a skyscraper. She didn't know the building, but she felt she needed to go there. She needed to go there right now.

Olivia's eyes opened with a clarity she'd never felt before. She pushed herself up from her kitchen floor, checking her watch before running to her room. It was just after two in the afternoon. She'd been out for a while, even though it had felt like seconds. She needed to go now. She had to get to San Francisco, to that skyscraper. Part of her hyped-up mind knew this was crazy; she'd just passed out again after seeing her home drowned in red. She should be on her way to the emergency room, but deep in her bones, she knew she needed to get to San Francisco. Her headache was gone, and she had to pack.

Olivia called her boss and left a message, letting him know she had to take some of her leave time and that her doctor could provide a note if needed. After she hung up, she realized she hadn't exactly made a request, just told him how it was going to be. That's how confident she was that she had to leave.

After packing, she paid for a train ticket online, because driving seemed less than safe with her symptoms. She had no idea how long she would be gone or where she would be staying, or even why she was bringing so many pieces of clothing, but she carried on anyway. Part of her mind—the part that still seemed to be thinking logically—knew she should be concerned, but she wasn't. The mystery building was singing its own kind of siren song, and she was not as strong as Odysseus.

The train took her to Emeryville and then Olivia caught a bus into the city, the sounds of Jefferson Airplane and then Jefferson Starship rocking through her earbuds. She laughed to herself that two iterations of a band steeped in San Francisco music history just happened to play during a random shuffle on her favorite streaming service.

San Francisco was shrouded in fog as she stepped onto its streets. The large hood of her rain jacket almost covered her eyes, offering what felt like a bit of protection as her legs moved her forward, that nagging feeling of need like a ticking bomb in her brain.

The fog misted Olivia's face as she briefly turned her eyes to the sky. She was now in the Financial District neighborhood, according to the map on her phone. A feeling of peace similar to the one she'd had outside her office settled around her. Her feet seemed to drift around a corner and then stopped dead in their tracks. Across the street, the shiny black building towered in front of her. That small, logical part of her brain screamed at her to turn around, to run, but her feet stepped off the curb anyway.

Olivia lugged her bags across the street and again came to a stop at the bottom of the stairs leading up to the building's entrance. It wasn't a new structure by any means but appeared to have received a face-lift in recent years, making it look more like a modern office building, perhaps for an expensive law or architectural firm that served a rich clientele.

It was covered with windows, but their tinting made it impossible to see inside. There was no sign explaining what it housed. A date on the black marble façade to the left of the steps read *Nov. 1968*. The modernization looked much more recent. Olivia backed up and strained her neck to count the rows of windows. It appeared to have eleven or twelve floors, but a bout of dizziness and the fog, kept her from being sure.

Something resembling a memory shot into her brain. She saw the short flight of stairs leading up to the entrance, but it appeared taller and more intimidating. She ascended, but each step seemed too large for her little-girl feet. Yes, she was sure she was a child in this memory. She studied the many cracks in the stairs. It was cold and pouring rain. There was such fear and sadness in her heart. Why? What was weighing so heavily on all corners of her mind? She almost saw it—the cause of that despair, but it flickered away before she could understand it.

In the memory, Olivia didn't want to go into that building. She wanted to escape the unknown that waited there for her. Two people were holding her hands. One of their hands was rough and large, the other softer. The softer one had long fingers, which twined comfortingly through hers, assuring her that everything would be okay. Her parents' hands. The love emanating from them felt so natural and true. She trusted those hands, so she went into that building without them having to force her, even though fear still followed her like a shadow.

Olivia gasped as she realized that outside of the memory, she had also ascended those formidable steps.

No, no, no!

She let herself in through one of the heavy glass doors.

She gaped at the sight in front of her, a blush flaming on her face, but icy anxiety flowing through her veins. And still, her body would not let her leave.

The inside of the building looked like a ritzy hotel mixed with an upscale restaurant—not at all what she would have expected from the outside. Beautiful marble tiles shone on the walls and under her feet. There were areas of plush carpet to the left and right, filled with padded dark wooden chairs and finely carved tables lit by the fashionably intricate light fixtures hanging above them on delicate wires. Soothing piano music played from somewhere to her right. The tiles she stood on sparkled as she peered down at them—her Converse chucks looked strange against their ornate backdrop. Olivia looked up and saw the tiles led in a perfect path to a large oak desk.

She gripped the handles of her two suitcases so hard it hurt, shifting her back just enough to reassure herself with the weight of her backpack still sitting there. This place meant something important, but it also exuded an eerie, controlling vibe, as if it had disconnected her from her real life when she stepped through its doors.

Olivia's eyes strayed to the left. Several small groups of people sat in the chic chairs, chatting, drinking from mugs and glasses, and staring at laptops, books, and phone screens. Some had plates of food. Her gaze paused on a small table occupied by a man who looked to be at least ten years her senior, and a woman who appeared to be younger than her by several years. They were watching her but trying to be inconspicuous about it. Olivia's heart picked up its pace. What was this place?

"There's another one." She heard the man comment to his table-mate. He didn't try to lower the volume of his voice. Others at the tables around him, most of whom hadn't seemed to notice her when she walked in, turned to look in her direction. Olivia frowned at the man in confusion.

The young woman, who appeared to be of Asian descent, with hair that was long, sleek, and black, and whose posture somehow looked both casual and straight as a board, sent her a small smile after shushing the man.

"Excuse me, miss. You appear to have just arrived." Olivia nearly jumped out of her skin as she heard the voice right next to her.

"Um, yes. What is this place?" Olivia met the eyes of the woman who had spoken to her. She was around Olivia's age and had glowing dark brown skin and brown eyes. She was taller than Olivia, nearly six feet. Her dark hair was in a neat bun, and she wore a tailored gray suit with a burnt-orange blouse underneath. Her eyes had a professional look, but also held a great deal of kindness. Olivia immediately felt like she could trust her, although she knew that was an insane assumption.

"I'm glad you arrived safely. My name is Ziya. Why don't you accompany me to the desk and I'll check you in? We'll explain everything."

Olivia followed Ziya, but not before glancing back at the man and young woman at the table. The woman had turned back to her drink, but the man was still watching Olivia. She found him annoying, only because he knew more than she did about this strange situation. And he wasn't trying to hide his attention, like the others in the lobby.

"Miss?" Olivia heard Ziya's voice again and turned to look back at the desk. A quick flash blinded her; she covered her eyes with a yelp.

"Olivia Murphy." Ziya stated, not as a question but as a fact. She was holding some kind of scanner, the size of a cell phone, in her hand. She seemed to be reading information off the screen.

"What the hell?" Olivia backed away from the desk, fear taking over. She didn't care what her body tried to make her do. She was out of here.

"I'm sorry about that. I should have warned you. Please, Ms. Murphy. I know all of this is very confusing, but if you trust us for just a bit longer, we'll explain everything." Ziya held up her hand, her face appeared just as friendly as before.

Olivia stopped. Her fingers were going numb from clutching her suitcase handles. She scanned the lobby, taking in the many people sitting at the tables. None of them seemed worried. They also didn't look like an obvious group of cult members, not that Olivia knew what that would look like. They gave the appearance of different groups of friends chatting in a coffee shop. It all felt too—normal, too casual and comfortable for a place she'd been led to without understanding why. She resumed her backward movement toward the entrance. Ziya did nothing to stop her, but concern filled the woman's face.

"Hi, I'm Jed Henley."

Olivia jumped, really done with surprises for the day. The man who had been watching her was now standing next to her holding out his hand.

His companion with the jet-black hair was standing several feet behind, a kind smile sitting on her lips. She pushed her hair over her shoulders, and it came to rest just above her waist. The young woman's eyes held so much more than kindness, and Olivia felt overwhelmed at how wise, but also sad, they were.

Olivia studied Jed's face. She tried not to find him obnoxious. Sort of. She knew her initial impression of him wasn't helping. He was an over-six-foot-tall Caucasian man who appeared to be in his mid-forties. Flecks of gray ran through his short, light brown hair, settling in more prominent patches near his temples. His eyes were a nearly impossible light blue. He had deep laugh lines that stood out with the grin he gave her, waiting for her to shake his hand.

Unfortunately, he fell into a category of men who had made Olivia feel awkward and less capable throughout her life, probably made worse by the father issues she still carried with her. But this man's eyes were welcoming, and his grin made it clear that he didn't take life too seriously. Maybe it also helped that his last name was the same as one of her favorite rock musicians from the 1970s.

"Olivia," she responded, giving his hand a quick shake, placing her fingers back into a fist at her side when it was done.

"Nice to meet you, Olivia," Jed said, putting his hands casually in his pockets and rocking back on his heels. "I know this must seem crazy. You were sort of called here, right? Felt like you had to come to San Francisco and to this building? It's been the same for all of us. They'll explain why. That's all they want to do."

"I'm Akiko Sato." The younger woman pushed around Jed, also putting her hand out. Olivia found herself feeling much more comfortable about shaking it than she had about shaking Jed's. "I know this is strange, but I promise you're safer here than you are out there right now. Let them explain. It'll answer so many questions about things you've been dealing with." She looked as if she wanted to add more but forced herself to stop.

Olivia watched them both for a moment, her suspicion hard to squash, but their faces appeared genuine. She turned back to Ziya and nodded.

Ziya motioned for Olivia to follow her into a large conference room just off a hallway to the right. Olivia insisted on bringing her suitcases with her.

"Can I get you a bottle of water or something to eat? We have a cafeteria-style café, and the food is delicious," Ziya said as Olivia sat down in one of the comfortable leather office chairs situated around the long, polished table.

"Water is fine; thank you," Olivia answered. She was hungry, but she couldn't imagine eating anything until she knew what was going on.

While Ziya crossed the room to a small refrigerator, Olivia took in her surroundings. Floor-to-ceiling windows looked out onto the now-dark San Francisco street. The blue-gray carpet with subtle geometric designs was common in any office space, and the walls were a standard beige. But there was something that kept the room from looking typical: overflowing shelves completely lined one wall, full of every size and color of book imaginable. A sliding ladder was attached to the shelves so even the highest works could be reached. Olivia longed to go to those shelves and spend hours studying their contents.

Ziya placed a bottle of water in front of Olivia and then took a seat across the table from her. At that moment, a door to the right opened, and a man and woman walked in. The woman was wearing a white coat. The man was wearing a slick black suit with a striking blue dress shirt underneath.

"Hello, Ms. Murphy. I'm Dr. Isabelle Cordova, and this is Mr. Davit Adamian." They sat down next to Ziya. "Mr. Adamian is the chief engineer of this institute—The Survivor Institute. I am the chief medical officer. I know you must have so many questions; we'll be happy to answer them to the best of our ability. We believe you may be the last patient we've been waiting for."

"What do you mean by patient? What is this place?" Olivia asked, her voice shaking. *Could I get around them and out the door before they would catch me?* she wondered.

"Ms. Murphy, to get to the point in layman's terms, The Survivor Institute was created to fix damaged human brains by inserting computerized patches, or chips." Mr. Adamian folded his hands and placed them on the table. "Unfortunately, after decades of use, many of our products have been malfunctioning and it isn't quite clear why. They were built to last for a user's entire lifetime. They are a self-updating technology, able to process infinite amounts of information, but they seem to be slowly breaking down. This has resulted in a number of less-than-pleasant side effects for their users. When they were programmed, the chips were built on a basic code that would cause the parts, and therefore the user, to want to return to their place of origin if something were to go wrong. This is why you and the other patients have been called to this building." He motioned around the room.

Olivia was sure her jaw must be resting on the table. "Are—Are you saying I have computer parts in my brain? That my brain was damaged and then repaired with computer parts? Look, I don't know what kind of sick joke this is—" She stood up, but a blinding headache burst into her head like a popping flash from a burned-out light bulb.

She gripped her skull, squeezing her eyes closed, and sat down again. There was a light touch on her arm and Dr. Cordova's voice was now coming from somewhere next to her, but Olivia couldn't understand the words. The pain subsided after several moments and Olivia dared to open her eyes.

She gave a small cry of terror when she found everything around her was once again covered in a shadow of red. Dr. Cordova's face, which was inches from her own, was the deepest scarlet. The doctor was giving someone firm orders for medical assistance. Olivia closed her eyes and opened them once more. All colors were normal and there was only the smallest ache in her head. Olivia sat back in her chair and said in a hushed voice, "I'm fine."

She heard Dr. Cordova speaking again, canceling the medical assistance request. When Olivia looked around, she noticed Mr. Adamian and Ziya were watching her, but neither seemed surprised by what had just happened.

"Ms. Murphy," Dr. Cordova was sitting in the chair next to her now, one hand resting on Olivia's arm, "this is why you were called here. You're having these symptoms, which I'm sure must be terrifying, because your implant is breaking down. We'll talk about your symptoms again soon, but for now, I just need you to understand what led to this."

At that moment, Mr. Adamian pushed a button on a remote that seemed to have just appeared in his hand. An LED screen rose from the middle of the table and displayed what appeared to be an MRI brain scan. Dr. Cordova nodded to the chief engineer, who pushed another button. The scan zoomed in, and Olivia could indeed see something that looked no bigger than a tiny circular battery, imbedded in the brain.

"This is a current scan of your brain," Dr. Cordova said in a voice just louder than a murmur, as if she were just now understanding the alarming gravity of the information she and Mr. Adamian relayed.

Olivia felt the blood drain from her face and tried not to pass out. But maybe she already had, and this was another nightmare? She took several deep breaths, digging her fingernails into the palms of her hands, hoping the pain would ground her. When she spoke, it was slow, because the words didn't seem to want to form. "H-How is that p-possible? I-I h-haven't had any scans done here."

"Actually, you did," Ziya spoke up, motioning to the device in her hand—the same one she'd used to scan Olivia's face earlier. Ziya's eyes were still kind and concerned. Her hand twitched as if she wanted to reach across the table in comfort.

"You'll see that our technology is quite advanced here—far too advanced to be released to the general public, or even standard science and medical professionals," Mr. Adamian said.

Olivia thought that was a selfish statement. Imagine what doctors could do with technology like this. But she said nothing to Mr. Adamian. Instead, she turned back toward Dr. Cordova and Ziya. "I just had a CT scan done in the hospital and they didn't see anything like that." She motioned toward the screen. "How am I supposed to believe that's really my brain?"

"The implants were designed to be undetectable by machines other than our own. Mr. Adamian can expound on that I'm sure, but there is something else I need to show you," the doctor answered.

Olivia was about to protest, demand more information about the scan, but Dr. Cordova slid a manila file onto the table—her hand leaving it only when it was directly in front of Olivia. The folder's tab was marked with Olivia's name and date of birth. Olivia opened the file like something might jump out at her. What she saw took her breath away.

On the right side of the folder was stapled a picture of Olivia as a little girl, maybe a toddler. She recognized herself in the photo, but there were things about her appearance that she couldn't comprehend.

In the picture, her eyes were closed, as if she were sleeping. Her forehead was bruised and stitched. Both of her eyes were black. An oxygen mask sat over her mouth, hiding the rest of her small face. Olivia numbly pulled the photograph up to study a second just beneath it. She sucked in air as she saw that this picture showed a large bloody wound on the right side of her little head.

"What is that?!" Olivia flung the folder away like it burned. She wanted to stand up, to run, but her legs wouldn't obey.

"When you were four years old, you were in a serious car accident with a family friend," Dr. Cordova explained in a calm, soft voice. "That person was drunk and hadn't secured you in your seat. Your parents were not in the car with you. They had not given the person permission to drive you home from the event you'd all been attending. The friend got away with only minor injuries. But your brain was damaged so severely in the crash, you were put on life support. Your parents were told you were brain dead and couldn't survive on your own. Through some in-depth research, they found our institute. You were brought here in a comatose state. At the time of your arrival, the institute's research had been going on for decades, but you were one of the first ones to receive the implant. You recovered well and were once again able to live a normal life."

Olivia couldn't seem to put together a coherent enough thought to ask any questions. It was difficult just to keep herself clear of the panic threatening to overtake her.

Dr. Cordova continued after a deep breath, "As was explained before, your implant, as well as those in the brains of the institute's other residents, is shutting down. Hence the strange side effects, or symptoms, as we're calling them, that everyone is experiencing. We believe these symptoms may be your brain's way of remembering and processing the trauma of your past as your implant slowly stops working. However, none of the institute's current staff worked here when the implants were designed, created, and placed. We have all the research, notes from when they were built, and medical charts needed, but there is nothing within that information that points to why this could be happening. We're working day and night on the best option to keep you all alive."

"Keep us all alive?" Olivia managed to repeat. She was still for a moment as the severity hit her. "Wait, this is killing us? The implants shutting down is killing us? Or is it our original medical problems, like the brain damage I knew nothing about, killing us? This—This is insane! Why didn't I know anything about this? Did they all know?" She motioned in the direction of the lobby.

Dr. Cordova's face was neutral, but her eyes held empathy. "The implants are hard-wired to your brains' synapses; there's no easy fix, like removing them and replacing them with new implants. Because your implant mended the damage in your brain, technically, both its shutdown and the original brain damage could kill you. And none of the institute's patients were made aware of the implants unless their parents or guardians wanted them to be. Your brains were healed through the implant placements, and all memories of your traumas and the surgeries were erased. The goal was to get you to live as of normal lives as possible. It does seem some guardians chose to tell their loved ones—" she sighed in a moment of hesitation, "things that weren't quite true to explain what happened—to make it easier on the patients."

"My parents never told me anything," Olivia said with a frown. *This can't be real, can't be real, can't be real.*

Cordova stared at her for a moment, maybe unsure what to say in response. Then she sped forward again, "Well, regardless of what happened in the past, we won't let any of you die! As I said, we're working every minute of every day to come up with a solution for a problem left to us by the institute's previous employees."

Here, Mr. Adamian cleared his throat and gave Dr. Cordova a look before saying, "Who created the problem doesn't matter now. We *will* find an answer. We're already making some very good progress."

Olivia's mind was reeling. She didn't know which thought to take hold of first. Her parents had known about this since she was four years old and said nothing. She'd told her mother about feeling strange and she'd heard the hesitation on the other end of the line, but still nothing. How could they have kept this from her? They never even mentioned the accident. Did this whole thing have something to do with the strain on their relationship, or had that already been going downhill before she had advanced technology implanted in her brain?

"I know none of this makes sense to you right now, but I want to schedule a larger block of time to sit down and answer questions, as well as interview you about any symptoms you're experiencing," Dr. Cordova said. "My medical team will also need to perform a basic physical examination and conduct a series of blood draws. Since we already have your scan, we won't have to do that again for now."

Olivia was silent as she considered each of the three people in turn. Dr. Cordova's expression was confident and empathetic, while Mr. Adamian displayed only calm professionalism. Ziya was looking down at the table, clasping and unclasping her hands. Her body language seemed to convey nervousness—or maybe guilt? But when she looked up at Olivia, she offered her a small smile.

"But we don't have to do any of that right now," the doctor said. "You must be hungry and tired. We have things all set up for you. You'll have a suite on the tenth floor, which is paid for. The whole building belongs to the institute. I believe you heard about the café, which is also paid for, but you will also be given a food stipend, so you can dine elsewhere in the city. We just ask that you don't leave San Francisco, or at least its surrounding area. Now that your implant has led you back here, we don't know if there will be even more adverse effects if you travel too far away. We will also put you on a regular schedule for treatments to calm your symptoms. The treatments are injectable and are like a band-aid. They're temporary, but they do seem to help. I can explain all that later. You will also have a miscellaneous stipend to spend on whatever you'd like, although we ask that it not be used on anything that could be considered inappropriate or illegal."

Olivia was so very tired. "And—And what if I don't stay?"

Ziya's eyes went wide at the question, but she didn't say anything. Mr. Adamian cleared his throat and looked like he was going to speak, but Dr. Cordova held up a hand and offered another weak smile. "This is scary and overwhelming, I know. And I need to stop rambling on about everything. I think I'm excited in a way, because you're the last one we expect. Now we know everyone is here and safe. But I need to not get carried away." Here, she paused and gave Olivia a little smile before saying, "But you understand, you can't leave. The symptoms of these shutdowns are debilitating, as you've seen. You're safe here with the temporary treatments we can offer. If you don't stay, your implant will shut down anyway, and it will be very unpleasant. Then, with no solution, you will die."

"Okay," Olivia murmured, the words "you will die" ringing in her ears. "But how can I believe everything you've told me is the truth?"

"You'll have to trust us, Ms. Murphy. And please, speak to some of the other residents. They'll corroborate what we've told you." Dr. Cordova motioned toward the lobby.

"Mr. Henley, who was speaking to you earlier, has been here the longest. His friend, Ms. Sato, arrived shortly after he did. They would be the best people to talk to," Ziya offered.

Dr. Cordova nodded, but there was something in her eyes Olivia couldn't interpret.

"Maybe you'd like to go out there now?" Dr. Cordova suggested. "Possibly get some dinner from the café? I can have one of the staff double-check that your room is ready. Everything else can wait for tomorrow."

And just like that, all three people stood up and made their way to the door, indicating the meeting was over. Although in that moment, Olivia couldn't imagine a future outside that conference room, she stood on shaky legs, grabbed her luggage, and followed, trying to ignore the loop playing in her head.

You will die, you will die, you will die.

CHAPTER 4

DR. CORDOVA USHERED Olivia back into the lobby, then disappeared somewhere. Olivia hadn't seen where Mr. Adamian went after he left the conference room. Ziya took her place back at her desk after asking a male staff member to load Olivia's suitcases onto a luggage cart and take them upstairs.

Ziya gave Olivia another smile. "It'll be a few minutes, but you're welcome to get some dinner like the doctor suggested."

Olivia nodded but didn't move. Despite the general insanity of the information Dr. Cordova and Mr. Adamian had just given, something else nagged at her. It was what she'd seen just before she walked into the building: the vision of her parents' hands holding hers, of the great sadness she felt, and the institute standing before her. It had felt like a true memory unlocked after decades. But how did that memory exist if she'd been in a comatose state upon her arrival to the institute as a four-year-old?

Before she could think too much about it, Akiko and Jed walked over. Their confidence of earlier seemed a little shaken.

"Go okay? It's a lot—at first," Jed said with a shrug as an afterthought.

Olivia narrowed her eyes at him. "Yes, yes, it was a lot. And I would *not* say it went okay. They just told me I have some kind of failing computer chip in my brain, which is killing me, or maybe it's my childhood injuries killing me. The pictures they showed me—" She cut herself off as she tried to tamp down sudden nausea. "But honestly, I'm wondering if I'm in a coma right now and my brain is making all this up as a way to cope."

"Nope, you've just joined the best trauma club in town," Jed said, a smile quirking up the corners of his lips.

Olivia couldn't deal with this guy, not right now. "Are you *joking* about this?"

Akiko gave Jed a little shove with the side of her arm and cleared her throat. She ushered Olivia back toward the table she'd seen them sitting at before. Jed followed in silence, surprising Olivia by pulling out her chair before choosing one for himself.

"Don't mind my awkward friend here," Akiko said. "He knows how to filter his thoughts, but he doesn't always choose to. We heard them call for medical assistance. Were you having symptoms?"

At Olivia's nod, Akiko continued, "I know they like to call them symptoms, but the term side effects *is* more accurate. Everyone's are different in terms of severity and what is seen, heard, and felt during a flare."

Olivia closed her eyes and leaned back in her chair, pleading with the universe to wake her up.

She felt a gentle touch on her arm and opened her eyes to see Akiko's hand resting there. "We're here and we understand," Akiko murmured. "I'm sure Dr. Cordova mentioned the treatments. They do help keep the symptoms under control for the most part."

"What are yours?" Jed's voice was full of curiosity.

"They're not something I care to think about, let alone talk about," Olivia answered with a frown.

His sudden grin made it all the way to his intrigued eyes. "Sorry. They're horrible, but they're also kind of fascinating."

Akiko shook her head at her friend. "He's a writer," she said, as if that explained everything. "You don't have to tell us anything you're not comfortable talking about."

Olivia's eyes flicked around the room, taking in quick glances of the other people sitting at tables in the lobby. A couple of them offered her small smiles, but most of them ignored her. "How many—like us—are there here?"

"You make number fifty-three," Jed answered.

Olivia felt her eyes grow wide. "They did this to fifty-three people?"

"Assuming there weren't more at some point," Jed said.

Olivia ignored that. "How was this sanctioned by oversight organizations?"

"They haven't exactly elaborated on that, but we checked, and the institute is licensed by the California Department of Public Health." Akiko grimaced. "It doesn't help that none of the people who worked here originally are still here. And this staff won't share any of the information the original group left behind. They say it could compromise our confidence in them and the solutions they're working on."

"And do you all have confidence in them?"

Akiko eyes went to Ziya at her desk and then back to Olivia. "We'll have plenty of time to catch you up soon. We'll answer as many questions as we can."

Olivia understood. Now was not the time to chat about that particular topic. She decided to ask about something that should be less controversial. "Were you also both children when this happened to you?"

Akiko gave a small nod. "I was one of the last ones to get an implant, and I was three."

"Three?" Olivia couldn't keep the shock from her voice. Sure, she'd supposedly only been a year older when she received her own implant, but three years old felt alarmingly young. They'd put computer parts in the brains of people who had barely had a chance to live.

"Yes," Akiko was saying. "I experienced hypoxia at birth and, as a result, my neurological development was not happening at what many would call a 'typical' pace. I wasn't meeting many milestones as a baby and toddler. The month I turned three, my parents found the institute and brought me here. I had the surgery six months later. It changed my life, allowed me to meet all developmental milestones from there on. My parents have been very open about it from the beginning. They explained it all as soon as I was old enough to understand. My brother and sister are younger than me, and they've always known. I grew up believing it was normal, although I realized after I got here that my parents tried to keep the information within our family as much as possible. I was a pretty quiet kid, so I hardly talked to anyone, let alone told them about the implant in my brain. That must have made it easier on my parents."

Olivia's mind spun in dizzying circles. How were she and Akiko here today, alive and sort of well? How could a tiny computer chip repair injuries to a brain?

Akiko nodded like she could read Olivia's thoughts, before saying, "It seemed like a miracle—until it wasn't."

Something profound and sad settled briefly on Akiko's face, but instead of saying anything else, she turned to Jed, who'd been listening, his expression more serious than Olivia had seen it so far. He gave Akiko a small, tentative smile. Akiko nodded and closed her eyes for a few seconds, clearly willing away tears.

Jed turned his attention to Olivia. "I was sixteen," he began in a relaxed tone. "My friend Brian and I had just gotten our licenses. We'd trade off driving around, doing nothing. We lived in a small town in Oregon, so there wasn't much to do anyway. He was driving that night, and we were acting like idiots. Except he was wearing his seatbelt, so when we rolled his dad's truck, he didn't get the brain damage I did. I was brought here and had the surgery. I don't know if my life has been normal since then. No, actually, I do know, and it's been pretty shitty. But maybe most adults think that when they have computer chips embedded in their brains that don't allow them to remember a portion of their lives," he laughed. "Then there's the added bonus of not being able to keep a romantic relationship, or any other relationship for that matter."

Olivia considered the man sitting across from her. He was such an interesting person. A mixture of awkwardly blunt, sarcastic, curious, and empathetic. Was that what writers were like?

"Sixteen seems pretty old for them to have successfully hidden this from you," Olivia couldn't help but say, part of her *still* wondering if her brain was making this all up. Was this just a very elaborate delusion? She dug the nails of her right fingers into the flesh of her palm as she balled her hand into a fist. Pain.

Jed nodded, and she thought she saw his eyes flick down to the movement of her hand. "They told me about the accident, but I just thought I was hurt, was in the hospital for a long time, and then got better, because that's what I remember. They never told me I'd had brain damage. After the implant surgery, I was taken back to a hospital where we lived in Oregon, but I don't remember traveling from California. I think they had me on some pretty heavy drugs. After my dying implant led me back here, my mom came here to visit and filled me in on the details. She felt horrible for not telling the full truth when I was a teenager, but that's what the institute staff advised her to do. They'd said knowing about the implant would be too traumatic—cause too many problems in my life. The implant's caused them anyway, even though I didn't know it at the time."

This statement sparked something in Olivia. She thought back on how unsettled she'd felt her entire life. How friendships were always difficult, even though she was constantly trying to escape the deep loneliness that surrounded her. How she'd always felt awkward in romantic relationships, never able to commit. She'd blamed it on her parents' divorce and her father's departure. "I think mine has done the same to me," she murmured, her eyes cast down at the table.

Silence settled over them, but Jed broke it with another casual statement. "Mine are screaming, scraping feelings on my skin, and seeing streaks of red."

Olivia felt the color drain from her face. "W-what?"

"Jeez, Jed. She doesn't want to talk about it." Akiko glared at the man.

"I'm not saying she has to talk about hers, but I'm okay talking about mine," Jed responded with a smirk.

"No wonder no one else ever comes over to talk to us." Akiko shook her head. "I'm going to go get a coffee from the café. Olivia, can I get you one?"

Olivia just shook her head and tried to give the woman a smile. It was late and she hoped she'd get some kind of sleep that night. Maybe she'd wake up back in her house.

"That's not true!" Jed called after his friend's retreating form. "Theo and Mira sat with us for at least fifteen minutes yesterday!" He laughed as Akiko waved away his words.

"It was ten minutes, and they won't be back!" she called over her shoulder.

Olivia was staring at Jed when he turned back to her. Yeah, she really wasn't sure what to make of this guy.

"Sorry, I love to bug Kiko, and she doesn't really care. She's been here seven of the eight months I have, so she's pretty used to it."

Olivia's jaw dropped for what felt like the millionth time that day. "Eight months? You've been waiting for them to fix this for *eight months?*"

"Yeah. Difficult process, apparently." He shrugged, his voice dripping with sarcasm. "I'm a freelance writer and editor, so I've been able to keep busy. Sorry about before. What I was trying to say was my symptoms are hearing screams—distant ones—seeing red streaks on things, and these scratching sensations on my skin, like I'm brushing up against something sharp. The treatments do help."

"I'm not sure I want to know how injections will be used to put a band aid on a failing computer chip in my brain," Olivia said, forcing herself to take a couple deep breaths.

"Dr. Cordova explained it to me when I got here. The injection contains nanorobotic technology. So, these tiny robots flow through your bloodstream, into your brain, and attach to the implant itself. They—"

Olivia held up a hand. "I said I'm not sure I want to know."

"Sorry." He offered her an apologetic smile. He was quiet for a few seconds before he said, "I also dream about forests a lot—dark, terrifying forests."

Olivia shivered, but she had to admit, Jed's confession made her feel a little more secure about analyzing her own experience. It was okay to talk about it with someone who was dealing with something similar, right? She took a deep breath and a chance. "I've been dreaming about oceans and rivers—maybe creeks. At times it feels peaceful, but then there's blood and terror. I don't understand what it means. I don't have any water-related trauma that I know of."

Jed lifted his chin in thought, his voice almost tranquil when he spoke. "It may be something you don't remember, from before, or something related to your accident. Maybe you were in a car driving by the coast or on a road next to a river when it happened. It could be the smallest connection your brain is trying to reconcile as the implant shuts down."

She stared at him for several moments. He looked uncomfortable with the prolonged attention. "How can you say that like it's a normal, acceptable thing? Doesn't this all terrify you?"

His face took on a sheepish expression. "Liv (she narrowed her eyes at the nickname no one called her), I know this is all new to you, but I've been here for a long time. Yeah, it's terrifying. I focused more on the fear when I first got here. I was also angry—at so many people, but I couldn't keep going like that. It was only making things worse. Now I stay busy working. And I analyze my symptoms and what I know of my past, because, since this is happening anyway, I want to see if there are any memories that'll come back to me. I try not to give into the fear unless I have a new reason to.

"Kiko was angry when she got here too, so I tried to be supportive. I tried to be positive, because I'd had time to get a little used to being here. At a month in, I was feeling hopeful a solution was just around the corner. But the implant wasn't a huge shock to her like it was to me. She had known about the operation for as long as she could remember, so there was nothing for her to adjust to in terms of having a computer chip in her brain. It was dealing with her symptoms and what the dying implant had done to her life that was difficult. Finding any hope seemed impossible for her because the implant had already done its damage."

A guilty look sprang to his face. "But *she* needs to tell you more of her story if she wants to. Anyway, my positive attitude was hard to keep up. After a while it just turned into acceptance so I could continue to move forward with my life. I think Akiko's gotten to that place too—as much as she can. So, if we ever sound a little too casual about this—this nightmare—just remember, we've been in your shoes. We understand how it feels, but we just can't stay in that mindset anymore."

Olivia kept her gaze down at her hands, which rested on the table. She clasped and unclasped her fingers, trying to keep her mind from drifting into darkness. Even with Jed sitting across from her, and the room filled with other residents, she felt so alone.

"It's nice that you had each other when you were first here," Olivia murmured.

"And now you have us too," Jed said, and she was surprised to feel him put his hand on her arm.

She slowly pulled away from him, avoiding his gaze as Akiko returned with her coffee and sat down.

"Coffee is my main vice," Akiko said. "And the problem is, I can drink it at any time of day, and the caffeine does nothing to me. It almost feels like a free pass." Then noticing Olivia's expression, she scowled at Jed. "I hope he wasn't too annoying."

Before Olivia could respond, Ziya called her from the front desk. "Ms. Murphy? Your room is ready. I can take you up."

Olivia stayed where she was, not sure what to do. Maybe she could walk out the door right now. It could be worth the risk to see if this was all a lie.

"Our rooms are like upscale hotel suites—one of the only good things about this place," Akiko murmured, her gaze holding Olivia's. "Do you want me to come with you?"

The idea was more comforting than going upstairs with just an institute employee. "If you don't mind," Olivia answered.

"Not at all." Akiko stood up in one graceful movement, taking her coffee cup with her. Everything about the younger woman seemed serene. But Olivia wondered what kind of pain she was forced to deal with on a daily basis.

"See you later," Jed said as both women walked toward Ziya.

"Try not to get in any trouble," Akiko responded. Jed just grinned.

CHAPTER 5

"YOU WEREN'T KIDDING."** Olivia exhaled a long, slow breath as she looked around her tenth-floor suite. It was like the swankiest hotel room she'd seen in movies. After Ziya left, Olivia roamed every space, touching surfaces and admiring small details.

The bathroom was all marble, with two vanity mirrors shining under the most flattering light. There was a jetted bathtub and an enormous stand-alone shower. A hint of lavender floated through the air. Before the hallway leading to the spacious king-sized bedroom was a living space with an enormous, soft sectional, a plush area rug, and the biggest television Olivia had ever seen. The small kitchen was covered in the same creamy marble as the bathroom. Pristine white subway tiles adorned the backsplash. The maple cabinets went all the way to the ceiling, providing more than enough storage for a large family.

"Yes, they go all out." Akiko surveyed the suite.

"This is what I imagine fancy Manhattan apartments look like— the ones people have professionally decorated. And we don't have to pay for this?" Olivia's eyes grew wide as she studied the high-end kitchen appliances.

Akiko shook her head with a small smile. It was clear she felt uneasy about the opulence. "I don't know how this place makes its money, because they can't exactly market failing tech, but they seem to have plenty of funding. Part of me wonders if they created something before the implants and that gave them the success and financial stability they needed to take a risk on a new technology. But they're not exactly open about where any continued revenue comes from."

Olivia nodded, finding it disturbing that not even the residents who'd been here the longest seemed to know how this place worked.

The bedroom was another breathtaking sight. Gorgeous floor-to-ceiling windows made up one wall, just like the first-floor conference room, though the view of the surrounding San Francisco buildings through the misty darkness felt ominous, as if she were entombed in this strange place.

The bed linens were the softest she'd ever touched, and there was a gas fireplace already burning next to an overstuffed chair and a bookshelf filled with an assortment of novels and nonfiction books. Maybe she should never leave this room. Maybe here she could pretend she was on some perfect vacation where all she had to do was read, rest, and dream.

"What do I do now?" Olivia asked, rejoining Akiko in the living area. She was still feeling jittery and had no interest in unpacking. If she stayed packed, she could get out quickly. Before Ziya left, she'd said someone from the medical team would be contacting Olivia as soon as possible, but she couldn't hazard a guess as to when that would be.

At least my symptoms seem to have calmed down.

Akiko turned from a window and gave Olivia another smile. "You wait. That's the most frustrating thing about this place—the waiting. They'll let you know when they're ready to interview you further. Then you'll be set up on a treatment plan to help proactively manage your symptoms. You'll be taken in for regular CT and MRI scans. They'll take your vitals every few days. But you'll continue to wait—to wait for them to figure out how to find a solution to this mess.

"I don't want to scare you, but it's better to be honest about what you'll experience. The treatments do help, but you'll still have bad days. You can get extra treatments on those days, but they might not completely stop the symptoms. Other days will just be quiet, but you can make them interesting. You'll wake up, spend time in the building, explore the city, maybe do something for your other life outside this place—like work if you're able to. Sometimes you'll feel like you're going crazy because you're so bored, but you just have to wait it out. Jed and I have discovered a lot of fun things to do around San Francisco, so we can give you ideas."

Olivia took all of this in as she breathed through the panic tightening her chest. How was she supposed to give up her life for an indefinite amount of time? Wanting to talk about anything other than their reality, and because she was curious, she said, "You and Jed seem really close. Are you seeing each other?"

Akiko's eyes showed her surprise and laughter followed. Her laugh sounded just as graceful and effortless as her movements looked. "No. I love Jed, but that's because he's looked after me since I got here. Maybe he had some older brother instinct that kicked in. Like I mentioned downstairs, we don't have a ton of close friends here. I wish that wasn't the case, but Jed doesn't seem to mind. The truth is that a lot of the residents have developed cliques. I think we've all just latched on to certain people who make us feel more secure. And that's the case for Jed and me. It's a good thing. I'm not sure who Jed would annoy if I wasn't around."

Olivia smiled at the affection in Akiko's voice.

"The other thing is that I was married before I came to this place, and I don't plan to have another romantic relationship during my lifetime," Akiko said, much to Olivia's surprise. But before she could say anything, Akiko asked, "Want to head back downstairs? You still haven't eaten. Tomorrow, we can get you some groceries to keep here for when you don't want to go out or eat at the café." She motioned toward the kitchen.

"That'd be great," Olivia answered. With one last look at her suitcases in the bedroom, she followed Akiko out of the suite.

When they had made their way back downstairs, Jed was sitting at the same table, typing away at a laptop. Olivia checked her watch. It was almost nine o'clock. She was hungry, but she was also so restless and wanted to be anywhere but in this building.

As if reading Olivia's mind, Akiko said, "Let's go out and see what's still open for food. A change of scenery might be nice."

Jed smiled up at them and closed his computer, shoving it into a laptop bag and putting the strap around his shoulder. Akiko called an Uber and they found a Mexican restaurant several blocks outside Golden Gate Park that was open until ten o'clock. During the drive, Olivia thought of so many questions she wanted to ask her new acquaintances. She was sure tonight was not the right time to ask all of them, but maybe she could get past a couple of the basics.

The restaurant was surprisingly busy, but they ordered and found a small table to wait for their food. Jed settled back in his chair, crossing his arms over his chest as he scanned the crowded space. "Quality people-watching tonight."

Akiko laughed, but her eyes were on the dark street outside the window next to them—her right elbow on the table, her chin resting on the back of her hand. Olivia couldn't help but notice again how unalike the friends seemed, even in their mannerisms—not to mention that they were from two different generations. It felt odd but comforting that they'd stayed close after so many months.

As Olivia took a deep breath and opened her mouth to ask her first question, whether the treatments caused any side effects themselves, she noticed red streaks appear on Jed and Akiko's faces. No, wait, they didn't just appear. The streaks were running down their faces—the color of blood dripping from their hairlines to their chins. Olivia's stomach churned as the headache she was beginning to recognize exploded into her brain, making her gasp.

She slammed her eyes closed. Her fingers rushed to the sides of her head. She willed herself not to pass out.

She felt Akiko's hand covering hers. Her voice was concerned but confident. "Fight it, Olivia. It'll pass. Stay with us. You can do it."

"Damn it. They should have given her the first treatment back at the cachot," Jed muttered, anger coloring his voice.

"Remember that they do that on purpose," Akiko responded in a murmur.

What was that word he said? Olivia tried to focus on their conversation, hoping to distract herself from the pain ripping her skull apart. *Something in another language? And what did Akiko mean?*

Olivia wanted to ask the questions out loud, but she was busy trying to keep herself from drowning in the pain. She wished she were back home. She wanted to curl up under her familiar blankets and hide from the world. She didn't want to pass out in a crowded restaurant, at a table with two people she barely knew.

Then just as fast as the pain had arrived, it was gone, leaving her breathless.

"Okay, Liv?" Jed asked with concern as Olivia opened her eyes.

Akiko squeezed her hand and Olivia nodded, but she felt like she'd run several miles. Her appetite was gone. She wasn't sure how she was going to get up from the table.

"Let's get you back." Akiko took Olivia's arm in her gentle grip and helped her up. "You can rest. Jed and I will ask about your first treatment. It's good to sleep after an episode."

She felt an uncomfortable combination similar to that of being drunk and exhausted at the same time. She stumbled a bit as they left the restaurant, both Akiko and Jed supporting her.

"I'm sorry about your food," Olivia managed to say as another Uber arrived and Akiko helped Olivia get in the back, while Jed took the front passenger seat.

"Don't worry about that," Akiko responded in a reassuring tone. "We can get something from the café."

Back at the institute, after both Jed and Akiko took Olivia up to her room, she fell into her bed. She remembered Akiko covering her with a comforter. She heard their whispered voices in her doorway for a few minutes. Then they were gone.

When her eyes opened next, her groggy mind registering a knock at her bedroom door. Dr. Cordova entered, saying soft words that Olivia couldn't hear. She felt a sharp prick somewhere on her left arm. A few more murmured words from Dr. Cordova and another female voice she didn't recognize. Then Olivia heard the bedroom door shutting again, and she seemed to be alone.

She held her breath, waiting for her body to seize, or break, or maybe implode as a result of the treatment. Nothing happened. Still, the idea of going to sleep after her first treatment was terrifying. How could she be sure she would wake up again? But her exhaustion was like a humid summer day, burying her in its suffocating stillness, and she was soon falling back into dreams.

CHAPTER 6

THE **MURMUR OF** *light fingertips on piano keys was coming from somewhere just behind her and also miles away—familiar miles she hadn't traveled in so long. It was a forlorn sound, so beautiful it made her want to cry. The music was simple—just a few chords that repeated two or three times. It reminded her of being a little girl and running through grass—running between trees in neat long rows. No, wait, she was a little girl, and the notes were swirling around her on a warm summer evening while she drank lemonade on an old wooden porch. The haunting music filled her existence. Who was playing it? Some corner of her mind knew. It was like the chords were part of her blood, her soul, but she couldn't reach their player.*

Olivia circled around, searching, but blackness stole any images she might see. Yet, she still felt safe. This was a place she knew. There were stars up above. Then she heard the water. Not a beloved ocean and not a terrifying river this time. It was a creek, not far from where she stood. She knew the creek too. She'd memorized its babbling tune and, for a moment, it seemed like the mournful piano was coming from under the water. The creek was safe. She loved it. She could go to it.

The trees she passed were part of a large fruit orchard. Yes, she was sure that was correct. She could still hear the creek and the notes calling from its depths. The tune was still beautiful and sad, but had it taken on a darker tone as well? One of anger and injustice? Just before she reached the creek, she saw the prone figure in the dirt. She stopped, but the music continued. One moment, the body was far from her, but the next, he was on the ground at her feet. There was blood all around. She couldn't see the man's face. She knew him. Didn't she? She screamed.

Olivia woke up shaking and crying. The headache was back, but it was dull. She could almost catch the fleeting chords from her nightmare. She glanced at the clock. Five-seventeen in the morning. Her bedroom was pitch dark. Someone had drawn the black-out curtains. She thought about getting up and wandering downstairs to see if anyone was awake, but sleep still wanted to claim her. She put her head back down on her pillow and closed her eyelids after just a few blinks.

She awoke again at nine-nineteen, still remembering pieces of the dream. Where was that place? And who was the man? It had seemed so real—like she had experienced it. But she couldn't have. She would know if she'd discovered a dead man in a fruit orchard. She took a quick shower and left her hair to air dry. She donned leggings and a long sweatshirt, because she had no desire to be anything but comfortable.

Just before she reached the door of her suite, a text message from her friend Stefanie dinged on her phone. *Hey! Haven't heard from you in a while. Can we get together soon? I neeeed adult conversation. I have kids' songs on a constant loop in my head.*

Olivia closed her eyes, leaning her head back against the wall, wondering when she would return to the normal world. She couldn't tell Stef what was going on, but she didn't want to put her off completely. So she typed, *That sounds great. Things are crazy at work right now, so I've been staying late. I want to see you, but can I get back to you soon?*

Yes, no problem! But make sure you're getting time to relax! Life can't be all about work, Stef responded almost immediately.

Olivia sent back a hugging emoji. If only she could be honest with her friend, but even if she took that risk, she would surely sound insane.

She slipped her phone in her back pocket and left her suite.

The moment the elevator doors opened on the lobby, she smelled coffee and saw Jed sitting at a table near the front windows, his fingers flying across his laptop's keyboard. She felt the quick blush of embarrassment at the thought that he'd seen her in such a vulnerable state the night before, but he must have had similar experiences with his own symptoms. She padded over to his table, wondering if she should interrupt him. He seemed to be deep into whatever he was working on.

But he looked up as she approached, giving her a small smile. He looked exhausted: dark circles under his eyes, and his hair a mess. Olivia wondered if he'd gotten any sleep.

"Morning. Doing okay?" He motioned for her to sit down.

Olivia nodded and sat in the chair across from him. She did a quick assessment of herself. Her headache seemed to be almost gone, but her movements still felt unsteady. "Better than yesterday. Sorry about that."

He shook his head, closing his laptop. "Don't apologize, Liv. It's happened to all of us. They should have given you your first treatment right after you got here, but Kiko said they eventually made it to your room?"

"Cordova did; I kind of remember." She yawned, not bothering to correct him about the nickname. A small part of her kind of liked it. "I had a crazy nightmare, but other than that, things seemed to get better."

"Nightmares are common. At least, they have been for me and Kiko." He nodded. His eyes studied hers for a moment before looking in the direction of the café.

There was no coffee cup on the table. She wondered if he was longing for some the way she was. "Where is Akiko this morning?" Olivia asked, scanning the room for the younger woman.

Darkness flooded Jed's face. "She's not feeling good, so she's staying in her room for a while. She wanted me to make sure you were okay though."

"Oh, I'm sorry to hear that. Her symptoms?"

"Maybe a small flare, but there's more to it," he murmured. She knew he didn't plan to elaborate. Olivia respected Jed's desire to let Akiko tell her story when she was ready.

Olivia sat back and tried to relax for a moment, but her curiosity soon got the better of her. "There's something I've been thinking about; something I wanted to ask you. Yesterday in the restaurant, when my symptom were flaring, you said something about how they should have given me my treatment already. You said a word I didn't understand, although my brain wasn't working well anyway. But it sounded like you were referencing this place. What did you call it?"

He folded the fingers of his hands together, sitting up straight while casually asking, "Feel up for a walk? Golden Gate Park?"

"Um, sure; let me just go up and get my coat," she said, understanding he would not be answering her until they were outside of the building.

1 0 1 0 1 1 0 1 0

An Uber ride later, they were walking in the park, each with a coffee in hand. Jed cleared his throat. "I said cachot. It's the French word for dungeon. It's what Kiko and I call the institute when we're outside its walls—just a code word of sorts."

"Why do you need a code word for the institute?" Olivia frowned at him. "And what did Akiko mean when she said they purposefully don't give treatments right away?"

He stopped walking and gazed at her for a moment, like he was wondering if she could handle what he had to say. "You've known something was wrong since you got here, Liv. You're right. Something is very wrong. Not just the fact that they installed tiny computer parts in our brains. Kiko and I believe it's something much bigger than that. But we haven't figured it out yet and we have to be discreet in any investigation or research we do, because we assume they're always watching and listening in that place.

"So, we try to only talk about our theories and research outside of the cachot's walls. And the thing is, even though we have no evidence of this, they could also be listening through our implants and having us followed. There's not much we can do if they *are* monitoring us in those ways, but it's been months and we haven't been penalized in any way. Ultimately, we want to draw as little attention to ourselves as we can out here, hence the code word. I'm sure you already understand the reason we chose dungeon: even though we're allowed to leave and travel in the nearby area, we're still like prisoners—being tortured by something we don't truly understand.

"And what Kiko meant is that they don't give treatments when residents first arrive because they're trying to keep them here. They told you staying was for your safety, right? Because the symptoms would escalate and they couldn't help you if you leave the greater San Francisco area? They want you scared—to build the foundation of their power over you. So, they let your full symptoms flare one more time before treatment, just to convince you that you can't survive without them. I've seen it happen with every new resident, and initially I refused to believe the staff would do something like that on purpose, but it's pretty clear now that they plan it that way." He paused, looking down at his coffee cup before adding, "And maybe we *can't* survive without the cachot's assistance, but we'll never know, because they never fail to keep us here."

It took Olivia a couple minutes to overcome the shock coursing through her. Jed walked beside her in silence, letting her find her questions. "But if you know that, how can you stay?" Anger made Olivia's voice shake. "Why don't you go to the police? If you feel like something sinister is happening—" She cut herself off, unsure how to finish that thought.

"We have no evidence," Jed murmured. "And if doctors outside of this place can't see the computer chips in our brains when they scan them, why would any law enforcement agency believe us? And like I said, we don't know if the cachot is keeping us alive. If the cachot is shut down without a solution, it could mean all our deaths."

Olivia gave a reluctant nod. They couldn't take that chance. "But this other thing that you think is going on, do you have any ideas of what it could be?"

He shook his head. "We thought our family members might know something—might break down and give us the information. But both Kiko's family and mine have stuck to the stories given to us by the cachot, so now we wonder if it's a secret from them too."

As they walked, Olivia tried to think of anything else to add, anything that would be relevant and helpful, but the situation seemed insurmountable, and she was still trying to come to terms with her small part in it.

"Tell me about your dream." Jed's voice broke the silence as they neared the Japanese Tea Garden. She'd never been before, but she recognized it from the images that flashed through her mind as her implant was calling her to San Francisco.

"What?"

"It would be interesting to hear another person's dream. Could provide some insight." He shrugged as if she'd already declined his request. He gestured toward the garden and Olivia nodded, keeping pace with his casual steps.

As Jed paid their entrance fee, Olivia couldn't help but turn her eyes to the large, transportive place just beyond them. Lush trees, flowing plant life, trickling water, and memorizing structures created a peaceful oasis just outside the ever-busy city.

Jed didn't push her about her dream as they took their time strolling every pathway. For awhile she let herself get lost in it all. There was something about that place, something that soothed her like she hadn't been in, well, maybe ever. She opened her mouth to speak almost before she realized she was ready to.

"Before I arrived at the—cachot, I sleepwalked to the river near my home," Olivia said. "I woke up standing in the water. I have no memory of walking there. It just seems to come back to bodies of water. In last night's dream, I was in an orchard and I was a child. It felt like a familiar place, although I don't remember frequenting any orchards when I was young. I heard this music. Forlorn piano music I swear I recognized. I walked through the orchard and came to a creek. There was a bloody body on the bank. I have no real-life memory of anything like that, but it *felt* so real."

He nodded. "My dreams feel that way too. They usually involve a car accident; that part makes sense. Then things get different. I crash into the woods, hear a woman's voice screaming. Then there's blood on all the trees—just running down the trees. I'm guessing that's related to the red streaks I see as part of my symptoms. Sometimes I try to seek out the female voice, but I can't find her. And there is the most intense feeling of adrenaline-soaked terror. Terror I can't begin to fathom in real life. My dreams are variations of that scenario. Sometimes it's just dark forests and I'm all alone. It's the being alone that scares me the most, because there is an almost palpable feeling of someone missing."

His dreams are just as traumatic as mine, and he's been dealing with them longer. How does he stay sane?

"My nightmares sometimes feel more like visions to me—like I'm not really asleep, I guess," Olivia added. "And I never dream about being in a car accident. There are no cars in the dreams at all. None of it makes sense."

"Yeah, I understand," Jed replied, turning his gaze up to the cloudy autumn sky. "Even though my mom and Kiko's family had no new information to offer when we asked, maybe yours would? Have you talked to them yet?"

"Not yet," Olivia answered with a grimace. She didn't think her strained relationship with her mother, and her nonexistent one with her father, would be made any better if she confronted them with the intense anger and confusion she felt regarding her implant.

Jed stopped walking and held her eyes with his. "A lot of the residents have—tough relationships with their families. Kiko may think no one else at the cachot wants to talk to me," here he gave a small smirk and she couldn't help but chuckle, "but most of them have told me their stories at one point or another. You're not alone with that familial strain—if that's your situation. You may not want to talk to them, but they may have something of interest to say now that you know about your implant."

"Maybe." She sighed and started walking again, hoping to change topics, or just not speak at all.

They stayed out most of the day, taking their time as they traipsed through several of the touristy parts of the city. Olivia was quiet for much of the time, but Jed didn't seem to mind. He told a few stories about his childhood and commented on things he and Akiko had discovered about San Francisco.

She found herself growing more comfortable with Jed as the hours passed and he just let her be, never pushing her to talk, but asking follow-up questions when she did. It was sort of nice to meet someone who didn't feel the need to hide anything or act a certain way, like others might. Maybe he did need a bit more of a filter, but Olivia was starting to think that wasn't a lack of maturity or couth, but more like a hunger for knowledge and connection.

For a very late lunch, they went to Boudin on the wharf. Every time Olivia felt the tiniest tinge of something in her head, she worried another symptom attack was coming, but since her treatment, they seemed to be staying under control.

When they were done eating, Jed called Akiko, who said she was feeling better but was spending the day in her suite. She spoke to Olivia briefly on speakerphone but didn't offer up any details of what was ailing her, so Olivia didn't ask.

"How often do you get symptom flares like the one I had yesterday?" she inquired of Jed when he'd hung up and put the phone back in his pocket.

"Not very often with the treatments. When I first got to the cachot, I was having them all the time, because the injections hadn't quite been perfected."

"The thought of having nanobots in my body freaks me out," Olivia said with a shiver.

"More than having a computer chip in your brain that cured your brain damage and erased a chunk of your life from memory, but is now breaking down?" he murmured, raising an eyebrow at her, a grin settling on his face.

"Uh no, I'd say I'm equally freaked out by both." She shook her head. "You know, maybe you do need some kind of solo hobby—to just give people a little break from your dark comedic honesty. Have you ever tried drumming?"

Jed gave a low laugh. "Ah, a Don Henley reference. The one constant in the life of sharing my last name with a famous musician."

"I can only imagine." Olivia laughed back. Then she took a deep breath. "Since you've been here for eight months, and since you and Akiko both believe there's more to this than they're telling us, do you think we stand a real chance of one day being able to leave and live normal lives?"

He was quiet for a beat too long before he answered. "I have to believe they're trying to find a way to help us, even if they aren't being truthful about how or why they're doing that. Somewhere along the line, someone must have messed up, but the current cachot regime doesn't want to come clean. I'm sure once they fix our brains, they'll figure out the legal issues, or how to get around them. Maybe make us sign NDAs or something similar. The residents will just be happy to get the hell out of there."

Olivia tried to push down her building anxiety. "So, if they're trying to come up with a solution, even if there is something bigger going on that they won't tell us, do you think we can trust the staff?"

"No," Jed said in a firm voice. "Don't trust any of them. Be respectful, be truthful, but don't trust. People who've gotten themselves into desperate situations will sometimes take even more desperate actions if they feel there's no other way. Akiko and me, you can trust. Most of the other residents are also trustworthy, but don't get any more involved with the staff than you have to."

She nodded. That wouldn't be an issue for her.

They picked up Italian food for dinner and took yet another Uber back to the institute.

When they walked through the doors, Olivia noticed Akiko was sitting at one of the more secluded lobby tables, set back against the wall farthest from the elevators. She looked up at them with a tired, grateful smile as Jed handed her a to-go container with fettuccine alfredo.

"Thank you so much. My appetite didn't exist for most of today, but I realized I was starving just before you walked in. I hung out in the pool for a while, but I just feel—restless."

Olivia scrunched her face at them. "There's a pool here? How?"

"Another positive, I suppose," Akiko tossed her a half-hearted grin. "It's an indoor pool with locker rooms behind the elevator bank. I'll show you soon. What'd you two do today?"

"Acted like tourists and had deep, meaningful conversations." Jed's voice was full of comedy, but he raised his eyebrows to let her know those conversations had involved the not-so-clear issues of the cachot.

"I see. More on that later. Are you feeling better today?" Akiko turned to Olivia, true concern in her eyes.

Olivia dipped her chin in answer. "No symptoms so far. Just a little tired."

"I'm glad. Within the next couple days, they should interview you about your symptoms, but I'm sure you'll need another treatment before then. Hopefully you'll get the schedule for that tomorrow."

"They don't seem to communicate much." Olivia frowned. "No one checked on me after last night's treatment."

"The staff here is smaller than you'd think, and they always seem swamped. Once they interview you and set you up on a schedule, the communication should get better," Akiko said.

Jed snorted a laugh. "Kiko, your optimism is inspiring."

Akiko kicked him under the table. He flinched but kept laughing.

Olivia was somewhat shocked to feel her face crack into a grin. She'd known these two for twenty-four hours, but she already felt more at ease with them than she did with friends she'd known for years. Common experiences certainly helped.

She looked past them as Akiko demolished the pasta. Olivia's eyes traveled to the desk where Ziya sat at her computer.

What are her hours? She's always there.

At the moment, Ziya was in what looked like a serious conversation with Dr. Cordova. Olivia blushed when the doctor threw a quick glance in her direction. But the woman's eyes kept on moving, as if there was no one there to see. A few seconds later, the doctor walked away, and Olivia wondered if this was what it felt like to not exist at all.

CHAPTER 7

RACING THOUGHTS MADE no room for sleep. What would the chip in her brain look like if it were outside of her head—if she were to hold it in her hand as someone must have done before they inserted it into her brain? How exactly had they put it in there? Olivia used her fingertips to search the skin of her scalp around her entire head, but felt no scars.

She'd always thought of brain surgery as precarious at best. The science behind it was baffling. And when she tried to move on from that, her mind focused on the question of how much longer her implant would last before it gave out altogether.

Olivia stumbled down to the lobby the next morning, needing the lifeblood that was coffee. Would every morning be like this? She headed straight toward the café, spotting Jed and Akiko sitting at a table; two empty plates were evidence that they'd already eaten. Jed was on his laptop and Akiko was lost in a book, her head leaning to rest on her right palm as she poured over the words.

A huge yawn escaped Olivia as she turned toward the café's menu, hung up high on the wall above the ordering station. She closed her eyes for a moment, then jumped when they opened again. A man in his late sixties was sitting at one of the closest tables, watching her with worried eyes. She hadn't seen those eyes, that face, in so long, she couldn't be sure it was really him. Surprise, sadness, and anger flowed through her. Then embarrassment replaced those, and Olivia felt her cheeks get red. She stared back at the man, her shock making it impossible to look away.

Her mind whirled, her eyes seeking the comfort of her new friends. They'd both spotted her and must have seen the strain on her face, because confusion shadowed theirs.

"Olivia," Edward Murphy said in a quiet voice, standing from his seat.

"Dad." She couldn't help but frown at him. When was the last time this man had reached out to her in any way? She couldn't be sure. He'd simply dropped out of her life. And yet, here he was. "What are you doing here?"

He didn't hide his hurt expression, but it was difficult for Olivia to have any kind of sympathy for him. He was an empty hole in the decades of her life.

"They called me—told me you were here." He motioned in the general direction of Ziya's desk. Then he sat back down, like all his energy had been drained.

"Why would they call you and how was it so easy to do? I don't even have your number," Olivia said, then cleared her throat, trying to regain her composure. "And just like that, you're here? Nothing in my life has ever merited that before."

"Olivia, I—There are things you don't understand." Her father looked down at his hands resting on the table. He was a real estate agent, so she figured he was good at selling things. She didn't know if she could believe the emotion in his voice.

"That wouldn't be the case if you and Mom had been honest with me, if you had mentioned any of this, if you hadn't disappeared when I was little." She forced herself to breathe. "Showing up now feels like you're trying to save face while I'm dealing with this mess."

He nodded. "I know it must be confusing and scary, living with what your mother and I did. It's been difficult for me many times over the years."

"So why didn't you ever contact me?" Olivia's heart felt like it might break out of her chest. She once again sought out Jed and Akiko, who were watching the conversation. She doubted they could hear much, because the café was filling with residents ordering their breakfasts and chatting to each other. No one knew Olivia's father or why it felt so painful that he was sitting there now, so they moved forward with their lives, while it felt like her own had frozen.

Her father sighed. "Can we talk?" He motioned out of the café, like he expected the busy lobby full of tables to be more ideal for deep conversation.

She wasn't sure how to answer. Something she remembered about Edward, even from her limited childhood memory, was that he was confident. She imagined he always got what he wanted. Turning him down might mean he wouldn't leave, or maybe he'd come back again. Olivia didn't know him, couldn't begin to know how he'd react. A tiny bit of her wanted to see what he'd have to say for himself. A big part of her just wanted to get through this awkwardness.

"Fine," she said, following him to a table next to the far wall of the lobby. Each step felt like her shoes were made of cement, anxiety squeezing behind her ribs.

They sat in silence for a few moments, Olivia gripping her hands together in her lap. Finally, Edward spoke. "You were so little when this all happened. Before it happened, you were such a ray of light to your mother and I. Always so happy."

"And I wasn't afterward?" She was surprised by the amount of venom in her voice.

He stared at her, a sad look on his face. An annoying feeling of guilt coursed through her, but she pushed it away. He didn't deserve it.

"After—After the accident, when we brought you here, I wasn't happy about any of it. I thought it was a mistake." Her father's voice was raw vulnerability.

Playing devil's advocate felt appropriate now. "But wouldn't the alternative have meant my death?"

His eyes bored into hers. She wished she could make her legs stand up and walk away, but something akin to how she felt when she first met Dr. Cordova and Mr. Adamian kept her in that seat—a bewildering force stronger than her own will.

"Olivia, you were the most important thing in my life from the day you were born. And I have to tell you," he lowered his voice, "from the day we brought you here at four years old until yesterday when they called me, my life has felt like one large mistake."

She was stunned but managed to regain her composure. "So, if bringing me here was such a mistake, why did you do it? And wasn't I still your daughter afterward? When you and Mom got divorced, why did you cut me out of your life?"

"We brought you here because your mother wanted to. I'm sorry, I don't mean to blame the whole thing on her. I know I was a grown man who could make my own choices, but your mother was very insistent. It was—difficult—to say no. And as you alluded to, we were both somewhat under the impression that it was the only way to—make you better. And to be honest, the decision made that day is a large part of what led to our divorce, which was still no fault of yours," he rushed to say.

"And afterward—Well, your mother seemed to still believe we'd done the right thing, although I swear, I'd catch moments of doubt in her eyes. But I was disgusted with what we'd done. My distaste for it grew over the following couple of years, because I felt like your life was one big lie, and I noticed ways in which it was already negatively impacting you. Your mother guarded you so fiercely that you were almost never away from her. It seemed like she thought I would try to take you from her. I guess I just found it all to be too hard, and your mother made it clear she didn't want me in your life. So, I left and after a little while, I stopped contacting you. But believe me, it was never easy. Every day has been torture. I think I eventually convinced myself that you wouldn't *want* me back in your life after missing so much of it. I told myself it was for the best to continue to stay away."

At some basic level, Olivia couldn't help but feel bad for her father if he was being honest. He'd made the decision to throw away his relationship with his only child. But it was still hard to trust that his words were genuine.

"That decision should have been left up to me," she said, trying to keep her voice even.

Edward cast his eyes downward. "I know."

Olivia paused for a beat before asking, "Do you know anything else about this place? I'm stuck here and don't have much idea of what I'm up against or what they're going to try to do to make me better. Do you know anything else that could help me? Anything about the institute in general or my procedure?"

Edward brought his eyes up to hers and shook his head. His face was full of despair. "I was told Dr. Cordova explained everything after you arrived. I don't have any other information to give you. We were told this wasn't a possibility. The implant was supposed to last your entire lifetime. I can tell you more about how we found the institute, but otherwise, I'm also in the dark. I'm so sorry."

It was jarring to see his eyes fill with tears.

"Does Mom know I'm here?" she asked.

He looked confused by the question. "I don't know. I'm guessing they called her if they called me. You haven't told her? She hasn't contacted you?"

"She and I don't have," Olivia paused, wishing she didn't have to discuss this with him, "the best relationship. It's been like that for many years now."

At this, Edward's eyes took on a new level of grief, and Olivia wanted to scream. He'd never cared before how she and her mother were getting along.

"I'm sorry, Olivia. If I could go back—"

"You'd what?" she questioned in a soft voice. "Stay? That's what you should have done. Maybe you thought the implant was wrong. Maybe you and Mom still wouldn't have worked out, but you wanting to get away from her and the choice you *both* made about *my* life, left me without a father. And it left me with a mother who holds an obvious grudge against me. You two got to make the decision that day, and there's been a storm cloud around me since then—for three decades, and I had no idea why!" Olivia wasn't sure how she managed to find the words to speak her truth, but it was a relief to set them free.

The wounded look on Edward's face grew even more severe. It was almost comical in a sick way. She still couldn't tell if he was for real. He turned to gaze out the window. "I should go. I'm sorry. I felt like I needed to be here for you, but maybe it wasn't the right thing to do. I'd like to talk to you more in the future, when you're ready." As he said this, he pushed a piece of paper across the table to her. On it was what she assumed was his phone number. It wasn't a number she'd ever seen before.

Then Edward stood up and attempted to give her a small, strained smile. She searched her memories for his father's face when it was joyful, but she couldn't find it.

He reached down to pat her hand before he turned and walked out the front door. Without a second thought, Olivia pushed back her chair, stumbling as it caught on the carpet. She grabbed the paper with her father's number and shoved it in her pocket. She marched to the reception desk and stood staring at Ziya until the woman turned to face her with a smile that faltered as she met Olivia's eyes.

Oliva brushed angry, embarrassed tears from her eyes. "It should have been my choice whether my parents were contacted. Whoever makes those decisions needs to ask first. We're all adults here."

"It's protocol for all patients, Ms. Murphy. Next of kin is always contacted after arrival," Ziya said, the empathy in her voice sounding more like pity.

Patients! Olivia grimaced at the word.

Fury was her overarching feeling now. She shouldn't *be* a patient. None of this should have ever happened. If they could have saved her without taking those memories from her—if she had known what happened all along, that would be different. Of course, Akiko's parents had at least explained everything to her, so maybe Olivia should be angrier at her parents than at the institute. But for now, she just wanted to be angry at someone in her proximity—someone whose emotions were reachable.

"Your protocols need to be changed. We're full-grown, damaged adults who had no say in the unethical decisions made in our lives when we were younger. We should be able to make our own decisions now!" She was seething, and although she was referring to herself as an adult, she wanted to throw a tantrum like a child. This was all so wrong!

"Liv." Jed's voice came from her right. She felt a hand gently touch her shoulder from the left.

She whirled to find Akiko standing there, Jed not far behind. It was Akiko's hand trying to comfort her, or maybe to stop her from losing it on Ziya. The younger woman's eyes were determined, even if the gesture was soft. It was clear Akiko wanted Olivia to stop talking. Olivia took a breath, attempting to calm her slamming heart.

"I am sorry your father's visit made you so uncomfortable, Ms. Murphy." Another voice came from the direction of Ziya's desk. Olivia was surprised to see Dr. Cordova when she turned back around. "We've found offering patients the option of talking to their families has brought comfort and more understanding in most cases."

At this point, Jed made what seemed to be a well-timed cough. Olivia glanced at him out of the corner of her eye and saw Akiko was glaring at him.

Dr. Cordova seemed oblivious and continued, "But we know not all families have positive relationships, so I do apologize. We also attempted to contact your mother, but we haven't heard back yet."

Olivia's cheeks flamed. The comment was a slap in the face, like the doctor had mentioned it just to be cruel. Olivia wanted to both lunge at her and shrink away.

Ziya was still behind her desk, watching the exchange, but silent in her deferment to Dr. Cordova.

Olivia felt like she could take on the world with her renewed rage. She looked Dr. Cordova directly in the eye. "I think you should check with *patients* from now on." She felt the close presence of

Akiko and Jed, taking a deep breath to signal to them that she wasn't going to bite the doctor's head off—no matter how much she wanted to. "As you said, we don't all have positive relationships with our families. With the toll the implants have taken on our lives, without us even knowing it, I'm sure this is painful for many people. And I'm sure many of us might not be able to deal with *more* trauma mere days after arriving here."

"I agree," Jed chimed in. "My mother and I have a good relationship overall, but our reunion was anything but pleasant. She felt horrible and I was angry. I would've at least liked to have known she was coming so that I could have been prepared—as much as it's possible to be prepared for that kind of conversation."

Olivia nodded, keeping her eyes on Dr. Cordova, but feeling grateful for Jed's support.

Dr. Cordova assessed them for a second. A trained, professional smile settled on her lips as her gaze fell on Jed. "We'll certainly take that into consideration. I'm sorry you both had unpleasant experiences." Then she turned to face Olivia. "Ms. Murphy, I'd like to see you this afternoon to talk more about your symptoms and set up a treatment schedule. I plan to give you your next treatment at that meeting. Three o'clock?"

"Sure," Olivia said through clenched teeth. The doctor seemed to have barely acknowledged their pleas, instead providing a reminder that the institute was absolute in its power to keep them alive. How many times had Dr. Cordova and her team pushed aside the worries of other residents?

"Excellent. I'll meet you here in the lobby." Dr. Cordova was gone as quickly as she'd arrived. Ziya gave them all a nod, her eyes flicking to Olivia's and holding there for a moment, then got back to work. Something about the look was odd, but Olivia didn't have time to think about it before Jed started talking.

"I told them how uncomfortable that meeting with my mom was right after it happened," he grumbled as they turned away from the reception desk, motioning toward the institute's front doors.

Getting out of the institute for a while sounded like the best option. Olivia's stomach reminded her that she hadn't eaten yet, but with adrenaline and all the feelings from talking to her father still rushing through her, she'd have to forgo coffee.

"You two need to take it easy. I don't think extra attention from Cordova is a good thing. She's the last one we can trust at the cachot," Akiko hissed after they'd left the building and walked a couple blocks.

"Now you have two of us to watch over," Jed responded with a grin.

"It's clear they know how this is affecting us. Adding estranged family members into the mix is cruel. Are they trying to be cruel?" Olivia asked.

"Possibly, as another power play," Akiko answered. "After eight months, it would have been easy for them to adjust their procedures if they wanted to."

"Where's the chief engineer I met with Cordova—Mr. Adamian? What does he say about all of this? Is he not involved in any of the day-to-day operations?" Olivia questioned.

"You won't see much of him," Jed said. "His job is either too demanding to have time for the residents, or he doesn't care, or he's not who he says he is. There's a team of engineers that works in the building, but you'll see the medical staff more."

Olivia sighed; so many questions without answers. They walked for a few more blocks and Olivia asked another question that had been weighing on her mind. "They're keeping us alive though, right? You indicated everyone is still alive."

"Everyone is still alive," Jed confirmed. "But we don't know how close anyone's implants are to shutting down."

He put his hands up in defense when Akiko shot him a glare. "They'll keep us alive," she said. "If they let us die, there will be reports and investigations, at least by families, if not by law enforcement. We *need* to figure out what we're missing. If I could just find her office. It's not in the clinic or the emergency room."

Olivia felt her face go white. She knew Akiko was referencing Dr. Cordova. "You don't want us to draw too much attention, but you're planning on breaking into her office?"

"She shouldn't be," Jed growled. This time he was the one glaring, his eyes firm on the side of Akiko's face. She refused to look at him.

Akiko sighed. "I've been looking for it for almost half a year now. We need to find the documentation the original staff left behind. Her office seems like a logical place to keep things, or maybe there's a database of information only she and Adamian have access to. I've been up to the twelfth floor, where both medical and engineering have their administrative offices, but I couldn't find an office that appeared to belong to Cordova or Adamian. The computers and filing cabinets in the open office spaces were all locked, and I didn't have time to even attempt to figure out any codes."

Olivia's mouth hung up. "When did you do that? How'd you get around without someone seeing you? They don't have any kind of security system?"

Jed muttered under his breath, clearly pissed.

"They *do* have a security system, so be aware of that. And I'm not telling you when or how," Akiko answered. "If I ever get caught, I don't want you to be incriminated too. I told Jed the same thing. I may not get another chance anyway. Usually there's at least a skeleton staff up there at all times, but everyone was at some big meeting.

"I've developed good relationships with some of the medical staff. I think a lot of them are uncomfortable with whatever is going on, but of course, they won't talk about it. For months now, I've been discreetly putting it out there that I'm looking for information. I just need someone to bite. Anything they could tell me would help."

"Wow, I don't know why, but I never would have pegged you for the spy." Olivia said in awe and fear, clocking Jed's grimace.

"Most people wouldn't; that's why I'm perfect for it," Akiko smiled as they stepped into a diner that looked like its décor hadn't been updated since the 1960s.

"It doesn't look like much, but you'll love this place," Jed said, clearly trying to change the subject.

"I'm fully aware of the danger, and I know Jed doesn't like it, but we need answers—any kind of answers," Akiko continued after the host had seated them. "Unless you two ruin my chances before that happens," she chastised with a joking tone.

Olivia watched as Akiko studied Jed, saw the exact moment when her eyes settled on his scowl. The young woman reached across the table to cover his hand with her own. "You know how much this place has taken from me and why I need to do this."

Jed was shaking his head, but then his eyes rose from the table to meet Akiko's and he sighed in resignation.

"We're here if you ever want to talk about your parents, by the way," Akiko turned back to Olivia. "We want to support you however we can."

"Thanks." But she had no interest in rehashing the conversation with Edward. Thinking about him reminded her of something he'd said: *And to be honest, the decision made that day is a large part of what led to our divorce…*

As the words twirled and spun on top of themselves in her mind, a deep throbbing began in the back of Olivia's head. She squinted her eyes closed against the sudden, horrific pain. When she opened them again, she was met with the sight she'd expected, but was afraid to see: Jed, Akiko, the buildings outside the diner windows, the street, the cars, were all soaked in red. Crimson covered everything, as if they lived in a child's haphazard paint-by-numbers creation.

"Damn it," she mumbled, cringing against the pounding in her head. She was surrounded by blood—drowning in it. She closed her eyes again.

Olivia felt Akiko's hand grab onto one of the fists she had clenched on the table. How was this happening in a restaurant again? Why did it almost feel—planned?

"They need to get her on a treatment schedule," Jed muttered, anger ringing clear in his voice.

"Cordova said this afternoon. Then things should get better," Akiko's soothing voice answered as she squeezed Olivia's hand. "We're here for you, Olivia. Just breathe. It'll be over soon."

CHAPTER 8

THE INTERVIEW WITH Dr. Cordova hadn't been at all what Olivia expected. As she woke up the next morning, feeling no motivation to get out of bed, she thought back on the two and a half hours she'd spent in the institute's clinic the previous afternoon.

Although Dr. Cordova met Olivia in the lobby and brought her up to the fourth floor, the doctor's medical team then took over, running a battery of tests and conducting the most thorough exam of Olivia's life. After a little over an hour, a nurse led her to a small office down one of the clinic's pristine hallways, where the doctor was waiting. After the incident following her father's visit, she had expected Dr. Cordova to be somewhat more guarded or cold, but instead the woman had been engrossed in what Olivia had to say.

"So, everything turns red? Not just certain things or people? And the color covers whole surfaces? Not just in drips, but completely covers? Do you hear any sounds?"

Olivia had focused on her breathing and answered the doctor's questions, but a heaviness had settled over her mind. She'd felt like she was regurgitating much of the same information over and over again. And just like when a word is repeated too many times, it seems to lose its meaning, Olivia's experiences had begun to feel faded and false.

"Based on the frequency and severity of your symptoms, you'll be receiving treatments every three days after this one. The evening seems to be the best time for most people, so we'll do that with you as well, unless a change becomes necessary. If that frequency isn't enough, we can increase to every two days," Dr. Cordova had said as she'd administered Olivia's injection.

Olivia had flinched at the unnerving warmth spreading from the injection site up to her head. "Every three days already seems like a lot."

Dr. Cordova had disposed of the needle with a shake of her head. "Most residents are on a schedule of every day or every other day, because their implants are already in worse shape than yours."

"Are you close to finding a solution? I think you and Mr. Adamian said there are some promising leads?"

Dr. Cordova had studied Olivia with a smile that was just slightly off. "Yes, there are. Every day we get closer, but testing is difficult, because we have to use computer simulations. At some point, hopefully soon, we'll feel confident enough to test on willing residents. We're doing the best we can, Ms. Murphy. We want all of you to get back to your lives as soon as possible."

I hope so, Olivia had thought to herself as she tried to gauge the sincerity in the doctor's eyes.

Olivia sighed as she came back to the present, stretching in her glorious bed. She'd never had sheets like these. She didn't understand thread count and had never pined after a specific number, but this number, whatever it was, was luxurious. So many things about the institute were too good to be true. She wondered if she'd ever find out how everything was paid for.

She made her way downstairs much later than she normally would, but it didn't matter. What was the point of keeping to a daily schedule? Time felt frozen in this monstrous place. She doubted she would ever have a surprise meeting with her mother in the lobby, so, besides discovering new-to-her things in San Francisco, what change would the days bring?

Olivia got in line, the end of which was stretching into the lobby, to order breakfast at the café. Many of her fellow residents must have also had late mornings, but she didn't see Jed or Akiko at any of the surrounding tables.

"You're Olivia, right?" A male voice made her jump.

She turned around to look at the man behind her. He was just under six feet tall with graying black hair, eyes that were a golden brown, and tan skin. His tight shirt made it evident that he was also in very good shape. He gave her a smile, but something in his expression made her uneasy. He was probably around her age or maybe a little older. He had several scars on his face, like fingernails had scratched deeply down his skin. He looked familiar. She must have already seen him around the lobby.

"Yes, and you're—"

"Samuel Murillo, but everyone calls me Sam." He stuck out his hand and she shook it. "I was in the lobby yesterday when your father visited."

"Oh." She wasn't sure how to respond to this comment.

"This place is insane, right?" he said without pause. His voice was instantly angry and a little loud.

"Um, yeah, it's been interesting," she said quickly, trying to turn away and end the conversation. While she didn't disagree with Sam, it seemed no one had told him it was better to be discreet about complaints against the institute while in the building. But the way he carried himself made it clear Sam was a very confident man, so maybe he didn't care about discretion.

"That's an understatement." Sam laughed and then frowned as he looked ahead at their slow-moving line. "Can you believe how long it's taking them to figure this thing out? They put these fucking chips in our brains and now they don't know how to keep them from shutting down? It doesn't make sense. I think they're hiding something from us."

That's a common thought, Olivia said to herself.

Sam motioned around the lobby. "And where did they get all this fucking money? A failed project brings in this kind of revenue? I've been here for two months and have been asking to see their financial reports at least once a week, but they ignore me. I used to be a financial advisor in Manhattan."

Olivia nodded, but she wished Sam would shut up. And why was he saying all this to her? He didn't know the first thing about her. Why would he trust her with his opinions? But then she realized, he was trusting most of the lobby with his opinions because of how loud he was. Olivia threw a look at Ziya, but the woman seemed to be busy at her computer. None of the other staff members were around. The residents closest to Sam were either staring at him with annoyed expressions or trying very hard not to acknowledge him at all. Olivia clearly wasn't the first victim of Sam's unregulated volume.

"I already told Cordova I'm going to sue this place for all it's worth for ruining my life. She promised me they were working as hard as they could to find a solution. That was back when I got here. Can you believe our families let these idiots touch our brains? I mean, I guess it was the original group of idiots, but it's not like this group is any better." He was gesturing wildly now, and his face was beet red.

Olivia found herself wondering if, despite how fit this man appeared to be, he was going to give himself a heart attack. Guilt quickly crept in at that thought. She understood his feelings, but she just couldn't attract the kind of attention that talking to Sam would bring.

"You know, I think I'm going to get breakfast somewhere else. Nice to meet you," Olivia said, motioning toward the line as she left it. She still didn't see Jed or Akiko, so she headed back to the elevator. *Why did I think coming downstairs was a good idea?*

"Don't blame you. This is fucking nuts," she heard Sam grumble as she walked away.

When Olivia passed the front desk, her eyes wandered to Ziya's face. She was surprised to find Ziya looking back at her, her usual smile gone. Olivia shivered and looked away.

1 0 1 1 0

The rest of the day in her suite was peaceful and full of small joys, making it almost possible to forget the computer chip in her brain. She ate, napped, read for hours, took a bath, and fell asleep on the couch. When she opened her eyes, the clock on the wall read 11:23 p.m. Her stomach lurched at her lack of dinner. Olivia knew the café was open all day, with a more limited menu at night. Akiko had explained the reason for this was the insomnia several of the residents experienced as part of their symptoms, resulting in irregular sleep schedules and the need for food at all hours.

Silence cocooned her as she left her room. The elevator was an eerie, reflective box as she made her descent. The doors opened on an empty lobby, save for a lone figure tapping away on his laptop at a table near the windows. Olivia wandered over.

"Hey," she mumbled, stretching as she yawned. Then she recognized the soft music coming from his computer. "Are you listening to the Eagles?"

Jed smiled up at her. "They're a good band. Despite the barrage of references I've heard about their drummer, I like their music."

"You promise you'd tell me if you're a cousin of his, right? I've never met a rock star before." She tried to keep her voice as serious as possible.

He laughed, leaning back in his chair and crossing his arms over his chest. "Do you like all music from the 1970s, or are they a particular favorite of yours?"

She shrugged. "I've always thought I should've been born maybe twenty years before I was. The '70s and '80s were the best two musical decades in history. I wish I could have enjoyed all of it when it was new."

"I don't know about the '80s, but I'll agree about the '70s," he said, still smiling. "It would've been pretty cool to see all those artists tour."

"To each his own, and yes, exactly," she said, a grin making its way onto her face. She was enjoying the banter, but her stomach chose that moment to emit a loud grumble.

"You should take care of that." Jed motioned toward the café. "Did you eat today? We didn't see you this morning."

"I came down a little late," she answered, not sure if she should mention her conversation with Sam. "Working?" She tilted her chin toward his laptop.

"Yeah; sometimes I get my best work done late at night. Go get some food." He shooed her away with his hands. "I'll still be down here for a while if you want some company."

She felt lucky to find macaroni and cheese and garlic bread on the menu. Not healthy by any means, but one of her favorite comfort meals. She ordered extra garlic bread in case Jed wanted any.

He gave her a grateful smile when she offered it to him and shut his laptop as she ate.

"What'd you guys do today?" Olivia tried her best not to shovel the food into her mouth. She hadn't been this hungry since she got to the institute.

"Saw two movies and went over to Rodeo Beach. Akiko wanted to sit by the water. How about you?"

"Not much. I was in my room for most of the time." Olivia hesitated, but decided it might be good to get Jed's opinion on Sam. She lowered her voice. "I had a one-sided conversation with Sam Murillo this morning. He was being a little too—vocal about his distaste for this place."

Jed's frown began as soon as she mentioned Sam's name. "I'd try to stay away from Sam. He's made several threats against Cordova. He's a bully in general—making demands and assumptions without letting the person he's talking to respond. I don't think he cares about how his actions could affect everyone else living here."

Olivia nodded. "Yeah, I tried not to engage him, but he mentioned that he was down here when my father visited, so he must be keeping an eye on things."

"He's always listening," Jed confirmed. "He's always looking for some kind of angle, something he can bring up as leverage in the future if he needs to."

Olivia would remember to steer clear of the man in the future.

After a few minutes, Jed broke the silence that had settled between them. "Didn't you say you dream about the ocean sometimes? Or have visions involving it?"

Olivia met his eyes, confused by the change in topic.

He sat forward, leaning toward her now. "I had a dream about the ocean last night. I was standing on the hot sand, looking out at the water. It felt so calm and—right. I saw Akiko down the beach a ways, and then I turned and saw—"

Before he could finish his description, they heard shouts over what sounded like a walkie talkie. Ziya came running out of the tiny office set into the wall behind her work station. She flew around the desk and headed for the elevator bank.

Seriously, does the woman ever sleep? Olivia wondered. *Or is that where she sleeps?*

Jed shoved back from the table, his chair falling to the ground with a heavy thud.

"Come on," he said in a commanding voice and pulled Olivia up with him. She was still trying to process the sudden movement as they charged into the elevator before the doors closed. Ziya was already inside.

"What's going on?" Olivia asked, but Ziya kept her eyes on the elevator door and said nothing.

Ziya stayed silent as the floors ticked by, her eyes blinking like she couldn't get them to focus. As Olivia studied the woman, she realized she was still holding Jed's hand. She dropped it, but he didn't seem to notice. He was also staring at Ziya. And was he shaking?

When the elevator stopped on the eighth floor, which was only residential suites, Ziya ran as if the ground beneath her feet was on fire. Her heels made muted thumps on the carpet as she disappeared down the hallway. Several residents had come out of their rooms and watched after her retreating form. Most were in their pajamas and murmured to each other in hushed voices.

"What's going on?" Jed demanded of the first group they came upon.

The man who answered looked to be in his twenties and wasn't familiar to Olivia. Would she ever meet all of her fellow residents? "It's Sam," he said. "They've been in his room for a few minutes. I could hear Dr. Cordova shouting all kinds of orders, but it's quiet now. I think he might be dead."

CHAPTER 9

JED AND AKIKO were stone-faced the next morning, and their utter lack of words was chilling.

"Now someone has died," Olivia said in a whisper.

Jed nodded. Akiko closed her eyes, her breaths uneven.

Olivia fought tears as red filtered into her vision. No headache this time, just a faint red tinge to the world around her.

Not long after Olivia and Jed had arrived in the eighth-floor hallway, Dr. Cordova had emerged from Sam's room. Her demeanor reflected exhaustion and defeat. She hadn't said anything about Sam, but they all knew.

Per the doctor's request that they all return to their rooms, Jed had taken Olivia back to hers without saying another word.

Olivia had tried to find sleep for several hours without success.

Now, the three friends sat silently at one of their usual spots in the lobby. Every other table around them was filled with residents and a few staff members. There weren't many words. Fear and confusion hung in the air. Dr. Cordova appeared, her eyes red.

She's been crying. Olivia hated how surprised she was by the doctor's very human reaction.

"Hi, everyone," Dr. Cordova's voice cracked as she addressed the room. "I'll be sending a message to all rooms, but wanted to address those of you who were down here. We'll be meeting in the large conference room on the second floor to talk about—about Sam. Let's meet at one o'clock. See you then."

In that moment, Olivia felt the splintering of the fragile dream of her life returning to normal.

Sam had died within these walls.

Maybe he'd had health issues. His glowering red face ranting about the institute floated through her mind. Maybe there was a chance it hadn't been his dying implant. But maybe it had been something much worse.

"He was just going off about that place," Olivia murmured to her friends as they walked to an early lunch. "Cordova didn't say how he died. You don't think they—" She cut herself off, not able to finish her thought because of how disturbing it was.

Jed didn't respond. His hands were jammed in his pockets. His eyes were dark.

"It seems a little obvious for the cachot to target Sam. Anyone who came into contact with him got an earful." Akiko stared straight ahead. "It could be that his was just the first implant to shut down."

"My implant is older than his," Jed muttered.

"Maybe that doesn't matter. They've never said—"

"Why are you bullshitting for them, Kiko?" Jed sent a glare her way.

Akiko frowned back at him. "I recognize they're keeping things from us, but like I said before, it doesn't make sense for them to kill us. Suspected murders would only create more of a mess for them. It's the only belief I have left, Jed. It's what keeps me from unraveling," she growled in Jed's direction.

The two friends were silent after that, and Olivia's anxiety was going through the roof. Her vision was still red. It was probably unhealthy to be so codependent after feeling alone for so much of her life, but the unit of Jed and Akiko was her lifeline now. She had to keep that unit stable. "Can we just wait to see what Cordova says this afternoon? I'm sure she'll have information for us. We don't know anything right now."

Akiko sighed and nodded before turning her head to look at Jed. He kept his gaze on the ground for a few more seconds, but then looked up and met her eyes. "Yeah, sorry." He took a deep breath before continuing, "But no matter what Cordova says, I think this is a sign. We need to work harder on figuring out what's really going on at the cachot. Sam went there thinking he'd get out someday and live his life again. No matter what killed him, we can't let that happen to anyone else. It feels like we have all the time in the world when we're in that building, even with the countdowns in our brains, but we don't."

Here he turned to Olivia. "We haven't shared this with you yet because it didn't get us anywhere, but on top of Kiko's clandestine adventures, I've already pulled a lot of historical information from city records: planning and occupancy documents, permits from when the cachot wanted to make changes to the building. It's all there, and it took me months to sift through everything in between my writing and editing jobs.

"Everything looks appropriate, although the truth has been stretched in certain cases. For example, our suites are called 'recovery rooms.' Nothing seems to be missing from the documents, except for a detailed account of what's going on at the cachot. The stated business mission and description is vague: an organization assisting in the recovery of patients suffering from brain damage, with a focus on memory care," Jed continued. "But there's no record of any city official asking the cachot to expound on that. I need to look harder, see if I can talk to any current city employees this time."

"When I first arrived, you told me the cachot is licensed by the Department of Public Health. I know we may not want to file a complaint for fear of getting the cachot shut down before we have a solution for our implants, but we can see what information that department has," Olivia suggested.

"We tried that." Akiko shook her head. "It's the same vague stuff the city has."

"And no one from the department has questioned that?"

"Not that we know of, Liv," Jed responded. "And I'm going to hazard a guess that someone is paying these government groups not to care."

Considering all the things that could shock Olivia about the institute, she wasn't sure why financial bribery was such a big one.

"I'm going to push a little harder to get something out of the staff," Akiko said

"Just be careful," Jed grumbled.

Olivia made a reluctant decision, hoping for a way to help. "I'm going to call my mom, and if I can't reach her, I'm going to call her husband. I don't want to call her, but I also don't want to talk to my dad again. I lived with just my mom for the majority of my childhood. She has to have something to say about this. And maybe since she was the driving factor in me having the surgery, she'll know more than my dad."

Akiko nodded, sadness in her eyes. Olivia turned her face toward Jed, but he was staring straight ahead again. Surely Sam's death had impacted everyone in the institute, but it seemed to have broken something in Jed.

The second floor of the institute housed the gym and large conference room, which was more like a small presentation hall, with plenty of tiered seats for all residents and staff members. As Olivia sat down, she was reminded of just how many people lived and worked in this ridiculous building, although she didn't know most of them. Nearly every chair was filled, and the occupants' faces held a mix of emotions ranging from fear and confusion to anger and sadness. The hushed tones of many different conversations flitted around the space, but like the flame of a candle being snuffed, they all stopped when Dr. Cordova entered the room.

She stood like a professor waiting to begin her lecture. A couple members of the medical team sat down in chairs behind her, but the chief engineer was nowhere to be seen.

"Where's Adamian? Isn't this something he should attend?" Olivia whispered to Akiko, who didn't look surprised.

"First, I wanted to let you know that Mr. Adamian wishes he could be here, but he's making himself available to Sam's family today. He's been on the phone with them off and on for hours," Dr. Cordova said as if she'd heard the question.

Olivia sank into her chair a little more.

Dr. Cordova took a shaky breath and looked to be fighting tears. "I know this is startling and confusing. Obviously, we didn't expect it. We have received permission from Sam's family to communicate his cause of death. For those of you wondering, his implant had not shut down."

There were some gasps and murmurs at this.

"He had a heart attack, and while my team and I tried diligently, we were not able to save him. We believe his symptoms in combination with his blood pressure, which was much higher than I like to see in someone his age, brought on the heart attack years sooner than it should have happened. If Sam's symptoms were severe enough to require more frequent treatments, he did not make us aware of that. He was on medication for his blood pressure, but we know so little about how implant symptoms impact other medical conditions, so the medication may not have been working as well as we thought. He was days away from receiving a regular exam." She looked down at the floor for a few seconds before returning her focus to the residents.

"I want to ask that all of you please keep us up to date on how you're feeling. If your symptoms are changing or becoming overwhelming, please let us know so we can adjust your treatments accordingly. If your preexisting medical conditions are flaring in ways that haven't been common for you in the past, please tell us. We will also be increasing regular exams for those who do have known medical conditions. You are here to be as safe and healthy as possible while we figure out a solution. And if anyone needs to talk to someone about Sam," she faltered, "or anything else you're feeling, we'll have counselors available."

She was silent again as she surveyed the room, trying to make eye contact with a majority of the residents. Her staff seemed to shift in discomfort behind her. The room was so quiet, Olivia could hear several of the people around her breathing.

Akiko was watching the doctor calmly. Jed was still, but his eyes were troubled. Olivia reached over and placed her hand on his arm, afraid he was going to fly out of his seat and demand Dr. Cordova explain what the hell had really happened to Sam.

"Please, please know we are doing everything we can to find a solution. We're running scans and data every day. Our engineers are creating and testing new chips around the clock, working to find replacements for the original ones placed in your brains. Sam's death was a horrible tragedy and we're determined to do everything we can to not let it happen again. We are going to give you your lives back."

Jed's hand curled into a fist on his leg. Olivia knew he'd been living through eight months of the same rhetoric, but she desperately hoped he wouldn't speak up.

"You've already decimated our lives!" A slim, brown-haired woman who was probably around Jed's age stood up in a rush. Her face was unfamiliar, like so many of those around Olivia. "You've completely ruined our chances of ever living them again!"

A redheaded woman in the next chair over grabbed the speaker's arm and pulled, urging her to sit back down, a frightened look on her face. Her companion glanced down at her, instant doubt clouding her features.

"Jillian, please. You know you can share your feelings here, especially in this time of grief." Dr. Cordova motioned for the brunette to keep going.

The redhead, who was still sitting, cringed as Jillian took a deep breath and did just that.

"Who's been here the longest?" Jillian's hands were wild as they waved around the room. "Jed, maybe?"

Jed said nothing, but Olivia sensed the tension rolling off him in waves. She moved her head to see Akiko's reaction. Akiko seemed far more relaxed, but her eyes were dark and never moved from Dr. Cordova. No one confirmed or denied the comment about Jed's tenure.

"Well, I've been here almost as long," Jillian continued. "More than half a year of my life gone. And what have you done to help any of us? Given us a band-aid treatment to keep our symptoms in check—to mask them. But really, do you have any idea how to solve this? How to help us stay alive?

"Many of us don't have lives left to speak of. And that didn't start with the beginning of our symptoms, or with us coming to the institute for the second time. It started the day your company put those fucking computer chips in our brains!

"I'm sure if you asked, if you demonstrated that you cared, most of us would give you accounts of just how shitty our lives were before coming here—how disconnected we felt from our families and whatever friends we managed to have. How many failed relationships we had, how awkward and unfulfilled we felt, how there always seemed to be some basic element of typical human makeup missing from us—something no doctor or therapist could help us understand. Is that what you want us to return to? How do you expect us to bounce back from the trainwrecks you've already made of us?"

Olivia had been watching Jillian but took the silence that followed her words to once again look over at Akiko. She was surprised to see tears in her friend's eyes. Olivia felt another rush of curiosity. What had Akiko been through?

Jillian's companion had managed to pull her back down into her seat, but Jillian looked like she'd still like to spit in the doctor's face.

Dr. Cordova's eyes were sad and tired. "If I could go back and change the past, I would. You know I wasn't here when the implants were placed, but once I started working here, if I could have known what would happen, I would have contacted all of you. My team and I would have worked with the engineering side to try to fix your implants before they began shutting down. If I had been here in the beginning, I would have tried to help ensure a better product was used in the first place, one that had the testing it required."

Now the doctor turned her emotional eyes back to the brunette. "Jillian, I do know about the negative experiences many of you have had throughout your lives. I listened to as much as you were all willing to share with me. But I truly believe that when we find a solution for this, you will all see and feel positive changes in yourselves—have futures full of purpose. It will be much better than before. We will all accomplish that together."

"Except for Sam," Jillian muttered, but Dr. Cordova didn't seem to hear her.

"For now, we'll keep you updated as much as possible. Sam's family will be coming for his body so they can hold his memorial service, but we're going to hold our own memorial here, which we'll also keep you apprised of. As I said before, please let us know if your symptoms or other medical conditions need additional attention. I know this whole situation is unnerving, but please don't be afraid to talk to us. It could save your life."

She gave the room a weak smile and then exited, followed by her team. The residents took their time standing up. Some of them seemed stunned and didn't speak, but many of them were murmuring again.

Jillian's voice cut through the room. "This is bullshit. I need some air, Mikayla." She stormed out the closest door, flanked by Mikayla, the redhead, who was trying to talk to her.

"I'm going to go lie down for a while." Akiko's voice was just above a whisper as they filed out of the conference room.

Jed met her eyes for a long moment and nodded.

"I'm going to call my mom," Olivia said without giving herself much time to think about it.

"You don't have to do that now," Akiko said.

"I think I do," Olivia responded. "We don't know if that was the truth, but it's all we're getting from them for now. Maybe I can get some other answers."

There was a chill in the late afternoon air as Olivia left the institute. She'd decided to take a walk for this conversation, feeling like she needed to anonymously blend into a crowd rather than be alone in her suite. She didn't know exactly where the walk would take her, just like the phone call, but her adrenaline was making her feel like she could conquer the world. Zipping up her jacket, she pulled her phone from one of the pockets.

She selected her mother's phone number from her call log, thinking back to the day she'd tried to tell Beth about her dream. That was before the institute and any knowledge about what was going on in her brain. It felt like years had gone by, but it hadn't even been a week.

There was no answer, and her call went to voicemail. She hung up without leaving a message and dialed her stepfather.

Unlike her mother, he answered right away. "Olivia, this is a surprise. How are you?"

It's not a surprise. You've talked to her. Has she heard from the institute? She must have, so you must have been expecting me to call, because you knew she wouldn't answer when she saw my number on her phone.

Will was a very intelligent man. He knew what was going on. But none of this was his fault, so Olivia kept her anger in check.

"I've been better. Can I speak to her please?"

He sighed, the sound full of hesitation. "Yes, just a minute."

Several minutes ticked by. Olivia wondered if her mother was just waiting for her to hang up. Then she heard Beth's firm voice come on the line. "Hello, Olivia."

Olivia knew she would have to get straight to the point. "Mom, I need to talk to you about my implant."

Beth was silent, but the call didn't end.

"I know they called you, because they called Dad, and he paid me a surprise visit."

"Did he?" her mother said, a note of curiosity in her voice.

"Yes. He said that while you both agreed I should get the implant to save my brain after the accident, you were the one pushing for it."

Silence again.

"But now my implant is shutting down, as I'm sure they told you. I have some friends at the institute, and their implants are shutting down too. We're all having horrible physical symptoms as a result, Mom. Painful, scary symptoms." Olivia sped forward in case her mother tried to interrupt her.

But there was no real interruption—just a simple clearing of her mother's throat.

"And now someone has died. A man died because his symptoms aggravated a previous medical condition. He was young—way too young to die. So, I'm just looking for answers. Anything you can tell me that might shed some light, maybe help us move one step closer to a solution. No one from the current medical or engineering team was here when the implants were placed, and they haven't explained why. Maybe—maybe there's something you've been told not to tell me. Mom, please, is there anything else I should know?"

The silence went on and on, but Olivia knew Beth was there, so she waited. Finally, there were words from the other end of the line. "I'm sorry to hear about the man who passed away," her mother said, real compassion in her voice. But that was gone with the very next sentence. "There is a reason I didn't call or come see you after the institute notified me you had arrived. The day you received your implant, and the days that followed, were a very—painful part of my life. You were young, so there was no way for you to understand and now—well, now there is nothing that can be done about that. I can't fix your implant, Olivia, and I don't have any other information that would be helpful."

Olivia felt like her heart was being crushed, both from anxiety and the immense grief of knowing that she was losing any kind of future relationship she might have had with her mother. There would be no going back from this conversation.

And with this knowledge, Olivia couldn't keep the anger from her voice as she spoke her truth. "A painful time in *your* life? Yes, I'm sure it must have been hard almost losing your only child in a horrible car accident. Then after my implant, your marital issues got worse, or maybe they were already bad before that. But *I* was the one in the car accident, the one who had a computer chip installed in my brain when I didn't have the capacity or ability to understand what was going on. And the way it altered my life from that day forward—"

"You can't blame your attitude about life or your personal choices on something that saved you when you would have otherwise died," her mother said. "You're an adult, and you've made your own decisions."

Olivia sputtered. "It isn't just me! The implants have affected everyone here! Most of us have had trouble making lasting relationships of any kind, of feeling connected to anything, and we had no idea why before we returned to the institute! Did they explain any of that to you when you brought me in? Did they mention the negative impacts this technology might have?"

"I'm sure they gave us the appropriate information, Olivia. That was over thirty years ago."

"How can you be so casual about this?" Olivia asked, then bit her lip to keep from screaming in frustration. The sounds of city life were loud around her, but she still lowered her voice so her plea would be harder to hear. "I'm dying, Mom. I didn't die when I was four, but I am now. All the residents at the institute are. We don't know when our implants will shut down, or if there will be a solution before that happens!"

Beth said nothing. Disgust coursed through Olivia's veins.

"Okay, we don't have to talk about this again, but even the most basic information might help. Is there anything else you can tell me about the accident or the research you did to find the institute? Any of the questions you and Dad asked, or the answers they gave you? Are there any documents you could send me? Medical records? A doctor's summary of the surgery? The names of the staff who used to work here?"

"It was decades ago," Beth said. "Unfortunately, many things got lost when your father and I divorced and we moved out of that house." Then she paused as if listening to someone. "Olivia, I have to go. I'm sure the institute staff will find a solution and all this worry will have been for nothing."

"But how was all the documentation lost? Wouldn't you have kept it in a safe place?" Olivia asked in disbelief.

But Beth had already hung up.

CHAPTER 10

THE WORLD WAS shrouded in fog. The institute's residents walked around like zombies in the days that followed Sam's death. Olivia tried to stay busy so the anger inside her wouldn't eat her alive.

When she'd told Jed and Akiko about her conversation with her mother, their jaws had dropped. Olivia asked whether they had any documentation from their families. They did not. Their families had given excuses for the missing records, just like Beth.

Now, a couple days later, the three friends sat in a small coffee shop in Sausalito, staring into their empty cups. It was the first time since she'd arrived that Olivia had crossed back over the Golden Gate Bridge to leave San Francisco, but they were still only about nine and a half miles away from the institute.

"I think my mom got rid of all the evidence from my implant surgery; she just doesn't want to say so," Jed commented. "She never thought she'd have to tell me about it."

"They're all hiding something from us," Olivia muttered. "If these surgeries saved our lives, why didn't they tell more of us about them? If the technology needed to be kept secret, I'm sure they could have trusted us to do that when we were old enough. And even Akiko's parents, who seem to have been honest with her, don't know where the paperwork is. All this missing documentation is too coincidental."

They sat in depressed silence after that. It was too much to believe that the residents' families might somehow be in cahoots with the institute.

Olivia was exhausted and emotionally drained by the time she went up to her room that night. She turned on the TV and plunked down in the recliner to watch a mindless reality show, but felt her eyes closing after a few minutes. She gave into it, the comfort of sleep wrapping its gentle arms around her.

She was standing facing the ocean. The air was heavy with mist. She could see maybe ten feet around her in every direction. The mystic sea lapped at her feet, its waves both booming and calm.

He stepped up out of the water, with a smile so bright it was almost blinding. He looked to be in his fifties. His hair was shot through with gray. Her heart soared at the sight of him. He was so familiar. She'd seen him on the ground in her nightmares, but she'd seen him bursting with life so many other times, she was sure of that.

"The Man from the Ocean," people had called him more times than she could count, although she couldn't recall who those people were.

She went to run to him, unafraid of plunging into the water. She threw her arms out, wanting to wrap them around him, breathe in his scent, as she had so many times. He'd lived far from the sea for much of his life. "Too far," he would say. He considered more than a couple miles away from the ocean to be too far. Because of this, there was forever a little grief in his soul. But somehow, he had always held a slight scent of salt mixed with sand.

She wanted to be closer to him, but she couldn't seem to move past the water line. Her feet wouldn't follow the commands her brain was giving. Panic sprung up in her. Tears welled in her eyes. She tried to cry out, but her voice was drowned by the ocean.

His smile remained, but she could see sadness in his eyes. He couldn't get to her either. Something was keeping him in the sea.

"They won't let you find me," he said across the water. His voice was quiet, but somehow still louder than the waves cascading around him. "They took me from you. They had no right. You were so brave. Now you have to fight to remember, sweet Olivia. Remember what happened. Remember who you saw. They will continue to try to keep me hidden. You have to fight to remember."

Tears were streaming down her cheeks, mixing with the dense air around her.

He was still smiling as the fog enveloped him, his hand raised in a frozen sign of goodbye.

She stood like a statue, wanting to scream, but wanting even more to remember who he was. He had been a constant in her young heart, but they had made her forget, because they were afraid. She hadn't agreed to forget him, but she had been so young. They had lied to her the day they took him away from her. She still heard his voice saying, "sweet Olivia." His voice had always been filled with joy when he called her this. This time his tone had been pleading. She had to fight to get him back.

The Man from the Ocean.

1 0 1 0 1 1 0 1 0

"Hi," she sat down hard in a chair late the next morning, her eyes latched on her phone screen. Jed and Akiko looked up from their laptop and book, respectively and typically, surprise written across their faces.

"You're alive," Jed quipped.

Akiko smacked his arm. "We were just a little worried."

"Personally, I wanted to break down your door, but Kiko said 'no.'" Jed smirked and Akiko rolled her eyes.

"That's all we ever do here, isn't it?" Olivia responded. "Worry that our symptoms will overtake us. Worry that we'll die before they figure this thing out. Worry that we will be eating the majority of our meals in this weird, dark place for decades to come with no answers. Well, I'm not letting that happen."

Olivia knew she sounded ridiculous; no one in their trio planned to let that happen. But after last night's dream, she was feeling particularly fierce. She was ready to lead an army right now, rather than just be part of one.

She scrolled like mad through a Google search, looking for any information on someone with the nickname The Man from the Ocean. She looked up her parents' names, her name, the name of the town in which she was born. There had to be something to find. But the pages of search results seemed to yield nothing, except a website for her father's real estate business, which she had never cared to look up before. She slammed her phone down on the table.

"Did you remember something?" Akiko asked, raising an eyebrow in curiosity.

"The Man from the Ocean. Does that mean anything to either of you?"

They both shook their heads.

"I think my implant erased him from my memory," she murmured, then recounted her dream from the night before. "He's the same man I've seen in previous dreams, the one bleeding on the ground. He said 'they' took him from me, so who is the 'they?' My parents? Anyway, the ocean made me think of his nickname: The Man from the Ocean. People used to call him that. But I don't remember why or who he was."

"Has the ocean played a big part in your life?" Akiko asked, leaning forward.

Jed did the opposite, settling back into the padded wooden chair and crossing his arms, but his face showed just as much interest.

"No." Olivia shook her head. "I've only been to the ocean a few times that I can remember, maybe twice with my parents. I don't remember them enjoying themselves there, but I loved it. The smell of salt and sea life, the sounds, the feel of the soft sand after a wave drenches it, the feeling of the water itself. I remember closing my eyes tight and just turning my head up toward the sun. I still do this now when I need to calm myself, and I think of the ocean. My first vision before coming here had to do with the ocean, and it made me feel so happy. I think that's a connection to this mystery man."

"A relative maybe? Or family friend?" Akiko suggested.

"But why would the implant have erased my memory of him? It doesn't make sense."

"Maybe he was the family friend in the car accident with you, and that's why he's bleeding in your dreams?"

Olivia frowned and shrugged. "I guess it's possible, but I felt safe and happy when I saw him in this dream—then it was complete sadness when I couldn't get to him. I need to figure out who he was."

"We'll help in any way we can," Akiko responded, but Jed was silent, his eyes masked with a distant look.

1 0 1 0 1 1 0 1 0

Two days later, Mikayla was dead. She passed out in the lobby during lunch and never woke up. Olivia recognized her as Jillian's companion from their meeting following Sam's death. Akiko explained that the two women had been in a committed relationship and were talking about getting married when they got out of the institute. They'd met within days of arriving and their connection had been instant, as if they'd already known each other.

"I thought Jillian would be the next to go," Olivia heard someone mutter in the lobby the day after the woman died.

"They couldn't be so obvious after Sam," someone else responded in a whisper.

Olivia turned to Jed to see if he'd comment. He met her eyes but shook his head, his face expressionless. He looked like he hadn't slept.

"It's time to go out," Akiko said in a commanding voice, standing up from their table.

"Now?" Jed raised an eyebrow.

"Yes, now." She was already walking toward the door.

The three of them headed into the frigid autumn morning. Sometimes it felt like they spent more time leaving the institute than being in it.

The cold air sucked all the words from their mouths. Akiko and Jed's faces displayed a jumble of emotions. Olivia was sure hers did too. How had another resident been allowed to die?

Dr. Cordova had already explained that a brain aneurism had taken Mikayla's life. She said the woman had been complaining of a severe headache for a day, but this wasn't abnormal, as headaches were one of Mikayla's implant symptoms. The medical team had given her an extra treatment and a higher-dosage pain reliever. Dr. Cordova reported that Mikayla's implant had not shut down, but the doctor seemed certain, even so soon after the woman's death, that Mikayla's symptoms had played a role in bringing on the brain bleed.

No one had seen Jillian since Mikayla passed out. Olivia hoped she had someone to be with her as she grieved. She thought about asking Akiko and Jed for the woman's room number, but would Jillian *want* a stranger in her space right now?

Countless fragments of thoughts played pinball through Olivia's mind as the trio continued to walk in silence. She was starting to memorize the streets around the institute; she'd traveled them so many times.

"I don't want to believe that they're doing this to us," Akiko whispered, tears making their way down her cheeks.

Olivia pulled her friend into a hug, and Akiko cried quietly for a few minutes. Olivia caught Jed's sorrowful eyes over their friend's shoulder. When Akiko pulled away and wiped her eyes, Jed offered a few quiet words, so soft Olivia couldn't make them out.

Was there any point to any of this? Would any of them make it out alive?

The colors around her slowly turned red, but once again, the headache stayed at bay. Olivia turned her face toward the sky, squeezing her eyes shut. The sun was behind the fog. She felt the mist settle on her eyelids, nose, cheeks, and chin. She breathed in the air and smelled the ocean. She heard the seagulls above her—then their screeches were all around her. She heard the waves crashing. She must be standing just above the water.

"Are we at the lighthouse?" she asked without thinking, without opening her eyes.

She was met with silence. Her cheeks flushed in embarrassment as she returned to reality, but when she did open her eyes, there was no judgment on her friends' faces, only that ever-present curiosity.

"That's gotta mean something," Jed said, checking his phone. "Let's go. It says the Point Bonita Lighthouse is open today."

They piled into an Uber, crossed through the ever-vibrant China-town, with its hanging lanterns and bustling shops and restaurants, and caught the 101. The cold morning was keeping some tourists away, but the Golden Gate Bridge was still teeming with life as they left the city.

The bridge was a blur as they sped over it, because she could still feel the lighthouse as if she were already standing there. She wasn't sure she'd ever been to the Point Bonita Lighthouse. Did she have some sort of connection to it? Something she couldn't remember? Or was it lighthouses in general? Did it have something to do with the mystery man from her dream?

They hiked the path that led to the light, which sat just north of San Francisco in the Marin Headlands. The moment they stepped foot on the white wooden bridge leading to the structure, visions of another lighthouse flitted through her mind. Memories? That building was blurry and distant. She couldn't see it well enough to feel any connection to it, and she didn't recognize the lighthouse she was standing in front of now.

Olivia turned her face toward the light, closing her eyes again, shoving her hands deep in her jacket pockets. She expected to hear the voice of The Man from the Ocean, but her mind was quiet. Opening her eyes, she stepped over to the railing, getting as close to the edge of the rocks as the barrier would let her. Olivia gazed out at the water, which churned as if it were a restless beast trying to free itself from a cage. What was she supposed to feel here? Was this supposed to answer all the questions raging inside her? She felt at peace, but nothing special happened.

Jed's eyes caught hers as she shoved wayward hair out of her face with a frustrated sigh. He looked lost in thought but managed to give what she perceived as a supportive smile, like he was willing something magical to happen in this moment.

Olivia's stare found the water again. Her mind stilled as she breathed in the crisp air. She felt the horizon beckoning her. Her body leaned forward, as if pulled toward the sea. Jed moved against her side but she didn't turn to look at him. She thought she heard Akiko's voice.

"Are you okay?" Jed questioned. She noted the smallest hint of concern in his voice, but she wasn't scared.

She felt herself nodding but didn't turn her attention from the waves. The water didn't seem to want to let her go. "Have you ever wondered what it would be like to swim out to the horizon? To just be there? To experience the peace but also loneliness of existing in the water? Would I be scared? Or would it feel like the place I was always meant to be?"

Olivia's legs pushed against the railing. She was ready to fly right over. Jed's hand grabbed her arm. She felt Akiko's firm grip on her other side.

"Stay here, Liv. Don't go." Jed's voice shook, his mouth near her ear. His words broke her from her trance. She moved her eyes to his, still feeling Akiko at her other side. Jed's expression was one of obvious fear. She realized she was in fact trying to climb over the railing. She stopped, taking a deep breath, and moved several steps back. No one around them seemed to have noticed what was going on. Jed and Akiko must have blocked her from view as much as possible.

"I'm sorry, I—" She shook her head. *What happened?* "It must have to do with that man. He's in my memory somewhere, but I can't get to him." A few tears made their way down her cheeks. Frustration once again burned through her.

"We should go," Akiko murmured, rubbing Olivia's arm.

Olivia nodded, not letting herself look back out to the sea.

The hike back to the parking lot (to yet another waiting Uber) and the drive back into the city, were quiet. They headed west to the San Francisco Zoo. After grabbing lunch, they spent the afternoon traipsing around the grounds, seeing as many animals as they could. The fog had lifted, but the air still had a bite to it. Olivia hugged her arms around her, warmth thawing her body as the three of them chatted and joked.

Her feelings and thoughts from the lighthouse were gone, and the trip felt like an escape. They were three regular people having a normal day, enjoying each other's company before returning to their real lives. In that moment, they didn't have malfunctioning computer chips in their brains and one of their fellow residents hadn't just died.

Akiko wandered ahead at one point and Jed reached for Olivia's hand. She took it, because it just felt natural and right to celebrate the joyfulness and normalcy.

They bought sandwiches at the grocery store and sat on the beach to eat as the sun finished sinking below the horizon. They watched people of all ages move around them. They created and shared the most perfect stories they could imagine for their own three lives—lives that could have been theirs if things had been different. When it had been dark for hours, they picked themselves up and went back to the institute.

Akiko waved and took the elevator upstairs after Olivia gave her a long hug, almost as if they wouldn't see each other the next morning. But then again, none of them could be sure what the next day would bring.

"Walk you upstairs?" Jed offered after they'd sat and chatted a little longer in the lobby.

"Sure." Olivia said, because it had felt like a rare perfect day she never wanted to end.

Exhaustion hit in the elevator ride up, but a small zing of electricity went through her as Jed slipped his hand back into hers. She looked up at him, but he was staring straight ahead. Did he look a little nervous? She couldn't deny that Jed was handsome in the somewhat disheveled, stereotypical way she pictured writers to be. She'd grown used to his quirks, although sometimes still wished he wasn't quite so honest. He felt like home to her, much like Akiko did. But could there be more than that? With death heading their way in an unknown amount of time, was it a good idea to start something? But then the thought came to her that their limited time was *exactly* why she should start something: to enjoy her life while she had it.

He walked her to her door, still holding her hand. She made no move to pull away.

"Today was a great day. It was almost easy to forget why we're all here. What just happened—" Her voice faded away. Reality seemed to be crashing back down now as she thought about Mikayla. Tears sprang to her eyes. She willed herself not to let them fall; not right now.

Then Jed's hands were cupping her cheeks. As one of her tears managed to trickle down, he caught it with his thumb and wiped it away before saying, "We can't forget. We have to remember in order to honor Mikayla and Sam. But finding some happiness is okay too. That hasn't been easy in this place, but knowing you has brought me happiness, Liv."

"That was beautiful." She smiled but couldn't stop the tease that followed. "The other Henley would be proud." She leaned toward him with a smirk.

Jed rolled his eyes with a grin, pulling her closer. He brought his mouth to hers, and at first it felt a little like floating on the waves. When she responded without hesitation, he deepened the kiss, his mouth more demanding. Fire was flying through her veins. She was positive in that moment that Jed was the only man who knew how to kiss. She never would have imagined that just hours earlier.

"Uh, okay," he said when they broke apart countless minutes later.

"Yeah," she replied breathlessly, noticing that he'd backed her up against the wall. She wondered if anyone had walked by. She was sure she wouldn't have noticed. "Do all writers kiss like that?"

"I didn't know *I* kissed like that," he laughed. "I think you're the one who deserves the praise."

"No," she answered with a shake of her head. "Expert kisser is not something anyone has ever called me."

"That changes now," he answered, moving his mouth back to hers.

Olivia wasn't quite sure what to say when they came apart again. Part of her was angry that it'd taken thirty-five years to have a kiss that good. And how much time would she have for more?

Jed spoke before she could express this thought. "Akiko told me to get over myself when I said I thought kissing you would make things weird, so I guess we can thank her. That was pretty fantastic for two dying people."

"And there it is," she laughed at his blunt comment. "I plan to stay very much alive, thank you." The words were hard to say, since she was sure she wouldn't be given a choice in the matter.

"That's the goal," he smiled, but something in his eyes had already grown dark.

Damn this place. It's impossible to forget for more than a few blissful seconds.

Olivia turned and unlocked her door to hide her frustration. She didn't want Jed to think it was directed at him. By the time she was facing him again, she knew the moment had shifted.

"'Night, Liv," Jed murmured, kissing her again, but it was nothing like before. His eyes held hers for a second longer before he walked away.

Olivia wanted to scream, to destroy the falsities around her. That kiss had felt like the truest romantic connection she'd had since—well, ever. How could part of her life just be starting when it was all coming to an end?

CHAPTER 11

JILLIAN DIDN'T COME out of her suite until Mikayla's brothers arrived to retrieve Mikayla's body, two days after the woman died. Jillian left with them. Olivia wondered if she would come back.

"She will. She'll assume she can't survive without coming back," Jed commented when Olivia mentioned her thought to her friends.

Olivia sent him an annoyed glance, wanting to believe Jillian could escape this place. Olivia knew it wasn't realistic, but it felt better to live in denial. She and Jed seemed to be doing plenty of that. They hadn't talked about the other night. They actually hadn't talked much at all. Did he think it'd been a mistake?

"Maybe she doesn't want to survive," Akiko whispered, depths of emotion in her words. A shiver went down Olivia's spine.

The three of them were having an early dinner in the lobby when Jillian returned, five days after she'd left. She was pale and weak, close to collapsing on the floor after she stumbled through the heavy front doors. Several of the residents closest to the entrance supported her body. Ziya, ever at her post, ran forward, speaking frantically into her cell phone, which appeared to be the institute staff's preferred method of communication over walkie talkies since Sam died.

Dr. Cordova and two of her medical assistants emerged from the elevator moments later. Jillian was loaded onto a stretcher, an oxygen mask fixed over her face. The doctor's demeanor was still professional, but her eyes were alarmed. The four people were in the elevator within seconds, presumably heading for the emergency room on the third floor.

Ziya sighed from where she stood. Her eyes swept the room and Olivia felt them pass over her before the woman returned to her desk. The residents who had helped Jillian went back to their seats.

"She tried to make it. She didn't want to come back," Akiko said, then got up and left the table.

Jed pushed up from his seat and made to go after her, but Olivia stopped him by grabbing his hand. He looked down at her with stricken eyes. Jed knew the story of Akiko's pain. Olivia thought maybe it was time she did too.

"Can I go? You two have supported me since I got here. I'd like to do the same for her if she's okay with that," Olivia murmured.

Jed nodded but didn't say a word as he sat back down.

Olivia sighed. They would need to talk about the other night soon.

Olivia found Akiko sitting with her feet in the heated pool. She was watching a few other residents swimming at the opposite end. Olivia loved swimming and had always felt at home in the water, but the fear of her symptoms taking her under had kept her out of the pool, except for once when Akiko swam laps with her.

"Okay if I sit?" Olivia asked softly.

Akiko nodded but didn't look away from the swimmers. Their laughs and splashing water filled the air around the pool. The carefree sounds felt wrong.

Olivia stumbled as she removed her tennis shoes and socks, pulled her pant legs up to her knees, then sat and breathed a deep exhale as her feet hit the warm water. She pushed her legs forward and backward in a slow motion, not sure how to begin the conversation.

"Jed's just confused, you know. Don't give up on him," Akiko murmured, looking down at her hands, which were now resting in her lap.

The topic surprised Olivia. She turned to study her friend's profile. "I haven't known him as long as you, but he doesn't seem like the confused type."

Akiko turned to look at her with a smirk. "He puts on a good front. I know I shouldn't even be talking to you about this, because it's between you and him, but you mean a lot to him. He talks about you too much to hide that fact. Unfortunately, he got in his head. I think he just isn't sure if pursuing something is a good idea, because—"

"We have failing computer chips in our brains and are hurtling toward our impending doom?" Olivia finished the thought.

Akiko laughed. "Yeah, that's the overarching problem."

Olivia nodded. "I get it. I just need to talk to him."

"If you two can find any bit of happiness in this place," Akiko said, "I think you should." She sounded as if she were trying to keep her voice firm, but the words shook as they drifted into the air.

Olivia stared down at the water, watching the ripples her legs made. She leaned forward with her arms on her thighs, deciding it was best to get to the point. If Akiko wasn't comfortable talking, that was fine. "Will you please tell me what happened in your past?"

Akiko twisted her long hair into a low bun at the nape of her neck and then let it go. It fanned out around her shoulders like a shimmering black shawl. She took another moment of silence and then began, "I told you the basics about my implant when you got here. I also told you my parents have always been honest about it. As I was growing up, I never felt out of place or lacking in any way. I felt loved. My parents did what they did to help me. I know I sound like I'm trying to defend their decision, and I guess I am. I probably wouldn't have lived past childhood if they hadn't made the decision for me to get an implant.

"I was twenty and in my second year of college when I met Daryll. It was what I've always thought of as love at first sight. He was two years older than me—the kindest, funniest man I'd ever known. I felt lucky to be in his orbit and somehow, he seemed to feel that way about me. We got married just after I turned twenty-three. We'd both graduated and were in jobs we enjoyed by that time. We bought a house. Everything seemed—wonderful.

"When I was almost twenty-five, we started trying to have a baby." Here she took a shaky breath and paused. After a few seconds of quiet, she continued, "I had—a lot of miscarriages. During that time, I also began experiencing my first implant symptoms, although I thought they were connected to the miscarriages at first. Head-aches, pain, blurred vision. They were tolerable, but they continued, so then I thought there must be something else going on. I saw so many doctors, but they couldn't find anything—nothing to explain my miscarriages and nothing to explain my symptoms.

"Daryll was so supportive, even though I know he was grieving our losses just as much as I was. He tried to keep his sadness from me most of the time. I was so anxious. I thought I had some horrible illness that they just couldn't figure out. Then, for a short time, my symptoms seemed to lessen. I felt like a new person. Our lives were more peaceful. And I got pregnant again. The weeks kept passing and I stayed pregnant. Then I was thirty-two weeks; I had pain and some bleeding." Akiko's voice caught. It was obvious she was trying to rush through this part of the story. "I went to the hospital and—" Her words ended in a shudder she tried to play off as a you-know-what-happened shrug.

"Daryll and I had both let ourselves believe it was going to work that time. I'd gotten so much farther than ever before. It was possible the baby could have lived if I'd given birth at thirty-two weeks, but she was—already gone. After that, Daryll gave up. It had been too much for him. Dealing with the grief he'd been squashing down until that point, the fresh new grief, and *my* just—life-shattering sorrow—was more than he could take. He left about six months later. Grief can be an overpowering thing. I've found it can make you feel like you're drowning on dry land, barely able to breathe. I think it was like that for him, but he didn't know how to talk about it.

"Not that I haven't been angry with him. I've felt every negative emotion toward him and—I still love him, which is difficult to deal with. But I'm the only one who knows even a part of what he was going through. It was the most awful thing a person can experience. I wished many times that I *hadn't* lived through it. So, I get it."

"Well, I don't!" Olivia couldn't stop herself from saying. "Your body and mind experienced all of that loss firsthand, and he left you!" She wondered how easy it was to hunt someone down in this day and age.

Akiko gave her a small smile. "Thanks. Trust me, I've cursed his name many times. Anyway, up until that point, my parents had assured me the miscarriages and my weird symptoms couldn't be related to the implant. The institute had promised them the chip would last for the rest of my life, no matter how long that was—that there were built-in fail safes to prevent problems. But after my last baby, we all started to wonder.

"My parents tried to contact the institute and received no response. When the implant led me back here, Dr. Cordova thought it was strange that the malfunctioning chip could have resulted in miscarriages, but of course, she couldn't say for sure. There are other women here who have had several miscarriages and never carried to term. But getting pregnant was never an issue for any of us. As woman after woman with similar experiences got here, it became pretty clear, at least to me, that there was a connection."

"I—I had no idea," Olivia stammered, shame running through her. What these women had gone through was unfathomable.

"You wouldn't have known." Akiko responded. "I don't like to talk about it; the sadness and anger is so all-consuming. A lot of the other women feel the same way. But at least we have each other to lean on when we need to."

Then Akiko said something Olivia knew her friend wouldn't normally feel comfortable expressing within the confines of the institute's walls: "All the losses of my babies, the horrible grief I endure, the loss of my husband—I know it was all because of this piece-of-shit failing computer chip in my brain."

Hot tears stung the sides of Olivia's eyes, but she wouldn't let herself cry. Akiko had been living a normal life. She'd been trying to create a future and a family. She'd deserved that happiness more than anyone Olivia knew, and it had been taken from her.

"Kiko, I—" she began, but what could she say?

"I was filled with so many emotions in my first weeks here, I didn't leave my room. But Jed was there. He sat with me while I cried or ranted. He was processing his own experience, but he never acted like mine was too much.

"Initially, it felt wrong to blame any of the staff for what I was going through, because none of them were here when I was a little girl. And then I thought that fact was strange. Sometimes, people are in careers for thirty or forty years of their lives, especially in the generations before ours. How was every staff member from back then gone? And with no explanation from the current staff. That's when I started feeling like something was—off," she whispered the last word. Her confession was heading toward dangerous territory.

Olivia leaned against Akiko in what she hoped was a comforting gesture. *We need to get out of this place.*

Akiko patted Olivia's knee and stood up with her usual grace, despite the pain still etched on her face. "Thank you for listening. I'm not happy you have to be here, Olivia, but I'm so glad we have you. Talk to Jed."

Tears once again sprang to Olivia's eyes. "Thank you for telling me." *How do I love these two so much already?*

Akiko dried her legs with a waiting towel, grabbed her shoes, and gave Olivia's shoulder a squeeze before walking away.

Goosebumps swept Olivia's legs when she pulled them from the water. She toweled them off for much longer than necessary. As she slipped her shoes back on, Akiko's story drifted through her mind. Her anger flared, but she tamped it down. Now wasn't the time.

Jed was at the same lobby table, now tapping away on his laptop's keyboard. Olivia's heart was thumping as she forced her body toward him.

"I just got a new editing project," he said, not even looking up to confirm it was her. "A set of short stories from an author I've worked with before." She could hear the excitement in his voice.

Olivia didn't want to have this conversation. Conversations like this were why she was still single. And maybe it was all the fault of her implant, but it didn't really matter at this point.

"Do you regret kissing me?" she asked as she settled into the chair across from him, cringing at the high pitch of her voice.

"What?" He looked up at her in surprise. "What kind of ridiculous question is that?"

"Jed." She was so used to him by now that she took no offense. But she did grace him with an exaggerated eye-roll.

"Sorry," he responded with a guilty smirk. "That didn't come out right. I meant, no, of course not, why do you ask?"

Olivia chuckled at the way he carefully enunciated each word. "You've been a little quiet with me, which is very unlike you."

He ran his hands down his face and sat back before answering. "I know this sounds like a cop out, but it's this place. It's our situation. On top of the very real possibility that our implants might shut down and we might die, now it seems like they're trying to—you know, hurry the job." He nodded toward the front doors, making Olivia think of Jillian's return, and lowered his voice to a murmur. "And here we are, still burdened by their lies, still waiting for something. I care about you, a lot, and I'd like to kiss you like that all the time, but—" he motioned around the room. "I didn't know how to talk to you about it and wasn't sure how you were feeling."

"So, you're spiraling like me?" Olivia leaned forward. "I wasn't sure how to talk to you about it either," she continued, turning her head to look out the closest window, "but Akiko gave me some encouragement."

He laughed. "Of course she did."

Olivia clasped one of his hands in hers. "I think we can figure this out. I care about you too, so much. Amid all this bleakness, I believe we can bring each other some joy. Maybe our lives won't last, but at least we'll have each other in the meantime."

"Now who should have been the writer? I'm sure all those '70s rockers would be proud, even the one with my last name."

She grinned. "Nah, I think this is pure '80s power ballad material."

He gave a dramatic sigh. "Yeah, you're right. Okay, knowing the ending of this situation has the potential to really suck, I'd like to have the meantime times with you."

"There's the Jed I know," she said with another smile. "I'm looking forward to the meantime times."

He moved his other hand to hers, running a thumb across her fingers. "Did Akiko," he hesitated for a moment, "tell you her story?"

"She did. I understand why it's painful for her to talk about," Olivia murmured so no one around them would hear. "So much loss; I can't imagine. And I'm sure her parents and siblings were there for her, but just from how she told the story, it sounded like such a lonely experience. And her husband…" She let her words fade away.

"Yeah," Jed's eyes were stormy. "I saw her walk by before you came back. Where'd she go?"

"I'm not sure. Probably working toward the cause," Olivia whispered, leaning closer to him.

"I wish she wouldn't," he said with a grimace. "It's too risky."

Olivia thought about the risk the two of them were taking by talking about this inside the institute, even with their vague words. "Yes, but she *needs* to do this, Jed. She's fierce and smart; she'll be as careful as possible. What about you? Found anything new in your search?"

"I'm waiting on a few people to get back to me, but it's clear I'm not their priority." Jed frowned. He looked around. "We can talk more in depth about this later, but I've been staying up to date on medical and technology journal publications. There's nothing to find. It's not surprising I guess, but no one is writing about these things." He motioned ever so slightly toward his head.

Olivia was distracted from her response by Akiko exiting the elevator. She made no attempt to scan the room for them as she normally would, but walked right by them and out the door, setting off down the street. Jed barely noticed in time to see her go. About five minutes later, a medical staff member Olivia didn't recognize, walked to Ziya's desk from the direction of the first floor's conference room. The medical employee, a young woman who looked to be in her later twenties, spoke to Ziya with a casual grin, typed something in her phone, and, with a wave goodbye, left the building as well. She went the same direction as Akiko.

"Interesting," Jed mumbled.

Olivia swept her eyes back to Ziya, but the woman was busy working, as always. "Very. Should I get us some dessert?"

Jed nodded. Olivia forced her legs toward the café, even though her mind was screaming at her to follow Akiko. But she and Jed would have to trust their friend knew what she was doing. And they'd sit and wait, for as long as it took for her to return.

CHAPTER 12

"ISN'T THIS PLACE cool?" Jed's voice was full of awe. He held Olivia's hand as they strolled by the cells inside the former federal prison on Alcatraz, an island just over a mile offshore in the San Francisco Bay.

"Yes, but also creepy," Akiko, who was walking ahead, responded.

"I don't know. It's kind of creepy," Olivia said at the same time.

The women shared a chuckle. Jed rolled his eyes. "The history of this island, even after the prison closed is tragic and astounding. All you can say is that it's creepy?"

Akiko raised her eyebrows with a savage smile. "I agreed with you—the creepy was just an addition."

Olivia felt a shudder go through her body. She swore she could feel the vague ghosts of countless humans all around her. It was an interesting place, but she'd had an unnerving sensation since they stepped off the boat that'd brought them to the former penitentiary.

"It feels a little haunted," she murmured to Jed.

"Yes! Isn't it awesome?" He looked positively giddy. "It sets my writer's brain into overdrive. Imagine all the stories—the lives of every soul who set foot on this rock! What was it like to live on a little island cut off from the city? Man, I wish I had a time machine."

Olivia smiled up at him. His happiness was infectious.

Akiko stayed in the lead as they descended a set of stairs into what was once the prison's exercise yard. A sudden bout of dizziness hit Olivia on the way down, so she took it slow. By the time she reached the ground, Akiko was already staring out into the San Francisco Bay through a doorway in the wall surrounding the yard. Olivia swept her eyes back to the building they'd come from. It was November now. The sky was filled with clouds that didn't seem to hold much threat of rain.

The cold was biting, even through Olivia's jacket. Hugging her arms around herself didn't help. The iciness felt like it was flowing through her now, and the strange feeling she'd had inside the building was even more noticeable.

As she and Jed joined Akiko by the doorway, their friend casually turned to survey the other tourists in the yard. Apparently happy with what she saw, she motioned for the three of them to face the water as she spoke. "I have some information. There are members of a resistance group within the cachot staff. They're working to bring it down. I'm still earning their trust, so they're not willing to be completely transparent yet. But they've seen my eagerness to get involved, so they reached out to me. They gave me what could be considered good and bad news, although the bad part is not a surprise. The good news is they don't believe the cachot is able to listen to or monitor us through our implants when we are outside of the building. It has something to do with the specific parts of the implants that are breaking down.

"Unfortunately, the bad news is the staff *is* monitoring us when we're inside the building; even our rooms are bugged. So, we have to be really careful with what we say there. Another thing is that Dr. Cordova is a lot more connected to this mess than she lets on. She may not have worked at the cachot when the implants were placed, but she was directly trained by some higher-ups who did. She knows the truth about everything, but she's purposefully hiding it from us based on orders someone is giving her, although the resistance members wouldn't tell me the identity of the person in charge. But it was that person who ordered Cordova to have Sam and Mikayla killed."

Olivia's voice came out in a whisper. "That confirms our fears."

"Could it be our absentee lead engineer?" Jed suggested, putting a soothing hand on Olivia's back.

"No. They said Adamian isn't who we think he is, and that's why he's never around."

"Not particularly helpful, but also not surprising, I guess," Jed responded with a sigh.

Akiko nodded and continued, "The resistance members are okay with me telling you both all of this, as long as you don't repeat it to anyone. They want to be able to trust you too. They asked me not to identify them. But, for at least one of them, maybe you don't need me to." She stared meaningfully at her friends.

Olivia understood right away, so she was sure Jed did too: the employee they'd seen leave the cachot just after Akiko the other night.

"We were wondering about her, but we thought we got it wrong!" Oliva said in surprise. "She came back so quickly, gave Ziya a container of food, then ate her own food alone in the lobby and left. You didn't come back for another hour, and then you went straight up to your room. It didn't seem like enough time for a meeting."

"That was by design," Akiko responded.

"So, will they get us out of this nightmare?" Jed asked. "Should we be getting ready for something to happen?"

"They weren't comfortable giving me the specifics of their plan yet. But their goal is to get the rest of us out of the cachot safely. They said they'll do anything they can to prevent another death."

Jed looked far from convinced. "Who is this group? Members of the original staff? Hopefully they know they have to have a solution for our implants before they shut down the cachot."

Akiko shook her head. "The people I've spoken to couldn't have been part of that original staff; they're too young. But I'm assuming there is some connection to the first employees, yes."

Jed ran one of his hands through his hair. "Kiko—"

"So, what do we do now?" Olivia asked, cutting Jed off. It was clear he was uncomfortable with the cageyness of this resistance group, but this lead was a hell of a lot better than anything else they had.

"We wait," Akiko said, rushing on before Jed could get a word out "I know it sucks, but I'm trying to feel grateful that this group even exists and that they were willing to talk to me. And they said they'll give me more information when the time is right. I understand it's hard to believe, but I'm sure about them. I just need you to trust me," Akiko said.

A small headache began at the back of Olivia's skull as she gave Akiko a weak smile. "Of course we trust you."

"Yeah, our trust in you is never in doubt, Kiko. Just please be careful," Jed said, then noticed Olivia wince with the pain already growing in her head. "Wanna head back?"

"Yeah, maybe so. I think I need a treatment," Olivia said, massaging the areas behind her ears, wishing for relief.

Akiko walked back toward the stairs. Jed took Olivia's hand, but she found she couldn't move—couldn't make herself turn from the doorway, from the view of the water. A sinking feeling filled her mind. Out of nowhere, waves churned around the island. Seagulls squawked overhead and fog rolled in. Then Olivia was alone in the yard; Jed, Akiko, and the other tourists had disappeared. And still, she was trapped in that doorway. Her heart slammed in her chest, but when she heard the man's voice from behind her, she felt at peace—until she registered the words he was saying.

"Do you remember the night he killed me? You were so young, but you'd followed me out there. You saw him running. Do you remember who he was?"

"What? No!" she answered in alarm. "I don't remember anything like that."

"That's because they've taken it from you—taken me from you. Try to remember. It's there. The memory is coming back to you. You'll find my killer buried in your mind," The Man from the Ocean said.

Olivia closed her eyes and inhaled deeply. She saw The Man from the Ocean, lying prone next to a creek, just past an orchard. She saw him there, one of his hands hanging off the bank. Then she saw the blood surrounding him. He'd been murdered; of course he had. And she was sure she knew who'd killed him. She tried to drag her eyes away from him, to see if someone was running away, but she was too scared. This night was too scary. A scream filled her thoughts, spread through her like a wildfire.

She exhaled and her eyes snapped open. The seagulls were gone, the waves had settled, and the smothering fog had dispersed. She was sitting on the ground now, Jed and Akiko crouching next to her.

"Liv, what happened? Are you okay?" Jed was cupping her face. Akiko had a soft hold on her arm.

"I'm okay. Someone killed him," Olivia murmured.

"Killed who?" Akiko asked.

"The Man from the Ocean. Someone murdered him. And he said I know who his murderer is." She recounted every piece of the vision.

"When you talked about him before, you said you thought the implant erased him from your memory. But you were in a car accident. Your experience had nothing to do with a murder," Jed said.

That's when an idea settled into Olivia's brain and her body started to shake. Looking at Jed and Akiko's faces, she guessed they were having the same thought.

"It's not possible, right? That our families and cachot have been lying to us about our pasts?" Akiko said, shaking her head.

"I think it's possible *my* family lied to me," Olivia responded, thinking of her mother's coldness and her father's evasiveness. "But why? Did I witness a murder? I never heard anyone mention a murder during my childhood." She paced across the prison yard. "The man in my vision asked me if I remembered who killed him. He said I have the person's identity in my mind. If there was an unsolved murder, why would someone want me to forget who the killer was?"

Akiko had pulled out her phone and was already calling someone. She walked away from them, back to the doorway in the wall.

Olivia turned toward Jed, who had his hands shoved in his pockets. His eyes looked far away and his face was pale.

"I've heard female screams in my nightmares. Did I tell you that?" he asked. "And the person screaming was clearly terrified. I've tried to believe it was a random way my brain was interpreting things. I tried to ignore it. My mom supported the cachot's narrative that it was one of my male friends driving the car, that I was the only one in any of the passenger seats. There was no woman or girl in the vehicle. But what if there was? Maybe the screams weren't random."

Olivia pulled one of Jed's hands from a pocket and wrapped her fingers through it. The confusion and fear on his face made it feel like her world was tipping.

Before she could go on, Akiko walked back to them, her eyes a storm. "I just spoke to my mother. She said everything she and my father have told me about my brain damage and the implant was true. But she didn't sound like herself. I could tell I'd caught her off guard. Maybe this is it. This is what they've been keeping from us—the *real* reasons we had to get the implants. But why…" Akiko's words trailed off, her body hunched in a look of defeat.

"Well, hang on," Olivia put her hand up, anxiety rushing through her. The throbbing in her head that she'd been able to momentarily ignore, was back in full force. Akiko had lost so much in her life. She'd always leaned on the fact that her parents were so open with her about her implant. Olivia didn't want to take that from her friend as well. She wanted Akiko to have that steady foundation.

"We don't know if my vision means anything, or that it means what I interpreted it to mean," Olivia continued, "I still don't know who this man is—was. I don't think we should throw away everything we've been told. Why would they falsify the reasons we got the implants? And why would anyone in my life want to keep a murderer's identity secret?"

But as Olivia said this, she remembered her vision from the day she'd arrived at the institute. But it wasn't a vision, it was a memory; she was sure of that now. When she was a toddler, she had walked into the institute for the first time, her parents holding her hands and leading her on. And she'd had no injuries, just a great sense of sadness, a deep chasm of it looming inside her. Because the person Olivia had loved the most was dead.

Olivia's headache had evolved into a pounding drum. She closed her eyes and gripped her head in her hands, taking deep breaths, trying not to cry. *I just had a treatment this morning. Why do I need another one so soon?*

"Let's get her back. Olivia, hold onto Jed," Akiko instructed in a quiet voice.

Olivia felt Jed's arm go around her and did her best to stay at his side, but the pain in her head was so bad, she wasn't sure how she was still alive. She heard several people ask if she was okay on the way back to the ferry. She wanted to cry out at the innocent, but totally inane question.

Jed and Akiko murmured around her as they sat huddled on the ferry on the way back to the mainland.

"Kiko, what if none of it is true? Lies upon lies," Jed said. "What does this mean for us—for all of us?"

"I don't know," Akiko mumbled back. "I don't know."

Her friends spoke in choppy thoughts every few minutes, but their words became more nonsensical and deluded, as if they were sinking in the ocean waves. Olivia was aware of leaving the boat and being helped into a car next to Akiko. After that was only darkness.

1 0 1 1 0

"If she wasn't due for another treatment for a couple days, why did this happen? We were out on Alcatraz! What if we hadn't been able to make it back? She passed out before we even got here!" Jed's voice was seething from somewhere in the distance as the world materialized around Olivia. Her head felt heavy and her thoughts were blurred, like she was waking up from a night of too much drinking.

Olivia was in her bed in her suite. She forced her eyes open, and it felt like they'd been closed for days. The lights in her bedroom were on, but dimmed. She moved all parts of her body from her head down to her toes to make sure everything was working. Olivia took note of the IV attached to the back of her left hand and followed its tube up to the bag of fluid hanging on a mobile metal stand next to her bed. It felt so close to a hospital setting that she expected to hear the beeps of other medical machinery, but there was just the sound of Jed's voice coming from the direction of her living room, followed by Dr. Cordova's response.

"If the situation had been that dire, we could have rushed a medical team to you." The doctor was attempting a soothing voice, but there was an obvious underlying tone of a professional trying to defend herself.

"If it had been that dire, she might have died! Then your fucking medical team wouldn't have done any good!" Jed growled back.

"Jed." Akiko's quiet but firm tone was a warning.

"It's okay," Dr. Cordova said in response. "I know this was very stressful. I know how close you've both become to Ms. Murphy."

There was no sound for several moments. Olivia wished she could see Jed and Akiko's expressions.

"Dr. Cordova, I'm sorry, but how close we are to her is inconsequential," Akiko said—probably to keep Jed from screaming in the woman's face. "This is how any human should react about another human who has just been on the brink of death, as we all have been at least once during our time here. What we're hoping for is answers. Answers about an operation or some other procedure that could fix our brains, perhaps to replace the malfunctioning computer chip or make it unnecessary. Answers about why the treatments seem to have different levels of effectiveness for different people, or why they sometimes don't seem effective at all. Answers about why the engineers and doctors here haven't discovered some kind of mobile treatment that we can give ourselves should these types of emergency situations arise when we're out of the building. Answers about whether we might be able to someday leave this place and go back to our lives. It's been so long and it seems like things are only getting worse. Is there anything, any small thing, you can tell us?"

"I can assure you that the medical and engineering teams are still putting everything they have into finding those answers, just as they always have been. And as soon as we can tell you anything, we will," the doctor answered, having to raise her voice to make her words heard over the loud scoff coming from Jed. "I understand this is horrible, and I want to end it as soon as I can. But *you* must understand that with none of the institute's original staff to provide us with guidance—"

"What about the documentation? Computer files? Testimonials in video or audio form about what tests they performed before putting these computer chips *in our brains*. Maybe what bugs they came across and how they fixed them? You told us you had the research, the medical charts, etc. when we got here!" Jed cut her off. "They may not offer an answer as to why the implants are shutting down, but there has to be *something* in there that would help!"

"Even if we find something helpful, we can't just share it with all of you," Dr. Cordova said, a hint of annoyance in her voice. "We don't want to give you false hope. I'm sorry, but we have to test every theory in our lab and then on willing participants before we can move forward and give it to you as a viable solution. These chips took many years to develop…"

"Are you implying that finding a solution will take many *years*?" Jed's voice rose an octave.

"I hope not, but I can't say for sure," the doctor answered.

Shut up, Jed. We don't know what they'll do to you, Olivia pleaded in her head.

As if he'd heard her, Jed went silent, but Akiko spoke up. "Honestly, a little false hope might be better than no hope. I know you're all doing your best, but, especially with the deaths of two of our fellow residents, most of us feel like we have nothing to go on."

Dr. Cordova sighed. There was a slight shake to the sound, like she wanted Akiko and Jed to know the weight she carried.

Wow, that woman is good at playing the victim in her own horror story, Olivia thought to herself.

"I'll talk to my team and see what we can share," the doctor said.

"Thank you," Akiko sounded grateful. She was the better actress of the two women. "Is there anything else that needs to be done for Olivia?"

"She needs the IV for two more hours. I'll take another look at her before I go. One of my medical staff will come remove it. Other than that, she should just rest."

Then there was the sound of the doctor's high-heeled shoes punching into the carpet in the hallway as she made her way to Olivia's bedroom. Jed's heavy footfalls and Akiko's light ones were right behind.

"Good to see you awake, Ms. Murphy!" Dr. Cordova beamed down at her. "How do you feel?"

Olivia wasn't sure how to answer. She was groggy and weak, but at least the stabbing pain in her head was gone. "Better than before."

"That's wonderful news." The doctor smiled as she checked the IV. "We can talk more when you're back on your feet. You've had a treatment. And Dr. Henderson will remove your IV in two hours. You were severely dehydrated."

"I was?" Olivia was surprised. She was always good about drinking water, and her symptom flares had never caused dehydration before. As Olivia opened her mouth to mention this, the doctor's phone rang.

The physician rushed out with a wave and a, "Call the medical team if you need help before the two hours are up!"

"Who is Dr. Henderson?" Olivia asked in a mumble. "We've never met him or her before. Actually," she continued with a big breath, "doesn't it seem strange that we see Cordova all the time? She's so accessible, even though she's the chief medical officer. Shouldn't she be too busy to see a resident after a symptom attack? Why wouldn't she have sent someone else to administer my treatment, like this Dr. Henderson?"

Jed sat down on the side of Olivia's bed as he sent Akiko a curious look. "Yeah, since you arrived, she does always seem to be around. Maybe you're just special," he said with a wry smile.

"Ugh, she's the last person I want to be special to." Olivia rolled her eyes.

Akiko sat on the end of the bed and gave a nod of agreement. "I think she just likes to be in control. She's not—" Akiko stood abruptly, grabbed Olivia's phone from her nightstand, and asked Olivia to put in her password. Akiko's finger then flew around the screen. She walked to the Bluetooth speaker mounted on the wall, turning up the volume as the song *Don't Bring Me Down* by Electric Light Orchestra blared around them.

Jed raised an eyebrow as Akiko sat back down.

"I don't know if this trick actually works to drown out words, especially with the tech the institute has, but it's worth a shot. If someone is listening right now, it's the only option we have," Akiko explained, turning her focus on Olivia. "I was going to say, Cordova's not the kind of person who delegates to others. But her accessibility is strange." She paused for a moment, a faraway look in her eyes, and then continued, "We have to find out more about that mystery man—about what happened to you. I think all of us have been lied to over and over, even after they said they were telling us the truth. We didn't tell Cordova about your vision, just that your symptoms flared while we were on Alcatraz. If she does in fact talk to you later, you'll have believably expand on that."

Olivia sighed as she tried, and failed, to sit up. "I wish I could tell you more about the man, but I just don't know. I know he meant a lot to me and I to him. I know he was murdered by a creek outside of an orchard, but I don't know where that orchard was. He looks like he could be around the age of a grandparent, but my father's dad died before I was born and The Man from the Ocean isn't my mom's dad. And obviously my parents won't tell me anything."

Akiko frowned, performing the familiar movement of winding her hair into a low bun and then letting it unravel. "I wonder if there's a way to encourage your visions? But then I worry the same thing that happened today will happen again. That flare was the worst we've seen it for you."

Jed shook his head. "I don't think we should do that. We wouldn't even know how to do it. We need your sources from that group to talk more, or we need to find whatever records the previous employees left behind."

"Are we back to the idea of me finding Cordova's office?" Akiko grinned and Jed rolled his eyes. She patted his hand to reaffirm the joke. Then she was serious again. "I'll reach out to my sources. We can't wait any longer."

Olivia thought for a few seconds. How could she bring about a vision? An idea popped into her head—a literal light coming on in the dark. "How about going back to the lighthouse? I felt something so intense there. Maybe it will trigger a vision."

Both Akiko and Jed's faces showed how little they liked that idea.

"You tried to climb over the railing," Akiko murmured.

"And you were talking about existing on the horizon," Jed said. "It was like you weren't in control of yourself. It scared the shit out of us."

"I know, and I'm sorry. Strangely enough, I remember that very clearly. But you'll both be there with me; we'll be prepared this time. If things get out of hand, I think you just have to interrupt my line of sight, get me away from the water. If I see him again, maybe he'll tell me more."

Her friends shared a long look before turning their faces back to her. Akiko nodded and Jed frowned. They were going back to the lighthouse.

CHAPTER 13

LATE THE NEXT morning, the trio took an Uber across the Golden Gate Bridge back to the Point Bonita Lighthouse. A light rain was falling. The driver's window was cracked open, and the sea air drifted around them. Olivia was sitting in the back with Akiko; Jed was in the front, looking out his window. Olivia took full, deep breaths, her nerves kicking in with the unknown of her immediate future. And yet, the closer she got to the ocean, the more she relaxed.

Olivia didn't notice when they climbed out of the parked car. She barely felt her steps as they crossed the white bridge. She tilted her head up to regard the top of the lighthouse, then stepped right up to the railing. Her fear was gone. Jed stood to her right, his body brushing hers. Akiko was on her left, her hands next to Olivia's on the railing.

Closing her eyes, Olivia let her mind focus on the image of the Man from the Ocean as she had seen him in her previous visions. When she opened her eyes again, she let her gaze settle on the horizon. Seagulls cried above her. Waves splashed up around the rocks. She was alone with the sea, but then his words were all around her.

"Livie, my curious girl." The man's voice filled her ears. "You've been beaten down and lied to your whole life for something that wasn't your fault. You've been punished for my death when you could have been the one to solve it. They were hiding things from you. They wouldn't let you speak about me."

"Uncle Jack," she murmured, his face flashing through her mind. Tears sprang to her eyes as she understood and remembered.

Jack was her great-uncle, her mother's uncle, who had emigrated from Northern Ireland when he was a young man. Jack had always felt more like Olivia's grandfather than her actual grandfather, Nial, who had been the first to immigrate to the United States. When Nial had moved to Los Angeles after Beth's high school graduation, Beth had stayed in Northern California and grown close to Jack. Jack had been overjoyed when Olivia was born.

Memories unfolded in what felt like a hurricane tossing its way through her brain. Uncle Jack in his Northern California mandarin orchard, the creek running through his property. Uncle Jack playing the piano—the same plaintive chords that Olivia had heard in her dream. An Irish love song maybe? Uncle Jack telling her tales of when he was a little boy in Northern Ireland, helping his father keep the family's lighthouse. Uncle Jack telling all manner of fairy tales and ghost stories until he was told to stop. Her parents always thought the stories would give her nightmares, but she loved them.

"How can I be remembering all of these things? I was just a little girl. And if you're dead, how are you talking to me now?"

Although she couldn't see him, she swore she felt him give a small shrug—a gesture that also felt so familiar to her. "Maybe because the floodgates have finally opened, love. And I'm not speaking to you, not really. I'm always looking out for you, Olivia, but your brain is hearing my voice through a combination of your memories and that piece of *shite chip in your brain. I don't know how it's possible, but I know the real me would have given anything to speak to you again."*

Olivia knew she was sobbing. She knew Jed and Akiko must be scared, but she couldn't go back to them yet. She needed to know more. "Who killed you? Why wouldn't my parents let me talk about it? Was there ever a car accident, or was my implant placed to make me forget you? Why?" The last word came out like a scream.

She heard his frustration, but not with her, never with her. "You know the answer to the first question, Livie. It's there in your memory, just like everything else. It will make more sense once that comes to you."

"I don't know how to remember!" she cried.

"You've remembered this much, sweet girl," he murmured in response. "They won't be able to stop you now. Just think. Think about everything you know to be true. It's there. It will come to you."

As he finished the last sentence, Olivia could feel his presence drifting away, like a ghost into the waves.

She came out of the fog and back to the world as it truly was, right away noticing Jed and Akiko holding her up. Her legs didn't want to bear weight.

"Liv, come back to us," Jed was whispering near her ear. She concentrated on the warm feel of his breath on her skin. She felt Akiko's firm grip on her arm. She felt her own tears wet on her cheeks.

"What happened? What did you see?" Akiko's words were soft and delicate, as if Olivia might shatter beneath them.

"You were crying, but you wouldn't answer us." Jed's voice cracked.

"I heard his voice," she said after several breaths, willing her heart to slow. "My Uncle Jack—The Man from the Ocean. He was my great-uncle, my mother's uncle, but he always felt like a grandfather.

He emigrated from Northern Ireland when he was a young man. He owned a mandarin orchard in Northern California. He was murdered in that orchard." Her sentences were choppier as she tried to calm her racing mind, squashing down the headache threatening to rip her brain apart.

She saw red expanding at the corners of her eyes, but she refused to let it spread. This was too important for a symptom flare. To Olivia's surprise, the pain in her head and the intrusive color both subsided. She'd never been able to do that before.

"It was just before my implant," she continued. "I saw who killed him. I followed him out of his house that night, through the trees. There was a creek running along the back of his property. That's where I found his body. The person who killed him was running away, but I still caught sight of them. I know who it was. It's right there on the edge of my memory. But I can't quite get a hold of it."

Olivia closed her eyes, inhaling and exhaling the crisp ocean air. The last bit of her headache floated away, like one of the seagulls in the sky above her. "And I think I can control my symptoms now."

Shock was written on Jed and Akiko's faces when Olivia opened her eyes.

"Okay, you'll need to circle back to that," Jed said with wide eyes. "Anything else you can remember about your uncle?"

"I was hysterical when he died, I know that much. Uncle Jack was my favorite person. My mind couldn't wrap itself around the violence and that he was just—gone. I kept trying to tell my parents who I saw running away, but the information upset them. They told me to stop talking about it. Maybe they thought I was making it up? But I wouldn't stop. So—so they brought me to the cachot. I know now that there was never a car accident. I don't know where they got those pictures in my file of my face all bruised and stitched, of the gash in my head, but they weren't real. My parents brought me to the cachot while I was very much conscious, my implant was placed, and I forgot. I forgot Uncle Jack, who killed him, everything." By this point, tears were running down Olivia's face again.

"Fuck," Jed said on a long exhale.

Akiko's face was dark. "And now we know for sure."

Olivia shivered, not able to meet Akiko's eyes. Lies upon lies, that's what Jed had said on their way back from Alcatraz. That's what their lives were.

"And what's this about you controlling your symptoms?" Jed asked, looking incredibly defeated.

Olivia shook her head. She didn't want to throw anything else at them right now. "It's just a feeling, and I'm not sure. We can talk about it later."

They ordered an Uber after making their way back across the bridge. Olivia almost laughed when she noticed it was the same driver who drove them *to* the lighthouse. Any consistency in their lives seemed strange.

"Have a fun time?" the man asked, raising his eyebrow in Olivia's direction through the rearview mirror. She was sure she still looked like hell.

"Yes, thank you," Akiko answered in her cool, pleasant voice from where she sat next to the driver.

"You all visiting?" he asked and Olivia felt a sadness go through her. How much easier life would have been if they were just three friends visiting San Francisco for fun.

"Nope, we live in the city," Jed said in a resigned voice. He squeezed Olivia's hand as she managed to give him a smirk.

"Nice, I'd love to live here. Too expensive though," the man muttered. "You're lucky."

Jed tried to hide his snort with a cough.

When they got back to the institute, Akiko disappeared into the elevator after a promise to see them for dinner. Olivia was amped up and decided to go for a swim. She grabbed her swimsuit from her room while Jed retrieved his laptop.

"Seems like a good time to get some work done," he said, settling into a lounge chair next to the pool, but Olivia found him throwing her glances every time she looked up at him from the water.

Olivia crossed the full length of the pool with long strokes of her arms, her feet slicing the warm water as she kicked. When she turned around, she pushed off from the wall of the pool, diving down. With her head submerged, she could hear the whispers of her uncle's voice again. She focused on the scene of his murder from inside her memories. She could see a retreating shadow, but who the hell was it? When would she remember? How would she break through that part of the darkness?

She opened her eyes underwater and looked up, seeing Jed crouched by the side of the pool. He was waving one hand at her through the small, rippling waves.

She broke through the surface, pushing her hair back, moving toward him.

"You were under there a long time. How long can you hold your breath?" Real concern was etched across his face.

"Sorry, it didn't feel like that long. The water seems to put me in a lighter version of the space I'm in for my visions." She reached the edge and put a soaked hand over his.

"You and water scare the crap out of me," he responded.

Olivia squeezed his hand, then went back to gripping the side of the pool, kicking her legs slowly. She thought about swimming in the ocean, remembering the time her parents had taken her to the coast when she'd been about six, just before the divorce. She'd felt so confident in the sea.

The memory of that day jolted back to her, strangely clear.

As she'd been running toward the water, her father and mother had been fighting, Edward motioning wildly toward Olivia, then swinging his hand back to point his finger savagely at Beth. Olivia had been running toward the refuge of the ocean to get away from the terror of the screaming match. The still air had allowed their undisrupted words to settle in her ears.

"You're her mother!" Edward had ranted. "She's putting her life at risk getting into the ocean, and you don't care! You should be watching her!"

"You don't get to put this on me!" Beth tossed back. "This is your problem now! You've disregarded my feelings for the last two years! Every day has been an agonizing mashup of anger and despair, and I won't let you tell me what to feel anymore! How am I supposed to keep moving forward in life? How I am supposed to try to forget that it was—"

Olivia had never heard her father sound as angry as he did just then. "Be quiet! This is *not* something we should be talking about. Ever!"

Beth's voice had been shaking as she responded, "You say that because you don't have this horrible push and pull inside you. This aching grief and guilt making me want to scream out the truth, even though the logical part of me is saying I can never do that! You have none of that! You think life can just go back to normal, but that will *never* happen for me, knowing what I know! And she knows too, and she always will, even if you don't think—"

"This conversation is over," Edward had stomped toward Olivia, who'd been watching them from where she was submerged up to her nose in the ocean, treading water.

Her eyes had traveled to Beth on the shore, now sitting on a beach blanket, looking down the shoreline. Edward had come to a stop where the waves met the sand, his hands at his sides, his stance stiff and uncomfortable. He'd called out to Olivia, and she'd swum back to him.

Realization brought Olivia crashing back to present day, knocking the wind from her lungs for a moment. She moved along the cement wall, tripping up the steps as she hurried out of the pool.

Jed handed her a towel, his face troubled. "What's going on?"

"It was someone my mother knew." The words fell from Olivia's mouth. She was aware institute staff could be listening to her, but right now she couldn't bring herself to care. "I just remembered an argument she and my dad had, and it makes a lot of sense. Someone she was connected to killed my uncle—her uncle. I accused someone important to her. She was never the same with me after my implant. It was like she wished I wasn't there. Maybe she was afraid—afraid the implant was going to stop working, afraid that I would remember who killed Uncle Jack. And this time she wouldn't be able to cover it up. That's why she distanced herself from me."

"And this person was more important to her than her own daughter?" Jed asked, incredulous. "So important she was willing to change the makeup of her daughter's brain to protect them?"

Olivia shrugged. "I guess so."

There was no hesitation from Jed. "You have to confront her."

"Based on our last conversation, I don't think that's going to go well."

Jed nodded. "Yeah, you're right. Well, if you're comfortable with it, maybe just see if you can get her on the phone and go from there? You don't have to throw blame. Just talk about what you've remembered. Maybe she'll slip."

Olivia sighed but pulled Beth's number up in her call log. The phone rang once and then went to voicemail. She frowned, pulling up her stepfather's number, but the same thing happened. "I can't get through. You don't think—they blocked me?"

Anger darkened Jed's blue eyes. "This whole thing is really fucked up. Okay, what about your dad? If you tell him you remember your uncle's murder, maybe—"

"Okay." She interrupted quietly, wishing there was anything else she could do. "Okay, I'm going to change and then I'll call him in my room."

She felt the tension in Jed's arms as he wrapped them around her. "We'll figure this out, Liv. We'll figure this out for all of us," he murmured into her hair.

And in that moment, she really wanted to believe him.

1 0 1 0 1 1 0 1 0

When she was dry, changed, and back in her suite, she put the crumpled paper with her father's number on her lap before carefully dialing the digits.

How am I going to do this?

"Olivia." Edward picked up after the third ring. "How are you, honey? Calling with good news, I hope!"

"Not exactly, Dad. I'm hoping you can give me some answers."

"Olivia, I already told you when I was there—"

"I know about Uncle Jack. I remember, Dad. I know there was no car accident, that for some reason my implant was used to cover up Uncle Jack's death. I need you to tell me why."

Her father was silent for so long that she pulled her cell phone away from her ear to make sure the call was still connected. When he spoke, his voice was raw with emotion. "Olivia—Olivia, we did this for you. I know it's hard to understand and hard to believe, but—but you were so traumatized. You loved Uncle Jack so much, and you saw him die by that creek. We found you draped over his body the next morning. You'd flung your arm over him, and your head was on his chest. Your eyes were red, and you woke up in a rage. You screamed and cried so much that you lost your voice for days. Then when you were able to talk again, you kept saying you knew who killed Uncle Jack. You were terrified and we were terrified for you.

"Your mother did some research to find ways to help you cope. She was looking into pediatric therapists specializing in intense trauma when she stumbled upon the information for the institute. The idea seemed so outlandish and impossible; I didn't believe her at first. So, we made the trip there. I wasn't sure, but your mother was adamant. She couldn't bear to see you like that. You couldn't sleep at night. You looked like a zombie during the day, insisting you knew who killed Jack. Your mother and I were trying to handle our own grief while also trying to keep you from breaking down at the intensity of yours."

"You didn't have the right to cover it up. That wasn't the right thing to do," Olivia muttered.

"Olivia, I can't express the pain, the absolute heart-shattering pain, that comes with seeing your child experience that kind of trauma—to see you stuck in that darkness while also experiencing delusions." Her father's voice broke, and she was sure he was crying.

"Delusions? What do you mean?"

Edward paused for the briefest of moments. "You were having delusions about Jack's murderer. You thought you saw someone that night who wasn't there."

She was sure that wasn't true. "Was the person I accused someone close to Mom? Someone she wanted to protect?"

"You don't remember that part then?" Edward asked, his voice full of empathy.

Olivia hesitated. She wished she could lie and say she did remember, but he could ask or say any number of things that would prove she had no idea. "No, I don't. But if it was someone Mom was close to, I was thinking maybe that's why she's resented me since then. She hated me for naming them. She didn't want them to take the blame."

"I'm sorry you've had that relationship with your mother; you didn't deserve it. You couldn't control what you thought you saw, and you were already so heartbroken over Jack's death."

"So, it *was* someone Mom knew?" Olivia pushed, hoping she was getting close to an answer.

"Yes. It was someone we both knew, Olivia. But what you thought you saw was not what happened. We couldn't let you accuse an innocent person, not that anyone would have believed a four-year-old traumatized by a violent death."

"If no one would have believed me, then—" Olivia began, but before she could finish the question, a face flashed into her mind. She saw that person running—running away from her dying uncle. She couldn't stop the startled gasp that came out of her as she realized this was the face of the murderer she'd seen that night.

"Olivia?" Her father asked, his voice full of worry again. "Are you okay?"

"I'm—I'm sorry, I have to go. One of my friends is having a bad symptom flare. I need to help get her to the clinic."

"Okay, honey, call me back when you can," Edward said.

She ended the call without another word. She composed a quick text to Jed and Akiko, trying to keep her fingers from shaking.

CHAPTER 14

THE SENSATION OF drowning without water was strange. There was no liquid to fill her lungs, and yet it was hard to breathe as she spiraled into the unknown depths all around her.

"Your father killed your uncle," Jed repeated for the second time as the trio picked at their food in a noisy Italian restaurant. They'd chosen that restaurant specifically for the noise level, which Akiko remembered from a previous time she'd eaten there.

Olivia barely moved her head in acknowledgement. Of course, she'd always known. The information had been buried in her brain since she was a toddler. But talking to Edward seemed to have given her access to the memory.

It was his face she'd seen in the shadows that night. In the days that followed, she'd named Edward as the murderer every chance she got. Her young mind had been so confused when her parents told her she was wrong. She'd *seen* him!

"It sounds like your uncle cherished you, cherished your mother, so why the hell would your father kill him?" Jed asked, not in a disbelieving tone, but in one clouded by shock.

"I wish I knew; not that that would make it any better. Maybe it was some kind of self-defense? In my visions, Uncle Jack seems like a gentle, loving soul, but maybe I'm remembering wrong. Maybe he attacked my dad, or me, or my mom?" Olivia tried to shrug as if the idea didn't upset her, but hot tears were stinging the corners of her eyes.

"You don't believe that," Jed said, reaching for her hand across the table. Akiko was still sitting like a statue in her chair.

"No, I don't."

Akiko took a breath and said, "Unless—Maybe it was your uncle trying to protect you or your mother that started it? Did your father ever try to hurt either of you?"

"I don't think so. My memory from the beach demonstrated that he had a temper, but I don't remember any violence. Not that a lack of memories means much, I guess." Olivia motioned toward her head. "Who knows what they erased with this thing. The divorce certainly makes a lot more sense now. How could my mother stay married to someone who killed her uncle?"

"Yeah," Jed agreed. "Although it sounds like they stayed together for a couple years after he did it, which seems odd. And why did your mom want to protect your father in the first place?"

"There must have been a reason," Olivia said. "Maybe she even— even supported, or wanted—wanted the murder." Olivia put her face in her hands for a moment, then picked up her fork to choke down her pasta, which she could barely taste.

"I'm so sorry," Akiko murmured. "This is—"

"Yeah." Olivia dropped her fork. It was pointless. "How am I supposed to get any real answers on this?"

Pushing that rhetorical question aside for the moment, Olivia brought up another topic she'd wanted to delve into. "I've been thinking about something else that might be easier for us to pursue. If I'm remembering what happened to me, others must be too, right? And I told you I think I'm learning to control my symptoms, although I don't quite understand that yet. But it can't just be happening to me. We have to talk to some of the others—see who else is experiencing these things."

Jed nodded. "But we can't make it obvious."

"Agreed," Akiko said. "We've been taking some risks inside the institute lately, and we can't keep doing that. We'll have to start with a couple people, then try to have them spread the word if we think we can trust them. But the conversations need to happen outside of the building."

A face popped into Olivia's mind. "What about Jillian? She was gone for five days after they came to get Mikayla's body."

"She barely survived," Jed pointed out.

"Right, but she *did* survive." Olivia said. "I doubt most of us could. I wonder if she learned how to control her symptoms while she was gone, but maybe it was just too long for her to keep it up. Maybe she started remembering her true story too."

"It's worth a shot, though I'm not sure if she trusts anyone enough to talk about it," Akiko said. "I know what room she lives in. I'll ask if she'd be willing to meet up with us."

The rest of their dinner was quiet, despite the loudness of the restaurant. Anticipation, anxiety, fear, and the scariest of all, hope, seemed to dance in the air around them.

After their car ride back to the institute, but before they set foot inside, Olivia hugged Akiko and said, "You do so much for us—for everyone here. I don't want you to feel like you always have to. I can go to Jillian's room instead."

Akiko gave her a small smile. "To be honest, it's about feeling in control. Like I'm helping, yes, but also in control of something. I've always thought I understood my life, who I was and what happened to me. And now I understand that I know nothing. So, I'm controlling my own truths of who I am and how I handle a scary, unimaginable situation. I need to keep doing that for myself. If it results in something that will help all of us, that's even better."

Olivia hugged her friend again, so grateful she'd met this powerful, brave woman.

Akiko, after giving Jed's arm a gentle squeeze, slipped through the front door.

Jed gave Olivia a tired grin, his hands in his pockets as he rocked onto his heels. He was quirky and kind, but not someone she ever would have pictured herself with. And she realized she'd never wanted anyone more.

"Can you stay with me tonight?" she asked, feeling the heat in her cheeks.

His eyes warmed as he pulled her close. "Should I look forward to more clever references to a certain musician?"

Olivia's smile grew. "No, I think this night will be just for us."

Jed's eyes danced as he leaned down to kiss her. Olivia took his hand and led him inside and up to her room.

1 0 1 0 1 1 0 1 0

The next morning Akiko called their cell phones. Jed slept through his call, his arm thrown over Olivia, who was awake but curled into his chest, wishing she could stop time. Her phone rang a few seconds later.

"Can you meet me downstairs in about an hour? I'd like to go out for breakfast." There was a muffled tone of excitement in Akiko's voice.

"Did you two talk?" Olivia's heart pounded as she made her way into her kitchen to brew coffee.

"When we go out," Akiko answered.

"Okay, we'll be there."

"Ah, I see," Akiko's teasing tone made it quite clear she understood what had happened between her friends. "Good for you! Tell Jed I'll see you *both* in one hour!"

Olivia's face grew warm as she hung up the phone, but she smiled at Jed's still-sleeping form when she made her way back into her bedroom.

She sat down next to him on the bed, combing her fingers gently through his hair. He sighed and, with a yawn, shifted his body to look up at her. The obvious affection in his eyes, the slow smile on his lips, made her wish once again that time wouldn't keep barreling forward.

"Kiko wants us to meet her downstairs in an hour to go out for breakfast. I think her conversation was successful," she said in a murmur, careful not to elaborate.

"That can wait," he answered, pulling her down on top of him and kissing her in such a tender way that it brought tears to her eyes.

"For a little while," Olivia whispered near his ear with a laugh as he moved his attention to her neck. "It's only an hour."

"I can work with that." He laughed in a conniving way.

She gave a breathless chuckle before he once again found her mouth with his.

As they made their way downstairs exactly an hour after Akiko called, Olivia felt like she existed in some kind of bubble where absolute joy was in a constant low-key war with uncertainty and fear. Such a strange time in her life to feel so loved.

To their surprise, they didn't see Akiko in the lobby. Jed was just starting to talk about going up to her room when one of the elevators opened and Jillian walked out. She had her earbuds in and was checking something on her phone as she pushed open one of the building's front doors and walked off down the street.

A few minutes later, Akiko exited the elevator and strolled toward them, looking, in true Akiko gracefulness, like she was drifting just over the carpet rather than taking actual steps.

"Sorry, my treatment ran a little long," she said, giving them a smile. "Ready to go?"

"Everything okay?" Jed asked when they'd followed her out onto the street.

Akiko's casual façade was gone, anxiety now written across her face. "I hope so. Did you see her?"

"Yes, she left just before you came down," Olivia answered.

Akiko let out a long exhale. "Good. I was worried she was going to change her mind."

They got a ride to a diner on the other side of the city. It was full of tourists starting their adventures for the day. A November rain began not long after they walked through the door. The volume of the restaurant nearly matched that of the Italian place, making Olivia wonder if it would feel strange to eat in a quiet atmosphere someday.

Jillian was already sitting at a table in the back, nursing a mug of coffee. Olivia studied the woman as they approached. Her dark brown hair fell just above her shoulders, but there were silver strands weaving their way throughout. Her eyes were a beautiful shade of greenish blue, but right now they were sunken, dull, and rimmed in red. Her olive skin was dusted with freckles. There were dark sunglasses perched on the top of her head, even though the sky had been nothing but cloudy for the last week. She appeared to be in her earlier forties, but her hunched demeanor made it look as if she'd lived many more years. Olivia couldn't imagine the pain the woman must be feeling.

"Thanks for meeting us," Akiko said in a kind tone as she sat down next to Jillian and Jed and Olivia took the seats across from them. She didn't offer any hollow words about Jillian's grief. Olivia knew Akiko had experienced too much grief to try to sugarcoat it for someone else.

Their server came by to take drink orders, but Akiko asked for a few minutes. With how swamped the restaurant was, it would probably be longer than that.

"I almost didn't come," Jillian said on a choked breath, taking another sip of coffee, "but I know Mikayla would've wanted me to. Like all of us, she wanted to get the hell out of that fucking place. She didn't even care to know what was really going on, like I did; she just wanted to be free." Her voice cracked over the last few words, and her eyes came to rest on her mug.

Akiko nodded. "Tell us only as much as you want to."

Jillian looked up again, her gaze catching Olivia's before looking past all of them. "When you came to my door last night and handed me that note, asking if I was remembering anything from my past, asking if there was anything different happening with my symptoms, I was surprised. I wondered how you knew, but then figured at least one of you must be experiencing something similar.

"Lately, it's been like I'm able to—to lessen my symptoms. After Mikayla died and I left to stay with one of her brothers and his wife, I was so angry—just so angry and sad, that my symptoms would start, and I would just—ignore them. I refused to let them get ahold of me. And it worked—sort of. They dimmed, but they never completely stopped. I was able to stay away from the institute as long as I did because of that symptom control, but on the last day, it was too much, too painful. So, I had to go back there—to that nightmare of a place."

"The cachot," Olivia murmured, then realized Jillian might not know Jed and Akiko's word for the institute, but when she met the woman's eyes again, Jillian nodded.

"I was in a fog those few days following Mikayla's death, but after I got back and had that emergency treatment, I wondered how I'd survived being away that long," Jillian continued. "Since then, I've been—trying more—trying to see if I can stop my symptoms altogether. And I've been having a lot of luck. I've still been getting my treatments, so I don't draw attention to myself, but I haven't really needed them."

"That sounds just like what I've been doing," Olivia said with what almost felt like glee. "I found out the truth about my past, about why they really put the chip in my brain. I started being able to control my symptoms around that time. I can make them go away just as they start. I've still been getting my treatments as well, which doesn't seem to impact the process."

"You've never circled back to that with us," Jed said, tilting his head toward Akiko. There was no judgment in his voice, just curiosity.

"I was hoping to understand it better first, but I still don't." Olivia gave him a tentative smile, and he squeezed her hand under the table.

Jillian's eyes went wide. "How is it possible? Isn't it the failing implant causing the symptoms? How can we stop the symptoms if the implant hasn't been fixed?"

"I'm not sure, but I think we've been told a lot of lies about our implants, starting with why we got them. Have you—Have you discovered the truth about yours yet?" Olivia asked.

The woman's walls went up as soon as the question was voiced, her face becoming unreadable. But after a few moments, she took a deep breath, turned to Akiko, and murmured, "Can I trust all of you?"

Akiko put a hand over Jillian's, which was now resting next to her abandoned coffee. "Yes, I promise. The three of us are just starting to uncover the truth of the cachot. We know we've all been lied to. Anything you share with us stays with us."

Jillian squeezed her eyes shut and nodded, as if she was hearing someone speaking to her. When she opened her eyes, she turned them back at Olivia. "I haven't filled in all the pieces, but I'm starting to. I was told I developed schizophrenia in my early twenties, that the implant cured me. But a little while before Mikayla died, I started having dreams about my life. They started feeling more like visions because I would also have them while I was awake. Mikayla was there, which was baffling, because I first met her at the cachot, or so I thought. But I think I've known her a lot longer. I think we were a couple before.

"Mikayla's supposed story was that she was estranged from her family from the time she was a teenager. After her implant surgery as a young adult, the institute staff told her she had been a runaway with a major drug addiction. The implant had 'fixed' that addiction. They told her no one in her family wanted to talk to her, because they were ashamed of her. The institute gave her some financial assistance, helped her find a dump of an apartment. Then they just sent her off into the world.

"When Mikayla's failing implant called her back to the cachot decades later, Cordova tweaked the story. She said Mikayla's file showed the court had ordered Mikayla to go through a rehab program after some theft and vandalism convictions. Someone at the program knew about the cachot. Cordova told Mikayla her record stated she'd come to the cachot willingly all those years ago, to get help in erasing the addiction from her brain. But of course, Mikayla didn't remember any of this. She got back in touch with her brothers after she returned to the cachot, but they didn't have any answers for her. They confirmed they hadn't seen her since she was a teen. Her parents have both passed away.

"From what I'm starting to remember of my own life, my parents weren't happy that I was gay. They weren't happy that I was living with my girlfriend. They wanted me to stop seeing her. I believe Mikayla was my girlfriend. No, I'm *sure* she was. I can only imagine how I originally came to be at the cachot—and how Mikayla did. I have no idea how they got us there, because we were grown women. We were both young adults when we got our implants. But I think somehow my parents," she took a deep, shaky breath, "took matters into their own hands. They delivered us to the cachot somehow, forced us to get the implants. Maybe drugged us? Threatened us? I don't know. I haven't spoken to my parents in years, and they've made no effort to contact me at the cachot. All I know is Mikayala and I were happy. We loved each other—then and now." Tears were running down Jillian's cheeks.

Akiko put her arm around the woman's shoulders, and Jillian collapsed into herself, quietly sobbing.

Olivia felt herself go white. Was the institute full of people whose loved ones saw them as misfits—as defective? People whose "undesirable" qualities or experiences needed to be erased?

After a few minutes, Jillian turned to face Olivia again. "Since you can control your symptoms, do you ever think about leaving? If the cachot and our families did this to us on purpose, it's doubtful they're ever going to come up with a solution, if a solution is even needed. So, maybe if we can control our symptoms, we can just—go."

Stunned by the idea, Olivia's eyes flew to Jed, who wasn't hiding his anxiety well. "I—I haven't thought about that," she said. "But I don't think they'll make it that easy if they're trying to keep us here. And we still don't know if our implants really will shut down and kill us. I think we have to be sure." She turned her gaze briefly to Akiko, who gave a small shake of her head. She didn't want Olivia mentioning the resistance group. "We're working on some things. You'll have to trust us for now."

Jillian's eyes were dark and distant as she said, "I want to, and I'll try, but I can't stay at that place much longer. If something doesn't change soon, I'm leaving. And without Mikayla, I'm not sure I care much about what happens to me anyway."

CHAPTER 15

JILLIAN LEFT THE diner first, blending into the bustling crowd just outside the restaurant's windows. Olivia desperately hoped they would see her again. A few minutes later, they all received a text on their cell phones. The institute was requiring all residents outside of the building to return at once.

Jed ordered a car and they soon found themselves back in the large conference room on the second floor, where Dr. Cordova was openly crying about the sudden death of Mira Vargas, one of the institute's younger residents.

"Unfortunately, we have since learned from Ms. Vargas's friend Theo Koch, who is currently on the phone with her family, that Ms. Vargas was on her way to report the institute to the San Francisco police." Shock laced the doctor's tearful voice. "Her rideshare car was struck by an SUV running a red light and Ms. Vargas was killed instantly. The driver of her vehicle was taken to the hospital with life-threatening injuries."

"It's like they're not even trying anymore," Olivia heard someone mutter behind her.

Akiko's face was in her hands on Olivia's left. Jed was staring at the floor on her right. "Why do Mira and Theo's names sound familiar?" Olivia whispered.

"I think I mentioned them on your first day here," Jed mumbled. "Mira was so quiet, so scared of this place."

Dr. Cordova raised her voice over the growing volume of the crowd. "I just want to reiterate that I understand this is a scary, stressful time, but please don't attempt to involve outside agencies. There is nothing they can do. They don't have access to the technology needed to repair or replace your implants, and their intrusions will only decrease the time we could be spending on finding a solution. We will take care of you, but we can't keep you safe if you put yourself at risk like Ms. Vargas did today.

"Just like Sam and Mikayla's deaths, Ms. Vargas's passing is a horrible tragedy, and we will have counselors on site for you to speak to," the doctor continued. "I would also highly recommend that you leave the building as little as possible from now on. I'd like to avoid any more situations like this one."

This only increased the roar of conversation all around them. Dr. Cordova exited the room, flanked by several staff members, ignoring the questions being hurled at her. Olivia turned to seek out Jillian, but couldn't spot her anywhere in the room.

Akiko hung back to speak with some of the others, but Olivia and Jed pushed themselves out into the hallway.

"I think I'll try to get some work done in my room for a while," Jed mumbled.

"Okay, I'll wait for Kiko," Olivia said, squeezing his hand, understanding that he needed to be alone. "I'm sorry, Jed. I wish I had known her."

"She mostly kept to herself, but she was one of the kindest people I've ever met. She deserved to see the end of this." He gave her a weak smile and a quick kiss on her forehead. "I'll see you in a little while."

Watching Jed walk to the elevator, the doors closing behind him as he stepped inside, was one of the most defeating moments of Olivia's time at the institute. She could see the toll the murders were taking on him, but she didn't know how to help him through that terrible grief.

"He's met all of them—all the other residents." Akiko came up behind her. "He knows everyone's name. And I don't think he'd ever admit to it, but he cares about all of them. Because he got here first, he saw each and every one of us walking through those front doors. In a way, he's like the elder of this place, so I think the deaths are hitting him differently. Just be there for him. We all need to be there for each other."

Olivia wrapped her arms around herself. "Jed said Mira was very quiet, but it sounds like she was also very brave. I wonder what would have happened if she'd made it to the police."

"Me too," Akiko said. "Come downstairs with me?"

They took the stairs down to the lobby and settled into one of their usual tables after grabbing coffees from the café. Akiko's phone buzzed as she was taking her first sip. Her face remained neutral as she checked the screen, but Olivia saw something like muted triumph in her expression when she looked up.

"I've gotta do something. You don't have to wait for me, but I'll call or text you when I'm done." Akiko stood up, taking her cup with her.

"Um, okay. Want me to—" Olivia started, but Akiko smiled and gave an almost imperceptible shake of her head before walking away.

A deep sense of loneliness settled over Olivia, even though there were other residents milling through the lobby.

Wow, I really need to get out on my own more.

She closed her eyes, listening to the sounds of the people around her. Hushed conversations only allowed Olivia to catch a few words, but much of them involved Mira, Mikayla, and Sam. The residents were scared and confused; some were crying. Olivia's thoughts strayed to Jillian's idea of simply walking out the institute's front doors and never looking back. What would it be like to be free but leave those she cared about behind?

"Ms. Murphy." Dr. Cordova's voice came out of nowhere. Olivia's eyes flew open, and she jumped, slamming a knee against the bottom of the tabletop. Caramel-colored coffee spilled onto the table as her cup tipped over.

The doctor rushed to get some napkins, then helped Olivia sop up the mess. "I'm so sorry! I didn't mean to startle you."

"It's, um, it's okay." Olivia rubbed at her knee, sure there was already a bruise blooming beneath her jeans.

Dr. Cordova chose a chair across the table and sat down. "How are you, Ms. Murphy?"

It took a few seconds for Olivia's brain to catch up with the question. "I'm okay." She glanced over the doctor's shoulder, noting a few residents were furtively watching them. She was sure someone would help her if things took a turn.

"I'm glad. I know it's a scary time, but we'll get through it together. It's made me so happy to see you developing close relationships with Mr. Henley and Ms. Sato. Friends are so important in tough situations like this one."

Tough situations? You've got to be kidding me. A third person under your care just died because she was trying to report your organization to the police, and you took it upon yourself to kill her. And you're referring to it simply as a tough situation? Olivia so badly wanted to say those words out loud. Instead, she gave the doctor what she was sure was a weak smile.

"I actually thought I saw Ms. Sato here with you a few minutes ago, and I was hoping to talk to you both. Where did she go?" Dr. Cordova's voice remained kind, but there was a sudden sharpness to her eyes that made Olivia's breath hitch.

"I don't know." It wasn't a lie.

The doctor leaned in closer. "You understand, Ms. Murphy, how important it is for everyone to be extra cautious right now? I can't protect those who put themselves in harm's way."

Olivia narrowed her eyes as the thinly veiled threat sent not only fear, but also anger, coursing through her. She sat up straight, folding her hands on the table in front of her. "You said as much in the meeting. I believe we're all aware."

A beaming smile burst onto Dr. Cordova's face. "Good. I'm glad we're all on the same page." Then she stood up with a gentle rap of her knuckles on the table and walked away.

"You okay?" Olivia heard a voice ask from behind her, a tentative check-in from a resident she didn't know. She gave a small nod, but didn't turn around, then tried to look bored as she pulled her phone from the pocket of the jacket she was still wearing. She couldn't let her anxiety show in case anyone was watching.

"That woman is scary," someone else murmured from nearby.

Where are you? Please let me know you're ok. Olivia hurriedly texted Akiko.

Ten minutes ticked painfully by with no response, and just as Olivia was about to call, Akiko's response buzzed through. *I'm ok. Give me five more minutes and I'll meet you right outside?*

Allowing any more time to go by before seeing Akiko's face was a frightening idea, but she sent an affirmative response. As Olivia stood, she turned her attention to Ziya, but the younger woman was on the phone at her desk. Dr. Cordova was nowhere to be seen. Slipping out the front doors, Olivia walked down the block, trying not to look like she was waiting for someone.

When Akiko stepped outside a minute later, Olivia exhaled the breath she'd been holding. Akiko saw her almost immediately and began walking her way. Her stride was purposeful, and as she got closer, Olivia noticed the grin on her lips. They fell in step together, down the sidewalk and away from the institute.

"I need to tell you something," Olivia said.

"Me too! The resistance group is getting ready to move forward! They're going to get me into a meeting so I can help!" Akiko's walk was now almost more of a bounce.

Olivia frowned. "How? Where are they meeting?"

"I don't have the specifics yet, but I was told just now that it will be soon. They'll contact me when they're ready."

"Kiko, this scares me," Olivia said. "How well do you know the people you've been meeting with? I'm worried it's a trap."

Akiko pulled her to a stop. "We talked about this before. I completely trust my sources."

"I know, but listen, I think Cordova might be on to you. While you were gone, she randomly approached me in the lobby, scared the crap out of me, and started talking about the friendships I have with you and Jed. Then she asked where you were. Not Jed, just you. She made what was clearly a threat about how none of us should be taking risks right now, and I'm pretty sure she was talking about you! Then she got all fake happy and just walked away."

Olivia saw the flash of doubt cross Akiko's face, but it was gone in a second. "She can think whatever she wants, but she has no proof. I'm being extremely careful."

"I don't think she cares much about proof," Olivia responded.

"We're so close now." Akiko started walking again, and Olivia had to hurry to catch up. "I have to be part of shutting that place down."

"We all want to be! At least ask them if Jed and I can come with you to the meeting."

Guilt crept into Akiko's expression. "That means a higher chance of drawing attention to ourselves. And if—if you could not tell Jed about this for now—"

"What? No!" Olivia shook her head before Akiko could finish her thought. "I can't do that, Kiko. He'll be pissed. And if something happens to you—"

"I'll fill him in on everything as soon as I can, fill you both in, but we were just talking about how severely the murders are hitting him. I don't want to put even more weight on his shoulders."

"Okay, I understand that, but this just seems so dangerous. Kiko, we can't lose you." Olivia fought back fresh tears.

Akiko stopped again and pulled her into a hug. "You won't. You're never getting rid of me. But Olivia, I *have* to do this. I've been picked to do this. You know what my implant has taken from me. I do want to find happiness again someday. But we all need to get the hell out of the cachot first."

Olivia stepped away, running a palm down her face with an exhale. "Well, if there's anyone to lead us out, it's you. But you have to promise me you'll do everything you can to be careful. And you have to update us as soon as possible."

"Of course, I will. You know me, the secret spy." Akiko smirked back.

"Why do you have to be so loveable? It's annoying," Olivia said with an eye roll.

"I'm pretty awesome, huh?" Akiko grinned. "And I love you too, friend."

"Sure, Ms. Spy. Just remember the wrath I will have to endure if something happens to you."

Akiko's laugh filled the air around them as she laced her arm through Olivia's and tugged her back into a walk.

1 0 1 0 1 1 0 1 0

Olivia didn't tell Jed about the conversation as they lay in her bed that night, one of his hands loosely clasped with hers. The guilt she felt at hiding something from him was eating away at her, so to mask her anxiety, she had to fill the silence with words. There was a question she'd been pondering for a while.

"What do you think we'd be like if they took these things out of our brains?"

"Hmm?" he murmured.

"I mean, would we be different people? Would it change our personalities?"

She wanted to mention that remembering the details of her uncle's death hadn't made her feel any different, but thought better of it in case someone was listening. When Jed didn't respond, she turned to look at him, but he was already asleep.

What felt like minutes later, Jed jerked up next to her with a strangled cry.

Olivia's hands flew in his direction in the dark. "What is it?" she asked, trying to slow her heart.

"I know what happened," he answered, his voice matching the shaking of his body. "The truth. I remember now."

Olivia's heart continued its jagged pace. She pulled him close, rubbing one of his arms, desperate to ease his trembling. "Can you tell me?"

"It *was* a car accident." He stopped talking then to take some controlled breaths. Several minutes passed before he spoke again, and during that time his body had stilled. "I was the one driving. I was a teenager. It was my girlfriend with me. She d-died. I crashed and she died. I can't—I can't remember her name. God, I can't remember her name." His voice cracked as sobs tore through him.

Olivia felt his tears dripping onto her bare chest and arms. He cried for so long that her arms grew tired from holding him, but she didn't let go. She understood the mind-shattering pain he was going through; nothing could make her let go.

CHAPTER 16

OLIVIA WANTED TO find Dr. Cordova's office so she could storm into it. She wanted to beat down the door, throw aside a chair, and yell until she was numb. The shock of remembering her uncle's death—of being certain her father was the one who killed him—was an intense kind of trauma she never thought she'd have to live through. But experiencing Jed's pain, hearing his guttural sobs, holding him as he once again found sleep, was something altogether more agonizing.

He woke up the next morning quiet and pale.

Olivia called Akiko, who was at Olivia's suite door in minutes. This time Akiko turned the music on to a cymbal-crashing symphony. When they'd gotten a full cup of coffee in Jed, as well as a few bites of scrambled eggs, he took a deep breath and met their eyes with his.

"She was my high school girlfriend. I was seventeen and had had my license for six months. Her mother didn't want her in the car with me—said someone so young and reckless shouldn't be driving her daughter. She was the youngest of three sisters," Jed said as his eyes got wide, remembering another detail. "Her mom always treated her like a little girl. She hated that.

"She ignored her mom, and we went to the movies that night. I don't remember what we saw, but whatever it was felt life-changing to two teenagers in a small town. I remember we debated the plot as we left the theater. She loved to debate, and I loved her." He managed a small smile at this. "And she was beautiful when she talked—so full of passion and confidence. All I ever wanted to do was listen and watch her face as it lit up.

"It was raining pretty hard when we left the theater. We were distracted by our talk—high off thinking we were the smartest people in the world. I took a turn too fast in my fucking truck, went down the embankment. We lived in the hills. There was forest all around our town. We skidded right down into the trees. I can hear her screams." Jed paused, squeezing his eyes closed before opening them again to continue, "I wanted to open my mouth, to tell her it was going to be okay, but the world was flying past me, and I couldn't move." A few tears streaked down his cheeks. Olivia reached her hand across the table and softly gripped his arm. He took a shaky breath and started again. "We hit a tree—so hard. I don't know if her seatbelt was on. They told me later it wasn't, but I didn't believe she'd ever forget that. I thought something must have severed it somehow, or that it came unclasped.

"I remember very little from after the accident, just some flashes of the hospital. I think I broke a couple bones, but I know there wasn't any damage to my brain. They didn't have to tell me she died; somehow, I already knew. I'm not sure what happened next. I don't know if I was charged or served any time. I don't know how I got to the institute or why I had the procedure done, but I'm sure it had to do with the accident—with her."

Jed frowned, lost in his thoughts. "They erased the accident, which seems merciful, but they also erased her. They just took her away. I have no memories of my time with her before the accident. I don't remember anything else about her family, besides what I told you, or how we met. I don't know how long we'd been dating. I don't know how well she knew my family. I still—I still don't remember her name."

He stopped and covered his eyes with a hand. Olivia wanted to punch something.

Akiko heaved a sigh. "Jed, I'm so sorry. Do you think you want to try to talk to your mom about it?"

"Yes. I have a lot of questions I want answers to. But—" he took his hand from his face and placed it on the table, "it's been so long—close to thirty years. What will this do to her? Talking about my *fake* accident wasn't easy for her. My mom, she's a good person. I killed someone. I can't—"

Olivia moved chairs to sit next to him, gently rubbing his back. "It was a horrible accident. I don't know the circumstances leading up to your implant, but it's your life. It was your experience. You deserve answers if you want them."

Akiko nodded.

Jed looked up, his eyes red and tired. "I'll have to figure out how I want to approach that conversation with her."

"Let me get you some water." On the way to the refrigerator, an idea popped into Olivia's head. As she sat back down, handing Jed his water, she asked, "Have either of you ever wondered if any of this is real?"

"You mean are we living in some kind of controlled environment, like *The Matrix* or *The Truman Show*?" Akiko said. "Yeah, Jed and I tossed that idea around a couple times after we arrived here. It was a little too daunting to think about, so we dropped it."

Olivia wished she hadn't thought of it as she tried to calm her already spiraling mind. "That's probably for the best."

"Great movies, though," Jed added, pushing up from the table. "Okay, I need to try to move on with my day. I'm going to take a quick shower."

As he walked down the hall toward the bathroom, Akiko's phone rang. She stood up quickly, excitement in her eyes. "I need to get this. I'll call you in a bit!" She was out the suite door before Olivia could say anything.

Wondering if she could get her mind to slow down enough for a nap, Olivia leaned back in her chair, but jumped as there was a loud thump against the outer wall of her room. "Jed!" she called, already striding toward her door, but she could hear the shower running, so he probably didn't hear her. "Jed!" she yelled one more time anyway. She flung open her front door and propelled herself into the hallway, already sure of what she would find.

Akiko lay crumpled on the floor, and Olivia's vision narrowed into a tunnel as she fell to her knees next to her. She felt for a pulse at Akiko's neck and let out a garbled cry as she found one. She pushed her friend's dark hair out of her face, checking her body for injuries. There was a large bump forming on the right side of her head, presumably from where she'd hit the wall on her way down. Although Olivia didn't see any other obvious injuries, she didn't want to move Akiko without being sure.

"Help me! Someone help!" she screamed, sure there had to be some residents in the suites around hers, cursing the fact that she'd left her phone inside.

Olivia heard her suite door bang open. Then Jed was kneeling beside her, his hair dripping and his shirt sticking to his wet chest. She noticed over the buzzing in her ears that he was talking to someone.

"Yes, she's just outside Olivia Murphy's suite on the tenth floor. It looks like she just collapsed," he was saying in a hurried voice.

He must be on the phone with the medical staff. Olivia could barely grasp the thought as it flitted through her mind.

"Akiko, can you hear me?" Olivia murmured.

"You're coming now, right?" Jed asked, his tone growing angry. "Yes, Ms. Murphy and I will be waiting with her."

When he hung up, Olivia shot him a glance. His expression said he was ready to fight someone. "What happened?" she asked.

"The nurse told me there are a lot of people experiencing symptom flares right now. At first it sounded like they weren't going to send anyone. But they better fucking send someone," he growled.

"It's okay. I'm fine," Akiko said in a voice just above a whisper. Olivia whirled back to her, supporting Akiko's right side as she sat up.

"Slow. Go slow," Olivia advised. "You've got a bump on your head. I don't know if you have any other injuries."

"You're not fine," Jed's voice didn't change. "Don't stand up!"

"She's not the one you're angry at," Olivia reminded him.

"Don't worry, I'm not going anywhere." Akiko's eyes were closed as she let her head lean back against the wall behind her.

"Someone will be here soon." Olivia was trying to soothe herself just as much as she was her friend. "Do you remember what happened?"

Akiko's eyes fluttered open, but she looked past Olivia and Jed. "Not really. I had just left your suite, felt a little dizzy. I remember stumbling, but nothing else until now."

"What about the call you answered just as you left?" Olivia whispered, retrieving Akiko's phone from where it lay on the floor next to her.

Akiko looked at the device as if confused, then gave her head a small shake. "I'm not sure. I think it was about the meeting."

"What meeting?" Jed responded.

Just as Olivia was wondering if Akiko would tell Jed about the latest development with the resistance group, even though it wasn't safe to do so, the elevator down the hall opened and several members of the medical staff rushed out with a gurney.

"No, I don't want—" Akiko started, but then lifted a hand to her head with a wince.

"We'll come down with you, Kiko," Jed said.

"We're taking her to emergency on the third floor, not the clinic," said one of the male nurses as he helped her onto the gurney. "We're a little overwhelmed at the moment. It might be better for you to wait here. We can have someone update you soon."

"Should I call 911 and have her taken to a real hospital then—if you're so overwhelmed?" Jed snapped back.

"Jed, stop," Akiko said, and Olivia shifted closer to him.

"Is that what I need to do? Are you scared of me calling for outside medical professionals?" Jed's body was radiating rage.

"Of course not," the same nurse frowned back. "Fine, just wait fifteen minutes so we can get her settled and then you can both come down. But you might have to stay in the waiting area."

"Okay, thank you," Olivia answered, grabbing one of Jed's hands, which was balled into a fist.

"I'll be fine. See you soon," Akiko said as they rolled the gurney back toward the elevator.

When the doors closed behind them, Olivia was ready to play a game for anyone watching and listening. "I realized I've never seen Akiko have a symptom flare before. She seemed fine in my room. But it must have been pretty bad."

"She's a master at hiding her symptoms," Jed grumbled back, still staring at the closed elevator door. "At least now she can get a treatment." He gave Olivia a pointed look. Neither of them believed Akiko had had a symptom flare.

Fifteen minutes crawled by. Olivia could feel every bit of tension flowing from Jed's body as he slammed his way through the emergency room entrance and into the waiting area. The nurse hadn't been lying: the place was overflowing with residents who were in various stages of symptom flares. Some were curled up in chairs, holding their heads, some were pacing, and others were prone on the floor. Sounds of crying and quiet pleas for relief filled the air.

"This place is a joke," Jed muttered. "They're not even equipped to help these people."

Dr. Cordova was across the room but made her way to them while checking on patients. "Are you both having symptom flares as well?"

Before Jed could say anything that might get him into trouble, Olivia answered, "We're actually just here to see Akiko. What's going on?"

The doctor looked haggard as she took in the residents all around her. "It started early this morning and seems to be increasing. I'm not sure why. We'll keep everyone updated. If you'd like to see Ms. Sato, check in at the desk and they can take you to her." And then she was gone.

After a surprisingly short wait time, a nurse, who introduced herself as Vandy, led them to Akiko. They passed residents in exam rooms and waiting in hallways. Nurses and doctors were jogging from patient to patient to record symptoms and administer treatments. Olivia looked up into Jed's eyes and saw fear there. In Akiko's room, a curtain was all that separated her from three other residents in varying states of consciousness in their own beds.

"No one has any idea why so many people are experiencing symptom flares right now?" Jed asked.

Vandy shook her head. "We're working on it and even have a group of the engineers down here to help, but no answers so far."

"Have the engineers recreated a model implant to study and tweak outside of a resident's brain?" Jed asked. "That's gotta be helpful in situations like this."

"I'm not sure about that, but I do know they kept Sam's," the nurse answered, then her face went pale as she realized her mistake.

Olivia was positive her face matched Vandy's. She kept a tight hold on Jed's hand as she said, "They kept Sam's? You mean, they—removed it?"

Vandy closed her eyes for a few seconds. A blush spread across her face. "I shouldn't have said that, I'm sorry. I'm so exhausted, I'm forgetting myself. I can't say anything else about that."

"You can't just—" Jed started, but she waved his words away.

"I'm sorry, I have to go. You can see her now." Vandy motioned toward Akiko's bed and raced away.

"Jesus, I—" Jed started.

"We'll talk about it later," Olivia murmured. They both took another deep breath and stepped around the curtain to move to the side of Akiko's bed.

Their friend's eyes were closed, but they opened groggily as Olivia placed a hand on her arm. "Oh, hi. This is the happiest I've ever been to see you," Akiko said in the softest voice Olivia had ever heard her use.

"Sorry the other times were kind of a letdown." Jed answered with a sarcastic smirk.

Olivia couldn't help but laugh, even though images of forceps removing a computer chip from a deceased brain floated through her mind.

"How are you feeling?" Olivia asked, then lowered her voice to a murmur. "Have they been treating you okay?"

"I'm all right, just a little dizzy. I haven't noticed anything out of the ordinary, but I've only seen a couple nurses and a doctor who wasn't Cordova."

"Do you think it was your symptoms?" Olivia kept her voice quiet. "I realized I don't even know what your symptoms are."

"It wasn't," Akiko whispered. "And you'll never know what they are, because I don't want to put those thoughts in your head."

"Understood. Did you get to finish your phone call?" Olivia asked.

"What phone call?" Jed frowned.

Akiko just shook her head.

Olivia sighed and raised her voice to a normal volume, ignoring Jed's confused expression. "And your head? Have they run any tests or said anything about how long you'll have to stay here?"

"They said I have a mild concussion. They're ordering some scans and bloodwork. It sounds like I'll be here until at least tomorrow."

"We'll stay with you," Jed said.

"Thank you. That would make me feel better." Akiko motioned for them to lean in, their heads close to her face so they could hear her. "It was her. As I left your suite, a wave of dizziness hit me. I tried to catch myself on the wall, but must have ended up hitting my head. I remember being on the floor. I heard footsteps on the carpet behind me. Cordova walked by and just kept walking. She didn't look at me. I don't remember her touching me or feeling any kind of pain with the dizziness. But it was her who did this to me; I know it was."

"She must have gotten in the elevator or stairwell just before I came out of my room," Olivia murmured. "Not to sound morbid, but why did she let you live?"

"I was wondering the same thing at first. And then I thought about the fact that she also let me see her. She wanted me to know.

She was sending a message. You were right, Olivia; she's on to me. And that makes next steps even more important."

"I hope someone will explain this conversation to me at some point," Jed muttered.

"Soon." Olivia nodded.

Akiko reached for their hands. "And you both need to stay safe. She's already murdered Mikayla to hurt Jillian. I'm guessing she'd have no problem killing the people I love."

CHAPTER 17

FOR THE REST of the day, Akiko drifted in and out of sleep. Jed left briefly to get his laptop, and Olivia to get a book. Jed brought in lunch, and Olivia grabbed dinner. They intended to stay the night next to Akiko's bed, but some of the nurses had to squeeze in yet another patient. The resident was in a significant amount of pain and had to be sedated so he would stop screaming.

At that point, one of the nurses told Olivia and Jed they had to leave. Jed refused. The nurse appeared ready to drag him out herself when Akiko said, "I'll be okay. She didn't do it then, she won't do it now. I'll see you in a little while."

"Call or text us if you need anything at all. And let us know your test results when you can." Olivia gently hugged her friend, making sure Akiko's phone was on the small table next to the hospital bed.

"We'll be back as soon as possible." Jed continued his glare at the nurse as Olivia took his hand and pulled him from the room.

"Kiko's right," Olivia said. "If Cordova was going to do something more extreme, she would have done it already. And maybe I'm being naïve, but there must be some good medical professionals here, ones that would protect Akiko if she needed them to."

The emergency room appeared to be calming down as they made their way out and down the hall toward the elevators. Olivia was just allowing herself to feel grateful when Jed doubled over with a gasp, clutching his head between his hands.

"What is it? Are you in pain?" Olivia didn't try to mask the panic in her voice.

"Just—symptoms. Bad." He forced out.

"Let's get you back inside." She put her arm around him so he could lean on her. But when she tried to turn him back toward the emergency room, he wouldn't move.

"*Not* g-going to l-let them touch me," he muttered, his breathing ragged.

With what happened to Akiko, as well as the rush of symptom flares, Olivia could understand why he felt that way, so she helped him down the rest of the hallway to the elevators. It felt like an eternity for one of the two sets of doors to open, but when one did, they stumbled inside, Jed sitting on the floor with his head leaning back against the wall.

"Take deep breaths," Olivia instructed. "Focus on how you feel about this place—about what it's done to us. Focus on your sadness and anger. Don't let them be buried by the pain. They're trying to control us with the pain. Don't let them. Focus on your feelings." This was the only way she could describe how she controlled her own symptoms.

His breathing slowed as his body visibly relaxed. "I hate this fucking place!" he yelled. "They had no right to do what they did! I want all the memories I deserve to have! I want to remember her name!"

By the time they made it to Olivia's suite on the tenth floor, Jed was upright and moving on his own. "It worked," he whispered. "You were right. It worked; I stopped them."

Words were elusive as tears streamed down her face. But it felt like they were one step closer to being free.

1 0 1 0 1 1 0 1 0

Time felt like it was taunting. They'd already gone out for a very cold walk around the block so Olivia could fill Jed in on Akiko's news about the resistance group. With the danger they were all in, it didn't feel right to keep it from him.

Jed's shoulders had hunched and his frown deepened as he'd taken in the information. "I understand why it's so important to her to help, but they're not keeping her safe. Cordova obviously knows something is going on. If the resistance group wanted to involve Kiko, they should've found a way to protect her."

"I agree," Olivia had turned her face up to the darkened sky for the briefest of moments, focusing on the breeze against her skin. "It doesn't give me a lot of faith in their efforts."

Now, hours later, Jed was pacing back and forth between his kitchen and dining table, Tchaikovsky booming from his Bluetooth speaker. "I know Cordova probably already would've killed Kiko if she was going to, but it doesn't feel safe to leave her there. It doesn't feel safe to leave *anyone* there."

It was almost midnight, and they'd moved to his suite on the fifth floor to be closer to the emergency room.

Olivia was watching him from the couch, commanding herself not to get up and join the hypnotizing movement. Helplessness was the theme of this place, and she was certainly feeling that now. "I know. But she still needed medical treatment, and we can't give that to her. We'll get her out as soon as we can. Maybe send her a text, see if she responds? Then we can call down to the emergency room to see if we can get some kind of update on the symptom flares."

Jed settled down next to her, grabbing his cell phone from the coffee table. He was typing out a text when he made a surprised grunt and said, "I don't have any service. No Wi-Fi, no data, no bars."

"What?" Olivia pulled her phone out of her pocket, noting the lack of icons at the top right of her screen. An unnerving feeling settled in her gut as her heart picked up speed. "Okay, we'll just call down." She picked up the landline phone on the side table, but there was no dial tone. She slowly lowered it back down into its cradle.

"What—" Jed began in confusion, but a hard knock on his front door made them both jump. He motioned for Olivia to stay behind him as he checked the peephole. "It's Ziya," he said. He pulled the door open like the woman might lunge at them. With this place, who knew.

"Mr. Henley, Ms. Murphy, I'm sorry to show up unannounced, but Dr. Cordova and Mr. Adamian wanted the staff to inform all residents that phone and Internet services for the building have been shut off due to the current situation. I know this isn't ideal, but they don't want residents and their families outside the building to cause a general panic while they get things under control. But with Thanksgiving being today," Ziya checked her watch, "almost yesterday, they will both do everything they can to get the phones back up soon so those who had symptom flares can call any loved ones they missed talking to."

"Thanksgiving?" Olivia murmured. "We didn't realize." She looked at Jed, feeling completely baffled. How was it possible to exist in a place that was so outside of time, she didn't even know when it was a major holiday? No one had mentioned it until now.

She thought about her mother then and the fact that she was supposed to have gone to Beth's house for Thanksgiving. *Did she think about me today?*

"Really? I'm sure my mom would have called me this morning." Jed shook his head like he was filing that away for later and asked, "*Are* things getting under control? When we were in the emergency room, it seemed like the majority of residents were being hit with flares."

Ziya's face stayed professional. "Yes, the situation is already making a turn for the better. Several residents have been discharged to rest in their suites. Others are showing great improvement with treatment. Dr. Cordova still doesn't have an answer for why this happened, but she expects things to be much better by the morning."

"That's good to hear, but I don't know that shutting down Internet and phones was the best response," Olivia said. "That's probably scaring people even more. And how *did* they manage to shut down our cell service? There are so many different carriers, and—"

"Dr. Cordova and Mr. Adamian decided it was the best way to keep all residents safe," Ziya interrupted. "Your cell phones will be reconnected along with the landline phones and Internet when the time is right."

"Okay," Jed muttered. Olivia knew he was fighting back less productive words.

Ziya nodded and seemed ready to move on, but Olivia noticed a slight hesitation in the woman's eyes. "Is there something else?"

"How is Ms. Sato doing?" Ziya asked in a whisper, even though Jed's music was still blasting in the background.

Surprise washed over Olivia. "Um, she's okay, we think. We haven't heard any updates since we had to leave the ER because of space issues, and we weren't able to text her with the phones being down, but Akiko's a fighter, so she'll be fine."

Ziya nodded again. "I'm sure you're right." She paused, then took a pronounced breath and continued, "Ms. Sato had asked me to look up some information for you, Ms. Murphy. When I called her this morning, before her—incident, I was going to give it to her over the phone. She wanted to tell you herself, but in case she doesn't remember, or doesn't get a chance, I wrote it down to give to you myself. It's another contact for your mother."

She reached in the pocket of her blazer, then held out a small slip of folded paper. It fluttered in the movement of air from the heater kicking on in Jed's suite. Olivia took it with caution, recognizing it as a page ripped from the generic writing pads placed throughout the institute's rooms. Why would she need additional contact information for her mother? "Uh, thanks. I—" Olivia looked up to the sound of Ziya's boots marching away down the hall.

"That was weird." Jed ushered Olivia back inside and closed the suite door.

"Do you think she's…" Olivia's question of whether Jed thought Ziya was in the resistance group drifted away as she unfolded the paper. The tiny print on the page did not reflect contact information for her mother; another name greeted Olivia instead. Ivy Lynch. Under the name was an address in the Northern California foothills.

"Lynch," Olivia murmured. "Lynch is my mother's maiden name. Ivy Lynch." The name rolled over her tongue and a fresh set of memories—memories of a kind woman with the brightest smile and warmest hugs—blossomed in Olivia's mind. A sob escaped her as she said, "Uncle Jack's wife. I didn't remember her until now. Aunt Ivy."

1 0 1 0 1 1 0 1 0

After the phones were turned back on around three in the morning, Dr. Cordova sent out a pre-recorded voicemail to all residents: "We've made it through the worst. No new patients have arrived at the emergency room in the last several hours, and many of those admitted earlier tonight have been discharged to their suites. Thank you for your patience and strength. We're growing ever closer to a solution. We'll have more specifics over the next week. For now, I encourage all of you to get some sleep."

When Jed called the emergency room, the nurse on duty confirmed that Akiko was resting comfortably.

"Wanna try for four hours of sleep so we can get there right when visiting hours start at eight?" Jed asked, but as soon they were in his bed, he tossed and turned, unable to settle.

Olivia felt like a zombie when she crawled out of bed just after seven o'clock. Memories of Aunt Ivy, Uncle Jack, and their orchard had shaken her awake whenever she'd managed to fall asleep. She checked the paper Ziya had given her for the millionth time, still not sure if the address was that of the orchard. She knew where the town was located, though, and she'd be willing to travel anywhere to see her aunt again.

I have to go, but I can't leave Jed and Akiko.

Olivia and Jed walked through the emergency room doors at exactly eight o'clock. As they stood at the reception desk to check in, Olivia clocked Dr. Cordova approaching them from a back hallway. Jed tensed when he saw her a second later.

"Can I speak to you two in private?" the doctor asked in a quiet voice.

"We were just checking in to see Akiko," Jed said, not making eye contact.

"I need to speak to you about Ms. Sato," Dr. Cordova said.

Olivia's heart skipped a beat.

"What's going on?" Jed wasn't trying to keep calm, and his increasing volume was causing others to stare.

The physician's expression was one of clear discomfort. "Please come with me."

Placing a hand on his back, Olivia gave Jed a small push to follow Dr. Cordova, who was already walking away.

"What the hell is going on?" Jed didn't wait for the doctor to close the door of the small conference room off the waiting area.

"Sit down, please." Dr. Cordova motioned to the two metal folding chairs across the table from her own as she took a seat.

The room was sterile, cold, white—not a place Olivia pictured anyone receiving news about a loved one. She looked up when she noticed Jed wasn't sitting. He stood behind his chair, arms folded, glaring at the doctor.

Dr. Cordova sighed up at him before clasping her hands together on top of the table. "Ms. Sato disappeared sometime in between the hours of three, when a nurse checked in on her, and five-thirty this morning, when the same nurse attempted to take her vitals. Because the nurse reported that *you* called right after three o'clock to check on Ms. Sato's status, we were hoping she might have contacted you."

Olivia was having trouble understanding what the physician was saying, her brain a jumble of images of Akiko in that hospital bed. "She's gone?" Her own voice sounded so far away.

"No, she hasn't contacted us!" Jed's voice cracked. "What do you mean she disappeared? She was here five hours ago! Was she even well enough to walk out on her own? Did she say anything to anyone? Did anyone see her leave her bed?"

"No, unfortunately much of the staff had left by then, because most of the patients had been discharged," the doctor explained. "The staff members who remained were catching up on paperwork and tending to the few residents staying overnight. When the nurse last saw her, Ms. Sato seemed to feel much better, but she was still tired and a little groggy, hence why she was resting when you called. She had a mild concussion but no significant injuries. Her scans and bloodwork came back clear. I believe she was capable of getting up and walking. And with the staff busy, it might have made it easier for her to sneak out."

Jed jammed his hands back through his hair. "You *believe* she was capable? Sneak out? Why are you making her sound like a criminal? The emergency room isn't that big! How could she have snuck anywhere? No one saw *anything*?"

Dr. Cordova shook her head. "I've spoken at length to each staff member. None of them saw her. And she made no mention of leaving to any of them."

"Jed, sit down," Olivia said when she noticed he was swaying where he stood. She took his hand and pulled him into the seat next to hers.

"Could someone have taken her?" Olivia asked. "Was there any sign of a struggle in her hospital room? Were there any other patients still in her room who might have seen or heard something?"

"Everything in the room looked as it should—undisturbed—like she simply pulled back the covers and left," the doctor said. "All other patients in her room had been discharged or moved to other rooms as space became available, so there was no one to see or hear anything. And do you know of any reasons why Ms. Sato would be abducted?"

Olivia studied Dr. Cordova's confused face. *She really would have made quite the actress.*

A memory from the night before materialized in Olivia's mind. What had Ziya said when she gave Olivia the note with Aunt Ivy's address? She'd wanted Olivia to have it in case Akiko forgot or didn't get the chance to give it herself. Had that been a clue that the resistance group was going to get Akiko out of the institute?

"I need you to be truthful with me," Jed said to the doctor, breaking Olivia from her thoughts. "Is she alive? Is she okay?"

Oh, he's doing this. Not an outright accusation, but close enough.

Dr. Cordova stared back at Jed for several uncomfortable moments, tilting her head the smallest bit to the left. Her eyes were dark, her expression unchanged. "How would I know that, Mr. Henley? Those are things *I'm* hoping to find out. It appears Ms. Sato left of her own free will, although since she was not officially discharged, she left against medical advice. If she did want to keep herself safe, leaving was not the way to go about it."

"If she did leave, I'm sure it was actually the *best* way for her to go about keeping herself safe," Jed muttered back.

Olivia tried to shut him up with a glare, but he didn't notice. *Akiko would kill me if she knew I was letting him talk like this.*

The doctor said nothing but continued to stare.

Just then, Olivia remembered something else. "Her phone! Her phone was on the table right next to her bed. Is it gone too?"

Dr. Cordova turned her attention to Olivia, her expression softening. "It is."

She has it with her! They could just call or text Akiko when the doctor was no longer around.

"We've tried to call her, from several different numbers, but each call went straight to voicemail without ringing," Dr. Cordova continued. "When we attempted to text her, the texts said undelivered."

Olivia's hope fizzled.

Jed dug his own phone out of his pocket. The reception throughout the emergency room wasn't great, but he was able to make a call. "Straight to voicemail," he confirmed.

"Of course, if we find out anything regarding her whereabouts, we will inform you, but we ask that you do the same," Dr. Cordova said. "While she was well on the road to recovery, it would be advisable for her to come back to finish the discharge process. And," she heaved a sigh, "we will have to inform her family that she is missing."

"They'll be terrified!" Olivia shuddered.

"I've never spoken to her parents, but maybe I should be the one to call," Jed offered.

"You may certainly speak to them afterward, Mr. Henley, but I ask that you let me notify them first. As the medical director of this facility, it is my responsibility."

Jed gave a reluctant dip of his chin as Olivia squeezed his hand in support.

"Now, I'm sorry, but I do have to go take care of that phone call and attend to other matters. Like I mentioned before, please let us know if you hear anything from or about Ms. Sato." Dr. Cordova stood and exited the room before either of them responded.

They double-checked Akiko's hospital bed, but the room was just as the doctor had said: vacant with no signs of foul play. After an Uber ride to the wharf, they purposefully blended into the crowd of tourists and noise.

"The group must have already gotten her out." Olivia said. "That has to be it, right?" She reminded him of what Ziya had said the night before.

"I hope so," he answered. "Cordova wanted to see what we knew; she doesn't have her."

Multiple calls to Akiko's phone went to voicemail, and every text they sent said undelivered. The last remaining shreds of hope seemed to leave Jed as he stared at his phone, willing his friend to contact him.

"Kiko's alive, Jed, I know she is!" Olivia said, and she truly had never been surer of anything in her life. "She's part of a plan. She trusts that group, so we have to trust her. She'll get in touch with us when she can—hopefully soon. Until then, we keep moving forward, because that's what she would want us to do. And that brings me to my own plan."

Jed stopped walking, his hands in his pockets. He looked to the right, watching groups of people walk toward the shops and eateries on the pier. When he turned his gaze back to her, his eyes were fierce. "I think I might know what you're going to say."

She nodded. "Ziya gave me that information on purpose, whether Kiko was part of finding it or not. They want me to go to Aunt Ivy. I need to see her. I'd like you to come with me, and I think we should leave today."

CHAPTER 18

"YOU'RE SURE YOU** want to come?" Olivia asked from where she sat on the chair in Jed's bedroom, her feet tucked up beneath her legs. Jed was tossing clothes in an open suitcase on his bed. This time Journey was rocking from the Bluetooth speaker, at Olivia's request.

Jed stopped packing and sent her a classic Jed smirk. "Ouch. I thought my vague, albeit imaginary, connection to an Eagle, and my charming qualities, would keep you interested longer than this."

She rolled her eyes with as much drama as she could muster. "Oh, your qualities are certainly interesting," she laughed as he frowned in mock hurt. "Sorry, I think I'm just second guessing everything. What if my aunt doesn't want to see me after all these years? What if Akiko comes back while we're gone and doesn't know where we are? What if you're only going with me because you feel like you have to?"

Jed pulled her onto the bed with him. "Besides the fact that I might be murdered while you're gone and wouldn't get to say goodbye to you, it would also be boring here without you."

"Wow—dark and awkward. There's the Jed I know," Olivia muttered as he laughed.

"And you were right, Liv, Kiko's part of a plan. I don't think she'll come back until the group puts something into motion. If she had nothing to do with the information about your aunt, they'll fill her in.

"As far as your aunt goes, you remember her having a joyful face and great hugs. That doesn't sound like someone who won't want to see you. Realistically though, it's a risk, but I think you could get some real answers and reconnect with a family member who probably misses you."

"Yeah, you're right." Olivia leaned into his chest. "I just don't think I've ever felt so terrified and excited about something at the same time. You said you wanted to call your mom to tell her you were leaving. Did you reach her?"

He shook his head. "I've left her two messages, but she's not calling me back."

Frustration laced Olivia's next words, "I hate that they get to be the ones to hide and coverup and lie, and we have to be the ones to figure out how to stay alive."

"I agree," Jed said. "However, and not to replace my preferred snark with too much sap, a small part of me will always be grateful for this terrifying place, because it brought me you."

"Oh, that is sappy," she said, a smile spreading across her face. "But I enjoy a good dystopian sci-fi romance."

Jed grinned, turning her face up to his. "A unique genre. What would I do without you in my dystopia?"

Tears burned at the corners of Olivia's eyes as she held his gaze. "You'd avoid a lot of Don Henley references."

He snorted a laugh. "That's true, but when you have a famous cousin, you get used to that kind of thing."

"You wish." Olivia gave him a push. "And you know there'd be hell to pay if you'd been lying this whole time about not being related to him!"

"I can only imagine." He chuckled and pulled her back to him, murmuring into her hair, "We should go."

They held hands as they left his suite. They'd be back of course, because of Akiko and the others. Olivia had hoped to confide in Jillian where they were going, but the woman had seemingly disappeared in recent days. Olivia wrote her name and phone number on a piece of paper and slipped it under Jillian's suite door, just in case.

As if someone might try to physically break them apart, Olivia and Jed tightened their grips on each other's hands as they rode the elevator down to the lobby and strolled past the reception desk.

They knew the moment Ziya's eyes settled on their luggage. "Are you going somewhere?" she asked in her typical kind voice. Olivia understood that if Ziya was in fact part of the resistance group, she had to play her part, or someone would find out where her loyalties stood.

"We'll be gone for a while, but we'll be back," Jed answered as they continued walking.

"Wait—what?" Ziya rushed to get around the side of her desk, lacking some of her usual professionalism. "But your treatments. And Dr. Cordova advised everyone to stay here. You can't—"

Jed stopped walking and turned to face her, still holding Olivia's hand. "Ziya, you seem like a good person. And I'm sure, like *everyone* else here, you have our best interests at heart."

Blatant sarcasm is not necessary, Henley.

"But this is something we're going to do," he continued, his tone firm. "We'll be fine."

Ziya's mouth was a deep frown, but she made no attempt to stop them.

Olivia's heart jumped into her throat when she heard the elevators ding. If Cordova was coming, they needed to get the hell out of there. With a quick nod to Ziya, she pulled Jed out the front door to an Uber waiting by the curb. The driver had already agreed to the three-hour journey, as long as they also paid for his trip back. Jed paid with his own money, having given up on the institute's stipend.

"I hope Ziya will be safe," Olivia said when they'd been on the road for a few minutes.

"She's smart and resourceful, and she never made it obvious," Jed responded from where he sat next to her. "She'll be fine."

About ten minutes into the drive, Olivia and Jed each received a call from Dr. Cordova, who left them voicemails asking them to return "for your own safety." They deleted the messages.

Their driver wasn't very chatty, which Olivia appreciated. His Fleetwood Mac playlist helped ease some of her anxiety while question after question about Aunt Ivy flew into her brain. Would she recognize Olivia after all these decades? How old was she? Why hadn't she tried to contact Olivia over the years? Would Olivia be traumatizing the woman with her sudden reappearance?

Never would Olivia have imagined that she could sleep on that trip, but as they left the city and passed through neighboring bayside communities, her eyes grew heavy. Fragmented dreams with images of swirling water and sun shining down on orange trees drifted through her mind like a seagull on the breeze. And she heard the music again—that same sad, beautiful music calling her home. She woke with a start as they passed by the capital of Sacramento and through its sprawling suburban cities.

As the car climbed into the foothills, and the landscape changed from houses and stores to fields and trees, they pulled off the freeway and drove down several long roads. Something pushed at Olivia from the past, and she longed to remember this journey—to know for sure that this was a core place from her childhood.

The entrance to the orchard was marked with a sign that said Lynch Mandarins. One side of it displayed a beautiful painting of a mandarin tree ready for harvesting. The sign didn't look new, but nothing about it was familiar to Olivia. Sudden doubt hit her. Was this somehow part of the institute's lies?

They drove down the densely packed dirt road, coming to a stop in an open area used for parking, outside a barn-like building. Olivia could see the orchard's trees stretching off into the distance behind it.

The memories slammed into her so suddenly she found it hard to breathe. It took everything Olivia had to not grab her skull in response. She'd been here countless times, in darkness and early morning light, in rain and beating sun. A feeling of peace surrounded her. It was so wonderful and heartbreaking that tears began making their way down her cheeks.

Their driver gave them a doubtful look in the rearview mirror. "All this way for a mandarin orchard?"

"I have family here." Olivia said, her voice shaking but confident as she wiped her tears away.

The man shrugged and watched as Olivia and Jed climbed out and removed their luggage from his trunk. They'd made a reservation at a nearby motel, but Olivia had been too anxious to go there first, so they'd have to order another ride when it was time.

As the driver pulled away, looking eager to get on the road, Olivia and Jed surveyed the area around them. The orchard was full of people bustling back and forth. Late November meant mandarin season was in full swing in Northern California.

Workers were transporting giant crates of mandarins in the back of a truck and moving among identical crates sitting in the barn.

Olivia could see patrons walking through the trees closest to them, and several customers were buying mesh bags of mandarins in a smaller building to the left of the barn. Children ran with friends through the chilly autumn air. Olivia even spotted a young woman, who looked to be a reporter, holding up a voice recorder as she spoke with an orchard employee.

Olivia was frozen, letting the feelings and memories wash over her, leaning a little on Jed for support. Who should she ask about her aunt? Then she saw the gentleman being interviewed notice her over the reporter's shoulder. He had to be in his sixties, and his skin was tanned from the sun, but his face went white as his eyes found Olivia's. He said something to the reporter and made his way toward them. His expression fit the old phrase about seeing a ghost.

"Beth Murphy?" he asked, his tone tentative and confused.

"I'm Olivia Murphy," Olivia answered.

The man stopped a few feet from her and shook his head, taking another look. "Olivia. I'm sorry. You look just like her—your mother, and maybe just a little like your father. You were just a little girl the last time you were here, after—" He cut himself off like he was afraid to ruin a secret.

"After my uncle was murdered," Olivia finished his thought. "You knew me back then? And my parents?"

He nodded, his eyes sad now. "Yes, you were up here all the time with your parents. I've been working here for forty years. S-sorry," he stuttered, realizing she didn't know who he was. "I'm Ron Mathison. I manage the orchard's operations, but I started here harvesting mandarins in my twenties."

Olivia shook his outstretched hand, searching her rediscovered memories for him. She found a possible match in flashes of a much younger face.

"This is Jed Henley," she said, turning to face Jed with a smile. He'd been standing at her side the whole time, but had waited until she needed him. Jed put his hand out for Ron to shake as well, which the man did with a warm smile.

"S-so, my aunt—" Her voice wavered. *If Ron manages the orchard, where is Aunt Ivy?*

"Ivy still owns the place," he said with a reassuring nod as he motioned toward a distant house set down a narrow dirt road to the right of the barn. "But about ten years ago she decided she couldn't do the day-to-day operations anymore. Did you tell her you were coming?" he asked, then seeing the answer written on Olivia's face, he added, "This'll be a great surprise! She's missed you so much."

Fresh tears welled up in Olivia's eyes at those words, but before she could say anything, Ron continued, "Head on over! She eats pretty early, so she's probably cooking dinner, and she loves dinner guests. We're all wrapping up here for the day."

"Thank you, Ron," Olivia murmured, trying to convey in her smile how grateful she was.

"Of course! It's wonderful to see you again, all grown up after all these years. I tried asking Ivy about you and your parents a couple times after Jack died and you all seemed to disappear, but she didn't want to talk about it, so I let it go. Hope to see you again while you're here!" He waved and walked back toward the barn, resuming his conversation with the reporter, who'd been snapping pictures of Ron's employees at work.

Olivia watched him go for a moment, wondering how many people had been ripped from her life when her implant was placed. She once again turned to Jed, taking his hand in hers.

"Nice guy," Jed noted. "This has to be a lot. Are you okay?"

"I think so. It's all just so insane," Olivia said, grabbing her backpack from where it sat next to their suitcases.

"Let me know if it's getting to be too much—if you just need some time to decompress," he said. Then, picking up their luggage and turning toward the dirt road, he asked, "Ready?"

Olivia walked a few steps and then stopped, her heart slamming against her ribs. "He said she's cooking dinner. That's not a great time to surprise someone. Maybe we should wait—"

He pulled her close and kissed her head. "He said she likes dinner guests, and you don't have to drop it all on her tonight. We don't even know what—condition—she's in."

"Jed, that doesn't help!"

"I wasn't trying to be rude, but she's your great-aunt, so it seems like she's gotta be pretty old—" He threw up his hands and took a deep breath. "What I *wanted* to say is that you can see how things go before you start talking about everything. Maybe she doesn't know about the implant or maybe she does. You can wait to talk about that part if you want. But you can't just show up here and then leave without seeing her."

Olivia stared toward the house, then looked back toward the barn. It did appear the employees were closing up shop. The reporter had gotten into her sedan and was pulling out of the parking area. Ron was nowhere to be seen. He was sure to talk to her aunt later, which would make things more awkward if Olivia left now.

She combed back through the images in her mind of her uncle on the ground at the back of the orchard, his blood pooling in the dirt, his hand stretched to the bank of the creek, as if with his last breath he was determined to be as close to water as he could be. She gave a nod of assent and forced her feet to move forward.

"I'll be here with you," Jed said.

"You have no idea how grateful I am for that," Olivia responded, and the clear love in his expression made her once again want to cry.

They made their way up the road and through the open yard, the orchard now off to the left. Their steps were slow up the old wooden stairs of the porch. Olivia could see a light through the lacey curtains hanging in the bay window near the front door. She couldn't find a doorbell and Jed shrugged to confirm he didn't see one either. Inhaling as she closed her eyes, Olivia raised her hand and left it suspended in air for a moment, before knocking three times.

Exactly eleven seconds passed before the door flew open like the person on the other side was used to welcoming visitors at all times of day. The grinning woman framed in the light of the house was in her seventies, with light brown hair cut short and slightly mussed. Her brown eyes were the definition of carefree joy.

Another flood of memories made Olivia feel like she was going to collapse under their weight. She had seen this woman hundreds of times when she was a small child. Her present-day self felt the love and safety Aunt Ivy had always made her feel when she was young. Olivia remembered the laughter too. Ivy had had boundless energy, as well as countless exciting, sometimes goofy stories she told in a highly animated way. Her stories were the stuff of legends. Olivia remembered now that her aunt had been an elementary school teacher, which was where much of her subject matter came from. Teaching had been one of the great loves of Ivy's life.

Ivy froze, her welcoming smile turning into a look of shock as she absorbed the fact that it was Olivia standing on her front porch. She wore glasses. Olivia remembered wanting to wear glasses when she was little, because her aunt had explained the glasses were a result of tired eyes from voracious reading. Olivia had already been reading by age four, and the comment had only made her want to read more.

"Hi, Aunt Ivy," Olivia whispered, every nerve in her body zinging with anxious energy.

"Olivia—is that you?" Ivy breathed, her eyes moving to Jed's face and then back to Olivia's.

"It's me," Olivia confirmed. "And this is my boyfriend, Jed." She saw a smile touch his lips as he registered the word.

Ivy nodded to Jed, then stepped forward and put her hands on the tops of Olivia's arms, giving them a gentle squeeze. "My sweet, inquisitive girl. Can I give you a hug?"

Olivia tried to say something, but the tears previously burning her eyes were now falling freely. Her great-aunt pulled her into a tight embrace. The woman's scent filled Olivia's nose and once again pushed her into the past. She remembered that scent of earth from gardening (one of Ivy's favorite pastimes) and coffee (her favorite beverage). She remembered this hug.

As they pulled apart, she could see her aunt's face was also wet, but the woman dried her cheeks with her sleeve and pulled Olivia forward, motioning to Jed to follow. "I didn't think I'd ever see you again. Come in. Please come in and sit down."

Ivy cleared some papers off her small dining table in front of the bay window, ushering Olivia into a seat. Jed left their luggage just inside the front door after he closed it, then moved to stand behind Olivia.

A mouth-watering aroma floated in from the kitchen, which was mere steps away from the dining area. "We didn't mean to intrude on your dinner time," Olivia said, wiping her own tears away.

Ivy waved her words away. "You could never intrude on anything, Livie. But speaking of which, I'll be right back." She hurried into the next room.

Olivia marveled at the nickname, remembering that it had been common for her uncle and aunt to call her "Livie" or "Liv" when she was little. It felt like fate that Jed had chosen to call her that without knowing about her past. Noticing that he was still standing behind her like a bodyguard, Olivia pulled Jed down into the chair next to hers. "I remember her. And I remember so much about this place, it's wild!"

Jed once again took her hand. She loved how much he liked to touch her. "She's happy to see you, so that's a good sign," he said. "She must not have been involved with your implant."

"Thank God," Olivia sighed.

"And she seems to be in really good health," Jed added cautiously.

"Yes, she does." Olivia couldn't even smirk; she was too overwhelmed.

"And you're sure you're okay with me being here if you two talk about what happened?"

Olivia frowned at him and he laughed out loud. "Got it. Staying here."

Ivy rushed back into the room with two plates piled high with ravioli in a creamy sauce. Beside the pasta were roasted, seasoned carrots, which were making Olivia's mouth water simply by looking at them. "I hope you both like butternut squash." She tipped her chin toward the plates as she placed them on the table, indicating the ravioli's contents.

"That sounds delicious, thank you." Jed nodded, picking the fork up from his plate with no hesitation.

Olivia experienced the strongest sense of déjà vu yet as she remembered sitting at this table for breakfasts, lunches, and dinners. She'd been a little pickier when she was very young, but her aunt had always managed to find something Olivia would eat. "Yes, but are you sure—"

"I made extra," Ivy answered with a grin, settling into a chair across from Olivia. "A few of the workers usually stop by after closing things up, so I always have extra. But with Thanksgiving being just yesterday and some of them still having family in town, they'll want to be heading home, I'm sure. Did you talk to any of them before you came up to the house?"

"I met Ron," Olivia answered, taking a bite of the food, and then having to stop herself from inhaling it when she realized how hungry she was. "Or—met Ron again, I guess."

Ivy sighed, searching her niece's face. "How much do you remember? You were so young."

Her aunt's words sent her into silence. A huge ball of panic began forming in her stomach. Did Ivy mean how much did she remember because of her implant, or how much did she remember because she hadn't been here since she was four? Did Ivy know about the implant?

"Livie," Ivy said in a gentle tone, holding Olivia's gaze, "I know what they did to you—after Jack—" She paused for a moment, fighting more tears. "Your parents told me it would erase this part of your life." She gestured around her house. "They didn't give me a say, of course. But that's why I assumed I'd never see you again."

Olivia tried hard to keep the judgment from her voice while she asked her first question. "So, you knew. And you were here all these years. Did you try to find me?"

Ivy let out a deep sigh and stared down at her lap for so long, it didn't appear she was going to respond.

"Maybe we should wait until the morning for you two to talk about this? It's been a long day, a long set of months. Maybe some rest would be a good idea," Jed suggested.

"Please stay here tonight." Ivy's voice was thick with emotion. "I have plenty of room. You had one of the little bedrooms at the back of the upstairs hall when you were a girl. It's yours for as long as you'd like if you're comfortable with that."

The air around them was thick with tension and the passage of time, but Olivia couldn't fathom leaving her aunt now that she'd found her. "Thank you."

No one made to get up from the table. Olivia forced herself to take some bites of dinner, her appetite waning. Jed had finished his, and Ivy insisted on refilling his plate.

"Have you come from that place? In San Francisco?" she asked when she'd retaken her seat. She offered a small smile at Olivia's surprised expression. "Your parents would only tell me it was in the city, nothing else. They called me one last time after your procedure to let me know it was done. I figured if you're remembering things now, you might have gone back there."

"Yes," Olivia said, clearing her throat. "It's called The Survivor Institute. Our implants are shutting down, and there's recall technology in the chips that pulled us back there. But because of the shutdowns, some of us are now starting to remember our pasts."

She purposefully left out details about the residents' symptoms and how their failing implants were killing them. Her aunt didn't need to know about any of that, or the murders the institute had already organized.

A mix of emotions played out on Ivy's face. "And what had your parents already told you about the surgery when you were growing up?"

Olivia pushed her food around on her plate. "They didn't tell me anything. They kept the implant a secret until last month, when I found the institute. The doctor in charge told me a story about my brain being damaged in a car accident, but now—now I think I know the truth about what really happened."

"So, all these years, you had no idea something happened to you? No idea about the implant at all?"

"None," Olivia said. "And like they told you, I had no memories of you, Uncle Jack, or this orchard, until very recently."

Ivy stood up and paced to the bay window, staring out at the mandarin trees. "I'm so sorry, Livie. This all goes back to that cursed man."

CHAPTER 19

"I'M SORRY?" OLIVIA asked, forgetting her food entirely. "What man?" Did Ivy mean her father? She didn't want to bring up the subject of the murder. Had Ivy believed four-year-old Olivia when she'd accused Edward?

Ivy came back to the table and settled into her chair, looking much older than she had a moment ago. "Darling, first I want you to know that I pleaded with your parents not to do this to you. I don't know what you remember at this point. I'm guessing you have memories of the night Jack was murdered. Maybe you remember who you saw out there that night?"

When Olivia nodded, her aunt continued, "Your father should have gone to prison. I believed you and so did your mother, but Edward continued to deny killing Jack. And your mother, she wouldn't do anything about it because she was scared—scared of Edward and scared of losing you somehow."

"You believed me," Olivia said with relief.

"Yes, Livie, but I had no proof, just the words of a traumatized little girl. Your father left Jack out there by the creek. I think he meant to hide his body somewhere, but got interrupted by you. Still, there was still no evidence that your father was the murderer. He got rid of everything: his presumably bloody clothes, the weapon. I've never understood how he did it all so quickly. He also wore shoes that were too small, so the tracks left in the dirt couldn't be traced back to him. Those shoes disappeared as well."

"Was my mother scared of my father because of the murder, or for other reasons too? And what was my father's motive in killing Uncle Jack?" Now that Olivia was able to ask questions of someone willing to answer her, she couldn't seem to stop. "Who is the cursed man? My father?"

Ivy shook her head slowly. "No, your uncle Jack."

"What do you mean?" Olivia gripped the table as her world tilted. "My memories of him have all been positive."

Ivy settled her bright, kind eyes on Olivia's and looked as if she were ready to begin a retelling of *The Odyssey*. "You *should* only have happy memories of him. He was a great man, and he loved you so much. But—I've always believed trouble followed your uncle wherever he went. He moved to the States when he was in his early twenties. His father was a lighthouse keeper in County Down, Northern Ireland. Jack wanted to follow in his father's footsteps; he loved the light and the sea as if they were parts of him. But he also believed all of Ireland should be one united country. You know that's been an underlying struggle throughout Irish history. So, he was getting into a fair bit of trouble with authorities on a regular basis by running with groups of people who believed the same thing he did—people who took actions to try to make change. After a while, his father told him to leave. Jack was devastated, because his country and that sea were his identity. But his older brother, your mother's father, had already immigrated to Northern California, so if he had to go, California seemed like the most sensical place to land. He never returned to Ireland."

"The Man from the Ocean," Olivia murmured.

"You remember." Ivy smiled, but looked a million miles away. "He was an orchard farmer, but most called him that old nickname. Not everyone knew his full backstory, but they at least knew about his country of origin and the lighthouse. I think he was afraid to be too close to the ocean once he got to California. He didn't know what feelings it would awaken in him. He'd tried to bury all of them. I always thought he chose these hills to call home," Ivy motioned around her, "because it allowed him to be close enough to the Pacific, an ocean to remind him of home, should he ever get the courage to go visit it. But he never did. He saw the sea as a living thing, essentially a physical piece of him. He felt like he had let it down, so he stayed in the hills. The creek out back seemed like it gave him just enough of a reminder of his past life to keep him alive, but not to overwhelm him.

"He bought this land in the mid-1960s with a loan from his brother. He started the orchard and found he was good at farming, so he kept going. I was born and raised in Los Angeles, but came up here in my early thirties when I got my teaching job in the next town over. I visited the orchard with some of my coworkers after school one day. I met Jack while buying a bag of mandarins and was instantly regaling him with stories of my second-grade students. He laughed so easily, and I loved that. He was about ten years older than me, and we'd had very different lives up until that point, but there was an instant connection between us. I loved him more than I could comprehend. We got married a little over a year later. We never had the desire to have our own children, but there was a bond between you and Jack from day one. You were two old Irish souls meant to find each other.

"But Jack had a lot of anger inside him. No matter how far down he tried to bury his trauma, it still festered within him. When his father died back in Northern Ireland, it seemed to cut all ties he had with his homeland. He tortured himself about never going back, even though it was never clear to me how he left things with his father. The orchard was thriving, but Jack wasn't settled. He sought out trouble and fights, and even when he didn't, they seemed to find him. Hotheaded wasn't a good enough word to describe his personality. But with family, it was like a switch flipped. With us, he was gentle and kind. We were the people who seemed to soften him. Maybe we were the only ones he felt safe with."

This seemed to be a natural place for Ivy to take a break, although she was still clearly lost in her memories.

Olivia gave her some time in silence and then tentatively asked, "So if that was the case, then what happened between him and my father?"

Ivy came back to the present. "Your father was never his family, sweet girl. Uncle Jack was very protective of your mother. From the beginning, he felt there was something off with your father. Edward was some kind of engineer, but he didn't seem to have a steady job. We didn't understand exactly what he did to make money. Your mother was over the moon for him, but his feelings for her never seemed quite as intense."

"Wait, an engineer? No, my father's always been a real estate agent. I think he's one of the founding members of his current firm," Olivia responded, sure there must be some mistake.

Ivy's face grew dark. "No, Livie, that's just what he's always wanted you to think—what he's wanted most people to think. Your mother told us he was an engineer, but because he was working on this big project that he couldn't talk, he just liked to tell people he was in real estate. He knew a bit about it because his own father had worked in real estate. But at least back when I knew him, real estate was never Edward's field."

An idea made its way into Olivia's mind. The possibility of it made her want to shrink and hide, but she tried to vocalize it anyway. "Wait, but the institute, he wasn't…" She couldn't even put the words together.

"You were so young when your father started that place—that horrible place." Ivy nodded slowly, as if it pained her to do so. "He started telling your mother and then us about it little by little. He said it would help people, ease people's pain, maybe even save lives. He said he was working with the country's top neurosurgeons, scientists, and engineers. His partner was a man named Dr. Garside. I don't remember his first name. I believe they met each other in college. He was some highly sought after surgeon in Los Angeles. We never met him."

Olivia was shaking her head. Out of the corner of her eye, she saw Jed's face pale as he tried to process the information.

"And Jack—he was furious and terrified. His underlying belief about the whole thing was that we as a human race should never try to alter our brains by inserting technology. He could only imagine negative outcomes there. I didn't understand it at all, but the idea of it *was* scary. Your father pushed the life-saving part, but Jack didn't go for it. He was a little—wary—of technology to begin with, but he felt this was something much darker.

"Then one day Edward told us they were looking for volunteers for the implants. They were hoping to reach out to different parenting organizations, because—they wanted to implant these things in children's brains and monitor them as they grew up. Your uncle was disgusted. Your father said over and over again that the chips were perfectly safe, that they couldn't fail, that they'd been tested for years. He said these implants would help offer children better lives. Your uncle reiterated what we all know to be true, that nothing is infallible."

"This can't be right," Olivia said. "We've been living in that place, and we've never heard any mention of my dad. He came to visit me shortly after I got there, but it didn't seem like anyone knew him. He didn't act like he knew any more than any other relative. He blamed the decision to get my implant on Mom, even after I told him I knew about Uncle Jack."

"I don't know why he would keep his involvement a secret," Ivy said. "He built that place from the ground up, so I doubt he's let someone else take over. And it was certainly *not* your mother's choice, although she did agree to it in the end. It makes sense, though, that he would tell you that, because from what I observed of your parents' relationship, he enjoyed playing the victim. He wasn't one to take responsibility when things went awry, so he would find passive aggressive ways to blame your mother. He also enjoyed gaslighting her until she assumed he always knew what was best for her and for you. I'm surprised Beth ever found the strength to leave him, but I'm glad she did. I heard she got remarried. Is she happy?"

"Yes. Will is a good fit for her. They've been married since I was in my twenties," Olivia answered, her voice flat.

Ivy heard the tone and asked, "How were things after your parents' divorce? Did they have shared custody?"

Olivia shook her heard. "My dad disappeared after the divorce, which makes even less sense to me now. If the implants were his creation, you'd think he would have wanted to keep better track of the one in my brain."

"I'm guessing he *was* somehow, and you just never knew it," Ivy said, and Olivia was quiet at that. "What about you and your mom?" Ivy continued. "Were you okay after he left?"

"We've had an—interesting—relationship. I always felt like I was a burden to her," Olivia said, feeling a sudden, annoying sense of shame. She didn't know how close Ivy and Beth had been and didn't want to tarnish what memories Ivy might have.

"I'm so sorry, Liv." Ivy reached for her hand. "It was that horrible situation, I'm sure. Before all of this happened—before Jack died, you were your mother's world. Not that it excuses how she's treated you, but she probably couldn't move past the trauma she experienced, and your connection to it. I wish I could talk to her, but I only had your parents' home phone number from when you were little. And that was disconnected long ago."

Olivia studied her aunt's tablecloth and Ivy's hand gripping hers on top of it. Somehow thinking about her mother loving her when she was little made not having that love now even more painful. Jed put his hand on her knee under the table, and she silently thanked him.

"I understand that Uncle Jack disagreed with the implants, but why would a disagreement lead to Dad killing him?" Olivia asked, pushing forward.

"So, it seems like the story, as you know it now, is that Jack died and that chip was put in your brain to make you forget the trauma of what you saw, but mostly, to make you forget who his murderer was. But—" She turned her head toward the wall, like she couldn't bear to look at her niece. "But Edward was planning on having the implant installed in your brain before Jack was killed."

"What?" Olivia's world imploded for the millionth time.

When neither Ivy nor Olivia spoke again, it was Jed who said, "It makes sense. He was looking for volunteers. He wanted parents to volunteer their children. What better way to earn support and trust from other parents than to put the chip in his own daughter?"

The room was quiet for several minutes, but a small movement of Ivy's head confirmed Jed's theory. Olivia focused on her breaths and tried to keep from spiraling. Jed moved his chair closer to hers.

Eventually Ivy continued, "Your mother didn't want you to get the implant. She was frightened, and it was difficult for her to reconcile with going against Jack. But again, Edward convinced her, and she told me and Jack that Edward would never do anything to hurt you. Jack was livid. Maybe others in his life had seen him that angry, but not me.

"And this is why I called him a cursed man: Your uncle was truly one of the best people I've known, but he couldn't stay away from trouble when it found him. He could have tried to call the police—the FBI or Child Protective Services maybe—tell them what was going on in your father's company. Maybe they wouldn't have believed him, but maybe they could have looked into it. But your uncle wanted to take matters into his own hands. He thought he could scare Edward into changing his mind about your implant. He couldn't let someone else handle it. He felt like he had to protect you all by himself.

"Your parents brought you over one morning and Jack screamed at your father, threatened him, told him he wouldn't survive the day he put a computer chip in your brain. You were outside on the swing we used to have in that tree." Ivy pointed to her front yard. "After Jack died and they took you away, I had it taken down." Ivy started to cry. Olivia got up and rounded the table to pull her aunt into a hug. Ivy's tears stopped and she patted Olivia's arm. "Thank you, Livie."

Olivia sat back down and Ivy continued, "Anyway, it was obvious Edward was angry, but he asked Jack if they could talk about it in the morning, after they'd both had some time to calm down. That night Jack and I had already been in bed for several hours when he told me he was going to take a walk down by the creek to clear his head. He hadn't slept at all. As far as I knew, you and your parents were in bed too. You might have better knowledge of the next part than I do, but you must have heard Jack leave our room, followed him outside.

"I don't know how far behind him you were, or how quickly it happened. I have no way of knowing exactly what you saw out there, but we found you with his body in the morning. You accused your father right away. You were screaming and crying, asking him why he did it. I was confused, because your father looked like he'd just gotten out of bed. Like I said before, he cleaned up all the evidence. I had no reason not to believe you, although your parents insisted you were just traumatized by Jack's death. But you'd never said anything against either of them before, and there wouldn't have been anyone else in the orchard that night.

"I was in a fog for some time after that. Your uncle and this life we made together were everything to me. The idea of life without him seemed impossible. But as time went by, I started seeing some light crack through the clouds in my mind. I noticed that your father seemed genuinely sad and shocked over Jack's death. I also noticed that you wanted nothing to do with your father. You would cling to your mother and shrink away from him. I heard you asking Beth why your daddy killed Uncle Jack. You told her over and over that you'd seen Edward that night, running away from Jack's body."

Ivy hesitated for just a moment, then kept going, "Well, one day I flat out asked him if he killed Jack. I knew they'd been angry at each other. I knew Jack had been ready for a fight. Your mother was standing in the room when I asked, but you were still sleeping upstairs. Edward, of course, got very angry with me and denied it. He said the trauma had made you confused. He said maybe you had seen someone else out there that night, but because you were so young, you attached his identity to the person. But I saw something in his eyes—something dark. I just knew he wasn't telling the truth.

"But like I said, no evidence. The sheriff's office had been out, their investigators searched the scene thoroughly, interviewed us, interviewed everyone Jack knew in the area. The only evidence to even show a second person by the creek that night were those shoe prints that couldn't be traced back to anyone in particular.

"The investigators seemed to spend more time talking to your father and mother than to me, but nothing came of that. They talked to you several times, and you continued to insist Edward murdered Jack, but there was just nothing to support it. You were also either crying and yelling or nearly comatose most of the time, so I don't think they trusted what you were saying. Their final report called you 'hysterical.' In the end, they figured it might have been someone trespassing on the property whom your uncle surprised. They said Jack may have even instigated the fight while trying to get the person to leave our land, without realizing the person had a knife. With the trouble that followed Jack around, it was almost easy to believe, but I still didn't."

"It *was* my father," Olivia said. "But how would we prove that now? If no one believed me when I was a little girl, there's no reason to think they'd believe me now after all these years—and still without concrete evidence."

"I don't know, honey." Ivy frowned; her face was full of despair. "I don't think we'll ever prove it."

Olivia felt the beginning of a headache. Red filtered into the corners of her vision. She heard the distant sound of waves. *No!* she demanded in her mind, and the symptoms subsided.

"Uncle Jack was right not to trust the implants," Olivia said. "They were never meant to help anyone. They were used to shut people up or force them to forget pieces of themselves—pieces their families viewed as wrong."

"That's horrible, Livie," Ivy whispered in a defeated voice. "I wish I could have done more to stop him."

"I'm just glad you're here and safe," Olivia responded.

Silence descended again until Jed spoke, "It's a little early, but maybe we should get some sleep, Liv? In the morning, you two can talk more and we can try to come up with a plan on how to move forward."

"Yes, of course." Ivy stood up. "Please, use your old room."

Jed stood as well, pulling his phone from his pocket. "I'll cancel the motel room."

Ivy motioned for them to leave their plates and headed for the stairs just around the corner from the entryway. Jed was already on the phone, but waved Olivia ahead of him, indicating that he'd get the luggage. As Ivy climbed the stairs, the wood beneath the carpeted steps creaked loudly. Olivia wondered if the sound was how she'd known her uncle was leaving the house the night he was murdered.

"You might be a little snug in a double bed, but you'll find all the sheets and pillows you need there." Ivy gestured toward a small room at the end of the hall, then toward the linen cabinet just outside it. "Things might be just a bit dusty. I have a lady who comes once a month to help me clean, but otherwise I don't go in that room much. It was—painful after you were gone."

"Thank you, Aunt Ivy," Olivia said, swiping at a few more tears. "I'm so happy I found you again."

Ivy's face lit up with a joyful grin. "Me too, Livie." Then she enveloped Olivia in a warm hug, her reluctance to let go obvious. "I'll always be here for you now."

That night, Olivia heard the piano music again in her dreams, but this time she looked up into Uncle Jack's face as he played. He smiled down at her and said, "Thank God you're home, Livie."

CHAPTER 20

N THE MORNING, Olivia's eyes drifted open as the sun peeked through the lacey curtains that matched those of the bay window in the dining room. She turned onto her right side and Jed, seeing she was awake, pulled her toward him with a sleepy smile.

Now, as the light traveled over the blankets on the bed, she thought about the room. She'd inspected it the night before, but saw everything with fresh eyes now. It looked like a time capsule from a little girl's youth—a little girl she still didn't know that well. Dolls and stuffed animals sat on the window seat. A tiny vanity was situated against the wall opposite the bed, where the house's roof slanted down. Under the bed was a large circular rag rug that looked like it was from the early 1900s.

Olivia wished she'd been able to grow up in this room—to make many more years of memories in this farmhouse and out in the orchard. Maybe she could have worked here as a teenager, helping her great-uncle harvest and sell the mandarins. She was sure Uncle Jack would be proud to see the orchard still thriving all these decades later. She wished she could experience that pride with him.

"It must feel so strange being back," Jed said into her hair.

"Strange isn't a descriptive enough word. I have choppy memories from inside this house, although none in this room so far. I see short, hazy bursts of a life without all the details filled in. I wish I could remember so much more, although I realize not many people can remember being that young.

"And I wonder, would I have grown up to be the same person I am now if that part of my life hadn't been taken from me? Would I be the same woman I am now if I had been given a chance to experience this life through all my years? What if I was supposed to be someone else entirely? It's like I'm two different people right now, but the second person, who was the original person, is mostly a mystery."

"I have similar feelings about my life," Jed agreed. "In my recovered memories of the accident, I'm wearing a letter jacket, but until I remembered that, I had no idea I played sports in high school. Was that how I met her? Was I any good? Would I have gone on to play in college? Did I even like writing back then—or is that something my brain came up with to fill the void that used to be filled by whatever my sport was? How can you feel like you've known yourself all your life, but also feel like you have no clue who you are at your core?"

Olivia nodded. "Exactly." Then she heard the creaking of the stairs.

"Why don't you go spend some time with her before I come down? It might be nice for you to have time to talk by yourselves," Jed suggested.

"Thank you." She left a kiss on his lips before she pulled away from him, leaving the comfort of the old bed. She pushed her arms through the sleeves of one of her cardigans, closed the door behind her, and headed down to the first floor.

The smell of fresh coffee greeted her. Olivia allowed herself to have a still moment just before she reached the bottom of the stairs. She closed her eyes, smelled the coffee, lost herself in the bird calls that filtered in through the screen door. Yet another group of overwhelming memories—happy mixed with horrible grief—came to her. She had to grip the banister to keep herself steady. Her very young childhood was all jumbled in her mind. Hopefully the memories would sort themselves out someday. Olivia wanted all of them back, but she wanted to be able to analyze them one by one.

"Liv?" Ivy was standing by the dining table, looking over at her. Olivia tried to paste a smile on her face. But it was clear Ivy wasn't fooled by fake smiles. "I hate what your father did to you. To take a huge chunk of your life from you, to take away people who loved you, to continue the lies for decades, until they were forced out into the open. I don't know what you're going through physically, but the toll it must take on you emotionally…" Her words faded away and she looked seconds away from crying again.

Olivia took the last steps in a rush to get to Ivy, clasping her aunt's hands in her own. "But I'm alive and now I've found you. I've been missing you and Uncle Jack for three decades of my life, and I didn't even know it." She gently pulled her aunt to the dining table and went to grab them both cups of coffee as Ivy sat down. Olivia then took a seat across the table, her fingers wrapped around her mug, needing to feel the extreme heat on her skin. She'd just seen a mug in the kitchen cabinet that said, "World's Best Uncle" and had had to squeeze her eyes closed to fight off tears of her own.

After a long sip from her own cup, Ivy found Olivia's eyes, a smile coming to rest on her lips. "You and your uncle could spend hours just sitting at this table, or the piano, or walking around the orchard—just talking about everything your curious mind came up with. He'd tell you all kinds of stories about his childhood, the lighthouse, and the ocean. You stared at him in wonder, asking question after question. It was beautiful to watch the two of you."

"I'd give anything to hear those stories again," Olivia said, trying to imagine her uncle sitting next to her at the table.

"Jack loved his time with you." Ivy appeared to hesitate before finally asking, "How many people did they do this to?"

Olivia leaned back in her chair. "It's never been clear to me whether there were people who didn't make it back to the institute, but there are fifty of us residents, or patients, living there now. There were fifty-three, including me, but three have since passed away."

Ivy put her coffee mug down with a clunk, her eyes wide. "Are the malfunctioning implants killing people?"

Shit. I really didn't want to get into this with her. But if I lie, she'll see right through me.

"Dr. Cordova, the chief medical officer, says no. She says the residents' symptoms, which are the medical side effects we all experience because of the dying implants, could have aggravated existing medical conditions, which led to their deaths. Except for Mira, who was killed in a car crash. We think all three of them were murdered—one for speaking his mind about the institute, one for being in a relationship with someone who spoke up, and another for trying to report the institute to the police. But we don't have any real proof.

"Dr. Cordova has been telling us that her medical team, and the team of engineers they work with, are trying to find a solution, something to keep us alive. But we no longer believe that either. Besides me, Jed and at least one other resident have started remembering what really happened to them—why they really got their implants. The institute has been keeping a lot of secrets from us."

"We need to report this!" Ivy stood up. "There has to be an organization that will shut that place down! All of the residents' implants can serve as proof of what your father and his colleagues did!"

Olivia gave a small shake of her head. "Somehow the implants don't show up on medical scans outside the institute. And all of our medical records are locked away where we can't find them, so there's actually no evidence. Plus, Mira was murdered because she tried to go to the police. If the three of us try to report the institute from here, I'm terrified the staff will kill the rest of the residents."

Ivy exhaled a shaky breath. "So, what can we do?"

Just as she asked this, Olivia heard Jed coming down the stairs.

"That's what we have to try to figure out," Jed responded as he padded over to the table, bending to kiss Olivia's cheek. Ivy got up to get him some coffee.

"Someone from the institute tried to call both of us again," Jed murmured. "Your phone's still on the charger upstairs. They didn't leave a voicemail."

"I'm so glad to be here with her, and to feel so close to Uncle Jack, but why did Ziya or Akiko send me? Was it really just to learn the truth about my father and reconnect with my aunt?"

Just then, Ivy came back in the room and handed Jed a mug of coffee. She sat back down, giving him a smile and a tilt of her head to indicate the seat next to Olivia. He settled into the chair, closing his eyes to take his first sip.

"The names I just heard you mention, are they people working against the institute?" Ivy asked, not even trying to pretend that she hadn't been listening in.

"Yes, Ziya is a staff member and our friend Akiko is a resident," Olivia said. "They're working with a resistance organization, but we haven't been given a lot of information."

"They're trying to get your father's attention," Ivy said with confidence.

Jed put his mug down with a curious glance in Ivy's direction. "What do you mean?"

"Livie, just like we talked about before, I'm sure Edward is keeping track of where you are. He knows you're here. This resistance group is trying to get his attention by sending you here. He's a possessive man, your father. He has to be in control. He demonstrated that with your mother. He wanted you to have your implant. He wants you at the institute, and he certainly doesn't want you here. It must be like a slap in the face to him—to have you back in the place he worked so hard to erase from your mind. Maybe they're hoping he'll come take you back."

"That makes a lot of sense," Jed commented.

"Okay." Olivia tried to think from the point of view of the resistance group. "So, for my father, it's about getting me back to the institute." Olivia realized they hadn't been calling it the cachot since they'd arrived at Ivy's house. "And for the resistance group, it's about getting my father to take me back there—Or maybe just about getting *my father* back there?

Jed's eyes went hazy. "Right. He came to see you after you arrived, but then he left. He hasn't been in the building. The group wants him in the building, and the only way they can get him to do that is by bringing you back."

"Their plan is to take my father down."

"Seems reasonable," Jed agreed. "Take down the one in charge and the organization will follow."

"So, they sent us here with that goal in mind? Isn't that putting us at risk, sending him here when he must know I've learned the truth? I don't think Akiko would have signed off on that," Olivia said, livid that someone was once again playing with her life.

"Yeah, maybe not," Jed said, sounding more resigned than angry. "But Akiko is one person with one opinion. I'm guessing this group has been working to bring your father down for quite a while. If this will help them finally reach that goal…" He left his thought unfinished, but Olivia understood where he'd been going with it: their safety came second.

"Well, we won't know anything for sure until it happens, and right now, you two deserve a little peace," Ivy said, pushing herself up from the table. "It's cold outside, but the sun is shining. I made croissants for the breakfast meeting I'm having with Ron and a few of my other employees this morning, and I always make extra. Why don't you take these and sit at the picnic table in the yard? You could also take a walk through the orchard if you'd like. I'll get you some thermoses of coffee." She strode into the kitchen before either of them could respond.

"I guess that's decided." Jed gave Olivia a small smile.

They were both still in their pajamas, but having a lazy morning felt like just what they needed. Ivy rushed back into the room, thermoses and a container of croissants in hand. Olivia took the thermoses after putting on her coat and handing Jed his. Jed grabbed the container on his way out.

Before Olivia could follow him, Ivy pulled her aside. "You asked me last night if I ever tried to find you after your implant surgery."

"Aunt Ivy, don't worry about that now. I was just upset."

"No, I need you to know that it was the most painful thing I've ever experienced—to not know where you were and how you were doing. I wanted to find you, and I should have tried, but I also knew you wouldn't remember me. I didn't want to confuse or scare you. And I didn't know what your father would do to you or me if I tried. But it was horrible, my Livie, horrible to know you were out there and I wasn't in your life."

Olivia threw her arms around her aunt. "I understand, and I'm not angry with you, not at all. We have each other back now, and I love you."

Ivy nodded with a sniff, pulling out of the embrace. "I love you too, honey—for always. Now go relax."

Olivia caught up with Jed and they sat down at the picnic table just as Ron and two other employees walked up the dirt road, carrying a laptop and large binder. Ron waved and called out a good morning before making his way up to Ivy's door.

"I'm glad this place is still doing so well," Olivia said, turning to look over her shoulder at the mandarin trees that expanded out behind her.

"Your uncle may not have expected this to be his calling, but he was clearly very good at it. Ivy must be too."

"And they've surrounded themselves with a dedicated team." Olivia motioned toward the house, taking her first bite of the croissant. Instant recognition hit her. "Wow, they're still just as good! I used to love these as a kid."

Jed also took a bite, his eyes growing wide with appreciation. "It's fascinating that most people can't remember their very young childhood years, but you have access to so many of those memories now, like you're experiencing that part of your life again."

Olivia noticed the unspoken emotion on his face, so she moved to the other side of the table to sit next to him. She put her head on his shoulder and her eyes on the trees. "It's different with you, isn't it? You remember what you thought your life was as a teen, but now you're having to learn an entirely different story."

"The truth," he agreed. "I always believed I was such an outcast as a teenager, but the things I'm remembering now—I think I was the opposite. I remembered last night that I played baseball in high school, before the accident." Olivia sat up to look at him as he continued, "I was good at it; I was going to play in college. I think there were already a couple of schools interested in me. I can remember my mom's pride. I remember my confidence."

"Anything more about your girlfriend?" Olivia asked in a tentative voice.

"No." He shook his head. "And I've tried to do research on the accident, but I can't find anything from my hometown's newspaper. It all feels very hushed up. I graduated high school before I turned eighteen and started college when I was nineteen, so there was a little gap of time there that seems to be void of anything. Somehow, I never questioned it until now. If I went to jail or prison, that could be when it happened, but that's such a short period of time." He leaned forward, resting his face in his hands.

Olivia rubbed his back. "Do you want to go to your mom's house? If she won't answer your calls, you could show up at her door. I can go with you."

"I do want to, yes. I plan to, but not right now. Your father is the key to everything. I think Ivy's right. The resistance group wants us to draw him out. Akiko trusts the resistance group, so I need to trust them too. We have to stay here."

Olivia took another bite and a long sip of coffee before saying, "Let's go for a walk after this. I'd like to go through the trees and down by the creek—like I would have that night."

"You sure that's a good idea?" He turned to face her, worry creasing his brow.

She shrugged. "It may not be, but I feel like I need to."

When they'd finished their breakfast, they left the thermoses on the table and set off into the orchard. Many of the trees had already been harvested, their branches empty of fruit. It made her feel a little dizzy to know she'd taken this same walk many times, over three decades ago.

"What do you want to do after all this is over? After we figure everything out and live to talk about it?" Jed asked.

"I'm glad one of us is being an optimist!" Olivia laughed.

He snorted. "And *I'm* glad it looks that way."

She closed her eyes for a moment as they walked. She didn't need her sight to make it down to the creek, sort of like she hadn't needed it the night her body took her to the river near her house. She'd toddled, then walked, then run this path when she was young. And right now, that felt like only yesterday.

"I want to live right by the ocean, right off a beach," Olivia said. "I want my backyard to border the sand, so I can go down to the water whenever I want. I still want to feel close to Uncle Jack, and I know I will if I'm by the ocean. But I doubt I could ever afford that." She gave a shaky laugh and opened her eyes, emotion clogging her throat.

"I'll make sure it happens, Liv," Jed murmured.

As they approached the creek, which was a little higher than she'd expected, the memories of the night Jack died tumbled into her mind. She once again leaned into Jed for support.

Her uncle had asked her to stay inside. He'd heard her coming down the stairs behind him. He'd looked up at her when he got to the bottom step, and she knew she'd tried to give him an innocent smile. Uncle Jack hadn't yelled or reprimanded, because he never did that to her, but he'd asked her with, what she now understood through an adult lens, desperation. He'd looked strange. Shaken.

"He knew something was going to happen," she whispered to Jed. "He wasn't just going out to clear his mind. I think he was either planning to kill my father or at least fight him. He knew I was following him—begged me to stay inside. I stopped on the stairs and waited for him to go out the door. I waited a while after that, just standing on those stairs. But something in my young mind must have understood the fear, or panic, that I was reading in his expression. I wanted him to be safe, so I went after him anyway. I had no idea my father was outside."

Jed held her as they stopped on the bank of the creek. Olivia knew it was where she'd found Jack—right in this spot. She knew it was where she'd seen her father running away into the trees. Olivia knelt and touched the dirt—the last place she'd seen her uncle as he lay dying so many years ago.

"I remember being so confused about the way he looked. I didn't understand all the blood—why he was just lying there—so the fear and sadness didn't hit me right away. He'd been stabbed so many times, but I couldn't comprehend that. Just as I got to Uncle Jack, I saw my dad running away, which I also didn't understand. I almost called out to him—almost asked him what Uncle Jack was doing. But it was like my mouth wasn't working. I wonder if things would have turned out differently if I had.

"Then, as I realized he was dying, I remember screaming, crying for help, but no one heard me. I don't even know if Uncle Jack knew I was there, because he was so far gone. My father must have snuck up on him for it to have happened so quickly. Uncle Jack never stood a chance. I couldn't leave him. I stayed with him and waited for someone to find us. No one did until the next morning."

Olivia expected to be sobbing as she relived that night, but an aching stillness settled around her instead. Her uncle still seemed to be there, in the dirt of his beloved orchard, wanting to feel water one last time. "Uncle Jack missed the ocean more than words could describe, but he did love it here. He was proud of the work he put into this place—proud of how it was thriving. He'd be so proud of it today. He'd be so glad Ivy refused to let it go. I can't believe they took him from my memories—that my own father took my uncle away from me."

Jed helped her stand up and pulled her into his arms, letting there be silence for several minutes. Then as he started to speak, his cell phone rang. "Probably Cordova again." But as he pulled his phone out of his pocket to check the screen, his expression changed to one of confusion. "I don't recognize the number."

Olivia's heart filled with hope. "Do you think?"

"Worth a shot." He said, swiping the screen, and putting the phone to his ear. "Hello?" He was quiet for a moment, but his lips turned up in a smile. "And where the hell are you?"

"Put it on speaker!" Olivia grabbed Jed's arm, her hope confirmed.

When he did, Olivia heard the tail end of Akiko reprimanding him for speaking to her that way. Olivia laughed with joy. It was so good to hear her friend's voice.

"You're on speaker now, Kiko, so Liv can hear you too," Jed grumbled.

"Perfect. Are you both okay?" Akiko's voice came across crisp and sure, per usual.

"We're fine, but what about you?" Olivia responded, her words not coming fast enough.

"I'm okay," Akiko said, her tone not betraying her true emotions. "I know the truth about my implant now. My brain damage made me—less desirable. It wasn't that they were trying to help me have a better life. They simply didn't want me the way I was."

Anger shot through Olivia as Jed asked, "Who? Your parents?"

"Yes," Akiko said.

"That's—That's insane!" Jed yelled. "You've always talked about how supportive and caring your parents are!"

"I know. But I think they were only that way because they *fixed* me. They wanted to put me up for adoption when I was born, but my maternal grandmother shamed them into changing their minds. I've never told you this, but my parents are both very active, very intelligent people. They didn't see me fitting into their life. They ended up admitting to it when I confronted them over the phone yesterday. It was like they just couldn't hold onto the lie anymore.

"They defended themselves by pointing out how much the implant improved my quality of life, how everything seemed to be going perfectly at first. They thought they had done the right thing. And I know they've felt guilty about the miscarriages and how they led to Daryll's and my divorce. They feel bad about the whole thing, but I'm so conflicted. Yes, the implant may very well have saved my life, and it gave me a 'typical' childhood, but from the beginning they've painted themselves as heroes, which seems far from the truth. Some people might call it semantics, but the reason behind my implant's placement still matters to me."

"Wow," Olivia said on an exhale.

"It's put me in a bit of a limbo situation," Akiko said. "I assumed after this was all over, I would go back to them, to live out my life with my familial support group, but I don't know that I can do that now. Maybe in time, but not right away."

"Kiko, I wish I could give you a hug right now," Olivia said.

Jed was silent and fuming.

"Soon enough," Akiko said, new warmth in her voice. "We have a plan and it should work. Olivia, I'm guessing you know about your father now? They just told me yesterday. I promise if I had known—"

"It's okay, Kiko," she said as her heart dropped. She didn't want to talk about this in their reunion conversation. "I know you would have told me. Yes, I know he started the institute. All this terrifying mess is because of him."

"I'm so sorry," Akiko sighed. "That must have come as a huge shock. We can talk about it when there's more time if you want to. For now, I need to tell you that while the resistance group gave you your aunt's information because they thought you'd like to see her again, and they knew she would tell you the truth about Edward, they are also trying to draw him out of hiding, to get him back to the cachot. He seems to want to steer clear now that there've been multiple deaths—doesn't want to acknowledge the blood on his hands. But he wants you back there, so the resistance group believes he will be paying you a visit soon to make that happen."

"Yeah, my aunt figured that out," Olivia said, her voice shaking. "I just wish someone had confided in us. He knows that I know. And with what he did to my uncle, and how little he cares about the residents—"

"You'll be okay," Akiko said, her tone as soothing as if she was putting her arm around Olivia's shoulder. "They're positive he won't hurt you or Jed, because he just wants to get you back to the cachot. And he won't want anything to do with your aunt, so try not to worry. I know, easier said than done, but try. There won't be any acknowledgment of wrong-doing or involvement on his part. He'll keep trying to cast blame on others, but you should say your peace if you want to.

"He knows the resistance group exists, but he doesn't know who they are. It's going to become an ego thing for him, because they got you out of San Francisco without him realizing it, and he'll be watching you carefully to make sure it doesn't happen again. That's our hope: that he won't be very far from you from now on. I have to go now. I promise I'll be in touch again soon."

"We love you," Olivia said.

"I love you both," Akiko said, and Olivia heard the smallest crack in her words before she ended the call.

"Thank God she's okay," Jed mumbled.

"Yes, and we'd better get to see her soon," Olivia agreed. "I just feel like I'm missing something here. I can understand why my father doesn't want me at the orchard, but if he knows about the resistance group, he knows it's a risk for him to go back to the institute, right?"

"I'm sure. It must just be an ego thing like Kiko said. And maybe he doesn't believe the group is powerful enough to do anything to him."

"Maybe," Olivia said. Her heart began to race as she thought about Edward showing up at the orchard. She'd longed for her absentee father when she was growing up, but now the idea of seeing his face felt akin to a nightmare.

CHAPTER 21

AFTER A DAY of walking through the mandarin trees, helping Ivy with chores around the house, and getting a tour of the orchard's operations with Ron, it was almost easy to feel like this could be Olivia's life—almost easy to pretend she would never have to see or speak to her father again. Maybe he would never show up. But guilt also crept through her like a fog settling over San Francisco Bay.

She and Jed could control their symptoms. That was why they were able to be away from the institute. Olivia was getting a chance to reconcile her past. But that wasn't the case for the other residents. They were still trapped inside those walls, wondering if anyone would ever find a way to help them—wondering if they would live or die. Some of them probably still believed the lies they'd been told about their implants. Who knew what lies Dr. Cordova was telling them now.

Even if Edward didn't appear, they would have to go back soon. It wouldn't be right to leave everyone else there. Not to mention, they still didn't know what would happen if their implants finally failed.

Two days after she and Jed arrived at the orchard, Olivia woke up with a strange feeling—like some sort of unknown threat trickling down her spine. There was only one imminent threat she could think of, so she took a deep breath and got out of bed. Jed was still sleeping, and Olivia wished more than anything that she could just stay with him.

Instead, she changed into some jeans and a sweater and left her childhood bedroom. The house was quiet, but she smelled coffee from downstairs. She walked cautiously down the hallway and stopped at the top of the staircase. This time no memories assaulted her. Her mind was fixed on the present.

"Aunt Ivy?" she called, but there was no answer. She again heard the sounds of birds, but they were muffled. She noticed as she reached the bottom of the stairs that the front door was shut tight. As Olivia stepped down onto the wood floor, she studied her surroundings, but nothing seemed out of the ordinary. Her eyes slid to the dining room table. A note on lined yellow paper sat waiting. Lifting it as if it might burn her, she read Aunt Ivy's flowing script.

Gone to town for some errands. There are cinnamon rolls in the fridge ready to go in oven. See you this afternoon. Love, Ivy

Olivia's skipping heart slowed for a moment, but then she heard a creak from the living room. She already knew it was him. After quickly folding Ivy's note, she secured it in her back pocket. Then with careful, slow steps, she made her way into the next room, which was lit up with the morning sun, its large windows looking out onto the orchard. She remembered that she'd often find Uncle Jack sitting in his old easy chair, looking out into the trees, as if he never quite felt comfortable taking his eyes off his land.

But this time *he* was sitting in Uncle Jack's chair. Fury spread through her. He had no right to sit there. Edward looked relaxed and casual, like a king on his throne. He gave her a small smile and a nod.

"How did you get in here?" Olivia asked. She made sure her voice didn't reflect fear or anger, but rather simple curiosity. "How'd you get past the crew?" It was Sunday, one of the orchard's more popular days. It was too early for customers, but the workers would already be down by the barn.

"Olivia," he answered as if she had asked a silly question, "I've been coming to this orchard since before you were born. There are more ways than one to get to this house."

"That's disturbing." Olivia stared back at him.

"This place is important to our family," he responded with a shrug—his demeanor unchanged.

"You're not a part of this family—haven't been for thirty years. This is Mom's family. You have no business coming here."

"You defend your mother because she treats you so well?" Edward smirked.

"I'm not defending her, although I understand a little more about what she's been through. I'm defending Uncle Jack and Aunt Ivy. You have no connection to them anymore." Olivia kept her tone even. "All you've done for years is lie—for most of my life you've lied to me. But Mom was too scared and Aunt Ivy never had the proof she needed to bring you to justice for what you did to Uncle Jack."

Edward looked surprised at this statement, but she understood now that, like Dr. Cordova, he was a very good actor—a sociopath who had done what he needed to do to get his way.

"I'm not sure what you mean. Sure, Jack was never very fond of me, but I didn't do anything to him. I advised him of the profit he could make if he sold this place. He acted like I had asked him to sell his soul. It was only a suggestion. That man had a fierce temper, but he never turned it on you, which is why you don't remember it. Ivy would never tell you how bad it was. She was scared of him and so was your mother. But you loved him more than anyone, so we kept coming here to keep you happy."

He feels just fine spinning his lie, even though he knows I know everything, Olivia thought, then said, "So, you had nothing to do with his death?"

Her father raised his eyebrow as if she were crazy. "I don't understand how my grown, intelligent daughter could believe such bullshit. Ivy has filled your vulnerable mind with lies—just like she did to your mother all those years ago. Ivy played a big part in the implosion of our marriage.

"The sheriff's office all but concluded Jack got into a fight with the drifter he'd been having trouble with for months. The man had wandered through two other nearby properties. Jack had chased him away several times, reporting him to the sheriff's office each time, but nothing was being done. Jack was pissed. He started patrolling the property every night, like he was some kind of trained security guard. The night Jack died, the guy was sleeping in the orchard, and Jack surprised him. The drifter had mental health issues and didn't think twice before stabbing Jack to death.

"But, like so many other times, you had followed Jack out to the trees when he left the house. You were there as he died. You saw the drifter running away, but your young mind thought it was me. The man had been identified before. From the description I heard, some of his basic features were similar to mine. You were four and you were confused. And after Jack's death, you were traumatized. You walked around like a ghost most of the time, when you weren't bursting into tears and throwing tantrums, accusing me of murdering him.

"We didn't know how to comfort you—how to help you move forward in life. That's when your mother, through her research, discovered the institute, and she thought the implant procedure would be right for you. I was hesitant and Ivy was livid that we would even consider it. Ultimately, I agreed with your mother, but Ivy wanted nothing to do with us after that.

"It was probably a relief to her that Jack was gone, because she no longer had to worry about walking on eggshells around him, waiting for his next random burst of anger. But she still thought it was immoral for us to erase him from your mind." Edward sighed.

"I know Ivy doesn't want to sully your image of Jack, but he was a very problematic man, Olivia. He resented his father for forcing him to leave Northern Ireland and their lighthouse. He couldn't leave his past behind, even though this orchard did very well. He couldn't feel grateful. He was obsessed with the 'transgressions' made against him. It's never surprised me that he got into a fight with the drifter, although it was poor planning for him not to carry a weapon of his own."

Olivia felt so much hatred for the man sitting in front of her that she seemed to have lost the ability to respond to his speech. Ivy had confessed that Jack was a troubled man who always seemed to attract negative situations. She hadn't tried to cover that up. But Olivia knew Jack had never displayed anger toward anyone he considered family.

Just as she opened her mouth to try to call her father out, she heard Jed's voice behind her. "Liv?" He was coming down the stairs and spotted her in the living room, but didn't know Edward was there as well.

Olivia held Jed's gaze as he reached the last step, hoping her expression was a warning. A look of confusion, then understanding settled on his face.

"Jed, please join us!" Her father called in a cheery voice.

Olivia felt sick. She wanted nothing more in that moment than to keep Edward away from Jed.

"Nice of you to stop by," Jed said, his sarcasm obvious as he came to stand next to Olivia, taking her hand in his. "Where's Ivy?"

"She's out talking to Ron. She left me a note that she'd be back in about twenty minutes for breakfast." Olivia squeezed Jed's hand to let him know it was a lie.

Her father laughed as if she'd told the best joke. "I know she's not here, Olivia. Her errands will keep her away for hours."

"What can we do for you?" Jed ignored Edward's response, his voice full of loathing.

"The institute called and told me you left." His eyes found only Olivia as he spoke. "I figured you must have remembered this place. They told me you need regular treatments for your symptoms, so I wanted to check on you."

"Bullshit," Jed spat. "We know all about you now—about who you are and what you've done to the residents."

Olivia squeezed Jed's hand again, this time in solidarity.

"What are you talking about?" Edward turned his attention to Jed.

But it was Olivia who answered, "We know you started The Survivor Institute—that you're not a real estate agent. You developed the implant technology that was used to erase the residents' memories. You initially played it off as a way to save people who had traumatic brain injuries or neurological conditions. But it was never used that way. It was used on people, mostly children, who were seen as less than—people who'd been identified as 'incorrect' for a variety of reasons. It was used by their families to isolate their supposed errors and erase them—to erase those people's true existences."

Her father's mouth was hanging open by the time she finished talking. "Are you hearing yourself, Olivia? That's insane! I'm a real estate agent, and I always have been! I have nothing to do with the institute! Is this something Ivy told you?"

His voice was so sincere, his surprise so real, that in the beat of silence after the question left his mouth, Olivia doubted herself. She had so many memories of Jack and Ivy floating through her mind. In those memories, her great-uncle and aunt always felt trustworthy. Ivy seemed genuine, but what if she'd made the accusations against Edward because she was enraged by Jack's death and Olivia's implant? No. What would Ivy have to gain from Olivia believing Edward started the institute? Why would she make up that particular lie? But—

"That's absolute crap," Jed muttered, and Olivia came out of her thoughts with a sigh of relief. "I don't know you, and I don't know Ivy that well either, but I know who to believe here. You're a great liar, an expert. Most people must fall for your gaslighting, but to someone who's just had to call bullshit on a huge chunk of my life, it's easy to see right to the truth of you."

Edward regarded Jed for a moment, his face blank, then shifted just a bit in Jack's chair, pulling a small item from his shirt pocket. It looked a little like a cell phone. He flicked the screen. Jed seemed to freeze where he stood, then crumpled to the floor. Olivia screamed, kneeling next to him to feel his neck for a pulse. She found one, but he made no movement when she gently shook him and called his name. Olivia jumped to her feet and stalked toward her father. She didn't have a plan, but she was done with his games.

"He's just sleeping for a while, Olivia, don't worry. I had to put a little pause on his brain so he'd shut up. To make this easier, I'm going to have to do the same thing to you."

She'd never felt rage like this before, but when she was within inches of lunging at her father, Olivia saw him swipe on his phone-like device. Her body stopped responding. Then her mind went black.

CHAPTER 22

OLIVIA WOKE UP with a headache reminiscent of those she would get with her symptoms. Panic filled her as she tried to open her eyes and the lids didn't seem to want to pull apart. She tried to move her right hand to her face, but discovered she was restrained to whatever she was laying on. Scrunching her face didn't result in the feeling of anything over her eyes. Her heart slammed like she'd just run several miles, so she took deep breaths and imagined the ocean.

My toes in the sand. The sun trying to break through the cloudy sky. The sounds of the waves and gulls.

When Olivia once again tried to open her eyes, they protested, as if she'd been sleeping for years, but then obeyed. The room was bright around her; she squinted until her eyes adjusted to the light. The commercial ceiling tiles surrounding fluorescent lights suggested she was back in a medical bed in the institute. Quiet beeps from somewhere nearby began registering in her ears. The sheet covering her smelled clean and felt crisp, but was heavy against her skin. Olivia discovered both of her arms were indeed bound at the wrists to the railings of the bed.

In a slow, careful motion, she turned her head from side to side. Jillian was in the bed to her left, but wasn't awake. However, the color of the woman's face and gentle rising of her chest showed she was still alive. There were a few other occupied beds in the room, but Olivia couldn't see them well enough to know who their occupants were. Her heart flipped when she realized Jed was in the bed to the right of hers. He was also restrained, and his eyes were closed. Olivia tried to speak his name. It came out in a crackling whisper. His eyes snapped open and he turned his head toward her. Jed didn't seem surprised by the situation, so he must have already been awake. His expression was a mix of relief and fear.

His words came fast. "Are you okay? I think I've been awake for about an hour. The machine told me your heart was beating, but I didn't know what he did to you—to any of us." He moved his head to include the others in the room.

"Okay—headache," Olivia croaked, wishing she could touch him. Jed nodded with a grimace as she continued, "That remote—his pocket. He said—about—about pausing your brain. Must be the implant. He knocked you out. Said—me too." She gasped for breaths, terrified by how difficult it was to speak a few sentences.

"I've never felt such a visceral need to punch someone repeatedly in the face," Jed said, shifting his body in his bed, as if trying to get closer to her.

"We're alive. We're—okay," she whispered, wishing she could remove the heaviness from her body. Maybe her father hadn't technically hurt her, but this didn't feel great.

Jed nodded, closing his eyes. When he opened them, Olivia saw him looking toward Jillian. "God, I wish they'd leave her alone."

"Yeah," Olivia said, thoughts of how much Jillian had suffered bogged down her already heavy mind. She drifted away again, exhaustion pulling her into sleep.

"Liv?" Jed's voice shook as he moved against his restraints.

"I'm okay. Just fell asleep again," she responded, turning her head to meet his eyes, relieved to note that her headache was gone. "Why are we the only ones awake?"

"I don't know, but I'm sure it's on purpose," Jed answered. "How did he get us back here?"

"He must have had help," Olivia said. Then terror washed through her body. "What about Ivy? Do you think he did something to her? I need to call her!" She struggled against the ties around her arms, thrashing back and forth as her strength returned. But when she scanned the area around her bed, she realized she had no idea where her phone was.

"Hey, hey," Jed said in a soothing voice. "I'm sure she's fine. Akiko said he wouldn't want anything to do with Ivy. And with how quickly he knocked us out with that remote thing, I'm sure she hadn't come home yet."

"And imagine how she felt coming home to an empty house, with no idea where we were or if we were safe. I just got her back." Olivia couldn't stop her tears. They streaked down her cheeks and she wasn't able to wipe them away. She heard Jed shifting in his bed again, but he didn't say anything—no false comforting words. The silence was what she needed in that moment. Olivia was scared and she knew Jed was too. She wanted to be optimistic, but neither of them knew if they would be getting out of this.

10101010

Olivia must have fallen asleep again, because when she opened her eyes, the lights were turned down. There was no clock anywhere, so she had no idea what time it was. The restraints were still on her arms. Her stomach growled and her mouth was dry. Olivia turned her head to the left and saw that Jillian still appeared to be unconscious. But on a mobile table in between them was a tray of food and a disposable water bottle from the café. A notecard was propped up against the tray. Even though the writing on the card was large, Olivia still had to squint to read it in the dim light.

When you're ready, push the call button on the side of your bed by your left hand. Let's have a chat.

The card was signed by Dr. Cordova. It was clear she wasn't getting the food or water until she pushed the call button, but the last thing she wanted to do was talk to the doctor. Olivia's father had left her alive, but who knew what Dr. Cordova would do.

Turning her head to the right, Olivia saw there was also a tray of food and water next to Jed, but his eyes were closed. His heart monitor was beeping in a steady rhythm. She stared at his chest for a long time, still needing to confirm it was rising and falling. Her gaze traveled to the ceiling tiles as she tried to come up with a plan. If she called Dr. Cordova and feigned horrible pain, would the doctor undo her restraints? Would Olivia be able to overpower her? It seemed like the only option.

Just as she was about to push the call button, the door of the room cracked and came open. The blinding light from the hallway came flooding in. Olivia froze and closed her eyes. The sound of light steps came toward her bed. Her heart was thumping in her chest, and the monitor betrayed her. Even so, she worked to slow her breathing.

"Olivia." The voice was a whisper, but when Olivia recognized it, she wanted to fly from her bed and throw her arms around the woman it belonged to.

But she gawked in surprise as she opened her eyes and saw a completely different person standing at her bedside. For a moment she was positive her need to see Akiko had her imagining things.

"Don't worry, it's me," the woman said. It was the medical assistant they'd seen in the lobby, the one who belonged to the resistance group, but she sounded like Akiko.

"Look." The medical assistant peeled back part of her hair from her scalp. Olivia could see a small piece of Akiko's black hair underneath. The woman then pulled some of the flesh from her forehead, the effect slightly nauseating. It was hard to see, but Olivia believed she spotted Akiko's skin tone underneath.

"I don't understand," Olivia whispered. She must still be dreaming.

"It's a wig and prosthetic skin," came the answer in a voice that was definitely Akiko's. "I'm also wearing contacts. I hinted to you that Karlene, the medical assistant you see right now, is on our side—a spy planted here by the resistance group. Have you ever noticed that she blended into the background a lot? That she never stood out? That was intentional. She worked and helped with patients, but her goal was to not attract too much attention from Cordova. The resistance group created these things," Akiko motioned toward her face and wig, "because I needed to be her in order to get back into the institute."

"B-but, aren't they watching this room? Won't they see you in here?"

Akiko shook her head. "They're jamming the video and audio in this part of the institute. It'll just look like the cameras in this room went out for a bit. It's also the middle of the night, and the team watching you has—coincidentally—fallen asleep in their control room."

Even with these reassurances, Olivia noticed Akiko was bouncing on the balls of her feet, the smallest movement that revealed she wasn't comfortable.

"So, you've met them now? The rest of the resistance group? Who are they?" Olivia asked.

"It's a group of scientists, engineers, and doctors who used to work for your father—for the institute—up through the placement of all the implants. A group of them was still here up until a few years ago, when your father could no longer keep it under wraps that the implants were failing. Dr. Rick Garside, the physician I was supposed to meet before Cordova paused my implant in the hallway outside your suite, was the co-founder of the institute—and he's horrified by all of this. He was your father's best friend when they started this place."

Olivia felt the blood drain from her face at the mention of that name. "My aunt told me about Dr. Garside. She never met him, but said he and my father were very close. How can we trust him now? His goals were the same as my father's!"

"I know it doesn't seem to make sense, and I wish I had hours to explain everything, but he *is* trying to help us. Your father ousted him, as he eventually did with all the original staff, by threatening Dr. Garside's professional credibility and his family.

"Garside told me your father was enraged when the failing technology started giving us symptoms—symptoms we didn't notice for a long time. The earliest recorded signs of them happened just a few years after some of us had our surgeries. Those times when we felt so awkward we were unable to cope in school or social situations? All of those romantic relationships and friendships we failed to keep because we simply couldn't make them work? Those were results of modified brain chemistry, Olivia; brain chemistry the implants altered as started to fail. Do you see? The implants haven't just been failing within the last year. They've been failing for most of the time we've had them in our brains!

"The group also thinks the implants not only changed the way we acted and felt on a socio-emotional level, but also the way our brains controlled how our bodies functioned. So, my miscarriages might have happened because the implant was physically changing the way my reproductive system operated. Every resident has probably experienced some physical change due to their implant, but maybe on a smaller scale.

"When Dr. Garside finally discovered what our implants were doing to us, he wanted to work toward a solution and then shut down the institute. But Edward refused. He enjoyed the experiment the implants were becoming—said they could learn a lot from the side effects in terms of how to make better implants in the future. They fought and Edward fired most of the staff in retaliation. He didn't have the power to get rid of Garside, so Garside stayed on, acting as if he'd come around to Edward's way of thinking.

"For years, Garside tried to work on a solution in secret, and eventually Edward found out. That's when he threatened Garside and his family. After every original staff member was gone, Edward hired the team that works here now, headed by Dr. Cordova. Mr. Adamian was just a decoy." Akiko paused to look toward the hallway, but hearing nothing, she continued, "I still have so much to tell you, but I can't be here much longer."

Olivia wanted to know why Dr. Garside had gone along with the implants in the first place. He was a medical doctor, but he didn't have any qualms with the misguided ethics of erasing chunks of people's lives? But maybe that would have to be answered in a longer conversation in the future. There was, however, another question on Olivia's mind.

"What's the real reason the FBI or some other organization hasn't shut the institute down? No one from the resistance group has reported what's going on here? Why isn't anyone else asking questions?"

"Edward is good at—persuasion—with money, threats, or harm. Over the years, he's managed to find the vulnerable employees in any number of oversight and law enforcement organizations. Garside said Edward calls them the 'weakest links of the human race,' and he makes sure those employees are too 'persuaded' to ask any questions."

Olivia groaned. *All those years I missed my dad, and I had no idea the kind of person I was missing.*

The truth of why the institute's staff kept prolonging the idea of a solution was now clear. "The current staff was never really trying to help us," Olivia said. "They just wanted to keep us here to continue my father's experiment. They figured some of us would die when the implants started shutting down for good, but they killed those who were making a problem for them."

Akiko looked at the floor for a moment, then back up, nodding. "And our implants didn't call us back here because they were shutting down; the institute staff sent commands to our implants to get us back here. They did it over the course of eight months to make it seem more natural." She fell quiet as Olivia took this in, then continued, "Dr. Garside and his team have found a way to neutralize the implant without having to remove it. It'll be done in a taper, so everyone who hasn't already remembered their real pasts won't have a suffocating number of memories hitting them all at once. We just need to get everyone out of here so we can get started."

Olivia felt hope bloom in her chest at these words. She motioned with her head to indicate those in the beds around her. "What about everyone in this room? How will we get them out? And why are Jed and I the only who've woken up?"

"They're keeping everyone in here heavily sedated with time-release medication through their IVs. But don't worry, we'll get them out." At that, Akiko walked to each side of Olivia's bed and cut her restraints with a small knife. "I'm so sorry about this," she said as she studied the marks the plastic had left on Olivia's skin.

Akiko passed Olivia the water bottle, then held it to help lips when Olivia's hand, sore and numb from the restraints, couldn't grip it. After putting the food tray on Olivia's lap with a muttered curse against Dr. Cordova, Akiko made her way to Olivia's IV and, with a gloved-hand, turned it off. She gingerly pulled the tiny tube out of Olivia's hand. "Karlene showed me how to do this, because she knew Edward was having you sedated. You'll stay awake now. And speaking of sedation, if you need to put someone out quickly, inject this into an upper arm. It will only take seconds. I'll put it here so they won't find it." On Olivia's ankle, Akiko taped a small vial and needle enclosed in a tube, pulling Olivia's sock up to conceal them.

"Thank you," Olivia mumbled, wishing more than anything in that moment that she could hug her friend.

"Things are happening soon, Olivia. Your father isn't in the building right now, but he's in San Francisco, and we expect him to return soon. He wants to make sure you stay here. We just need him in the building and distracted while we get the residents out."

Akiko made her way to Jed's bed, undid his restraints, turned off his IV, and pulled the tube from his hand. Within seconds, his eyes blinked open. "Kiko," he whispered in response to their friend's murmured greeting, although his face was full of confusion at the way she looked. Then he turned his head toward Olivia, a relieved smile settling on his lips. Akiko helped him drink his water bottle and handed him his food tray.

"Everything's going to be okay. The plan is in motion. In the meantime, you two need to keep yourselves safe." Akiko froze for a moment, as if listening to something. "Cordova's coming. I don't know when I'll see you again, but soon. I'm sure you already guessed that Ziya is a friend. She's helped Dr. Garside's group get a lot of its intel. While she has to keep playing her part, know that she's here for you." Akiko froze again, reaching toward a small device attached to her ear. "I have to go now." She made sure her wig and prosthetic skin were in place. "See you soon, I promise."

"I don't understand," Jed said, his voice still groggy from sedation.

"I'll fill you in," Olivia responded.

Akiko gave them each a smile and said, "I love you. Don't worry." Then she slipped from the room.

"What the hell? How long was s-she here? Why'd she look like the medical assistant? Where's she been?" Jed's words ran together as the questions tumbled from his mouth.

Olivia was about to answer him when the the door opened again. Her heart leapt in anticipation of Akiko coming back, but Dr. Cordova strolled into the room. Olivia cringed at the smirk on the woman's face.

"Nice and awake, I see," the physician muttered, her eyes noting their lack of IVs and restraints. She searched the room, glancing behind pulled privacy curtains and a closet on the opposite wall. "Where's your friend?"

Olivia shivered. The doctor might have just passed Akiko in the hall and not even known it. "You need to let these people go." She tried to flood her words with confidence, motioning her head toward Jillian's unconscious form. When Dr. Cordova didn't move, Olivia asked, "Does your experiment's inhumanity ever keep you up at night?"

The doctor didn't respond, but pulled a remote similar to the one Edward had used from her pocket. "I can pause you both in a second if I need to. I've been told to take the two of you back to your room, Ms. Murphy. You'll be held there for now so Ms. Sato no longer has access to you." She motioned for them to get up.

Olivia managed to swing her legs over the side of her bed and stand up without issue, but Jed stumbled, gripping his bed's railing to prevent himself from falling. Olivia rushed to support him. "Can't you give him some more time? He's only been awake for a few minutes!"

Her plea was met with the doctor's emotionless stare.

"What about the rest?" Olivia tilted her head toward the other residents. She saw even more of them now that she was standing up. "At least hold them in their rooms too."

Dr. Cordova ignored her again, walking toward the door, motioning with a flick of her hand for them to follow.

"What about everyone else?" Jed repeated in as loud a voice as he could manage.

The doctor swiveled around to face Jed. "I wanted to keep you here, and I have no problem doing so. You're lucky you're connected to Ms. Murphy, or you'd be just like that one." She shot a glare toward Jillian.

Olivia felt Jed twitch, the disregard for Jillian as a person hitting him hard. She squeezed her arm tighter around his back. *The resistance group will get them out. They'll all be okay,* she told him silently over and over.

Jed took a breath and nodded, taking a step forward. Olivia supported most of his weight as they followed Dr. Cordova out of the room, down the hall, out of the clinic, and to the elevators. Two expressionless men Olivia had never seen before waited there. When one of the elevators dinged open, the doctor, Olivia, and Jed, stepped inside. The men followed, putting a barrier in between the trio and the elevator doors. Dr. Cordova said nothing as the elevator moved upward toward Olivia's suite.

They saw no other residents during their walk from the elevator to Olivia's door. She wondered if everyone who wasn't under sedation was being forced to stay in their rooms.

The doctor opened the door to Olivia's room, which was shrouded in darkness. Olivia flicked on the light as she crossed the threshold. Everything looked the same, including some of her things sitting in the living room and kitchen, as if she'd never left. But any comfort this space had once brought her was gone. In that moment, Olivia missed Ivy and the farmhouse fiercely.

"You'll be locked in here and only allowed out when someone comes to retrieve you," Dr. Cordova said, already making to leave. The two men took up posts just outside the suite door. "There is still food and water in the kitchen."

"And my father? I'd like to speak to him," Olivia said.

"He'll be in touch with you when he's ready," Dr. Cordova answered, closing the door behind her. Olivia heard a click. Something made her try the handle anyway, but it didn't move.

Jed's face was pale when she turned back to him. After helping him to the couch, she ran to get him a glass of water. He gulped it down. "I feel like shit—like the worst hangover of my twenties."

"I think they were giving you a higher dosage of whatever they were using to sedate us. It needs to work its way out of your system."

Jed put the cup down on the coffee table before pulling her close to him. "Are you okay? And you know what I mean by that, because obviously neither of us is okay."

"Mostly," she answered, wondering how she was going to tell him everything Akiko had said without someone listening in. She still didn't have her phone, and the Bluetooth speakers that had once hung on her walls were gone.

An idea popped into her head and Olivia got up to grab a note pad from the kitchen. Using the shorthand she'd learned years ago as a secretary in her office, she wrote down everything she could remember from the conversation with their friend, careful not to use Akiko's name. She was hoping Jed would be able to decipher the words and was rewarded with grunts of understanding as he read over her shoulder.

His face was troubled when she stopped writing. "I wish we could do something."

"I know." She took his hand. "And I think we will. We just need to wait for now."

"You know I love you, right?" he whispered in her ear. "When this is done, I'm going to find you that house by the ocean. And you can make all the Don Henley references you want."

"I love you too," she whispered back. "And I'm going to hold you to that."

CHAPTER 23

THEY PASSED THE next morning with TV they didn't pay attention to, a few rounds of poker, and a fitful nap where neither really slept. In the afternoon, they grabbed novels off the shelves and switched up the genres to retell the stories out loud. They ate a simple spaghetti dinner that night, and he talked her through a new story he'd been working on. Jed was exhausted by nine o'clock, his eyes hollow and dark. Fear formed a pit in Olivia's stomach as he kissed her goodnight and went to her bedroom. Would they both survive to see the future he'd talked about? Would they keep their sanity, or would the institute break them before they could get out?

When she fell asleep next to Jed hours later, she dreamed she was at the orchard again. Uncle Jack was standing just inside the tree line. One moment, he was far from her, but in the next breath's time, she was at his side, where she always wanted to be. He turned to face her. His face looked so young, as if he'd just arrived from his Irish shore. Jack stared at her, wordless. Then Jack turned into Akiko.

"We need your help," Akiko said in a hurry. "Edward is back at the institute. We're trying to shut him down, but we're missing something, some part of the technology in his implant that we can't hack. And yes,

your father has an implant. Insane, I know. I've hacked into your implant to send this message to you, and I don't have much time, because he can probably trace transmissions. Karlene found out Edward is going to start killing the other residents, Olivia, starting with the ones who are still unconscious in the clinic. So, we have to act as soon as possible.

"We need you to get his attention. Get him to feel like you need his help. Get him up to your room somehow. We need him distracted so we can get the residents out. We only need a little time. While you're talking to him, see if you can get any information out of him—anything that might be remotely helpful in figuring out what we need to do to shut him down. We'll keep trying on our end too. I'll keep you updated." Akiko disintegrated in front of her eyes.

Olivia let out a strangled cry, jolting herself awake. Jed flinched next to her, putting his arms around her as she molded herself against him.

"What is it? A dream?"

"Not exactly," she answered, her breathing becoming steadier. She grabbed the same pad of paper and used her shorthand to record everything Akiko said. He squinted to read it in the pre-dawn light coming through her windows, holding it close to his face to keep any cameras in the room from seeing the words.

He turned the paper over and scribbled like he was being timed. She translated his shorthand to: *He has an implant? Why the hell would he put one in his own brain? What does 'shut him down' mean? They are manually turning his implant off? Instead of it shutting down on its own, like what's happening to us? Cordova used the word 'pause' before, and that must be what Edward did to us in Ivy's house. Will turning his implant off kill him too?*

She took a little longer to write, then passed the pad back to him. *I don't know why he'd have one. Something to do with control? If he has the tech in his brain, he has ultimate control over all of it? Or maybe there was something he needed to forget. I'm guessing they are manually shutting him down, which I assume would kill him. That's how they plan to stop him.*

"Jesus," he muttered. Then he wrote, *How are we supposed to get him up here? Cordova said he'd come up when he's ready. And what makes them think he'll say anything helpful to you? I don't think he trusts you any more than the rest of us.*

Olivia closed her eyes and looked up at the ceiling, wishing it was the sky. "I don't know." Then she wrote, *First, let's focus on a plan to get him here. And whatever it is will have to look believable to anyone watching us. It'll have to look pretty dramatic.*

Jed nodded, sitting up in bed, his eyes staring into nothing. She sat up next to him, trying to calm her mind. His hand reached for hers under the blanket. "Hand me that pad, again. I just thought of a new story idea, and I need to get it down before I lose it."

She did, and he spent the next twenty minutes writing. When he turned the paper to her to read, her eyes flew through his words. By the time she reached the end, she knew his idea would work. "It'll be a bestseller," she said, giving him a kiss.

1 0 1 0 1 1 0 1 0

Over twenty-four hours later, there was still no sign of her father, so they got started.

Jed lay down on the bed for a late-morning nap. Olivia sat next to him with a book she'd been trying to read since she arrived at the institute. About forty minutes later, Jed opened his eyes and muttered incoherently, his hands gripping his head as if it were going to explode. Olivia turned to him, asked if he was okay, tried to put her arms around him to pull him close. He yelled and pushed her away. Surprise and anxiety took over as she caught herself before tumbling off the bed. Olivia tried to talk to Jed again, but he snapped at her, told her to shut the hell up. He writhed on the bed, still holding his head.

Olivia raced from the bedroom into the living area, where the landline phone sat on the table next to the couch. She hesitated for several moments before dialing. Jed threw her book at the wall in between her bedroom and the living area. She jumped and hit the zero button, which, after a few seconds, connected her to the front desk.

"Hi, Ziya, it's Olivia Murphy," Olivia said, her voice shaking.

"Who are you calling? I need help!" Jed yelled from the bedroom.

"Ms. Murphy, you should not be calling me," Ziya responded, her confident tone dropping for a fraction of a second. She must have heard the noise in the background. "Dr. Cordova will reach out to you when it's time."

"I understand that, but I need to speak to my father. I need him and Dr. Cordova to come to my room right now," she said in a rush.

Ziya hesitated. "Your father—"

"Ziya, I know all about what's really going on, and he's aware that I know. I know he's in the building. I need to speak to him. Jed is in some—distress. I'm worried about him. I'm worried about—about me."

"Do you believe you're in danger, Ms. Murphy?" Ziya asked.

Olivia cleared her throat and went quiet. But a shout from Jed shocked her back into words. "I don't believe my father would be happy if I were harmed. I need him and Dr. Cordova to come to my suite *right now*."

"I'll alert the men outside your room," Ziya said, sticking to her part of the game.

"No, no, you can't do that! I don't want Jed to be hurt." Olivia's voice cracked with desperation. "I just need—a little help. Then I need to talk to them about my living situation."

"I—" Ziya started, but cut herself off like she was changing her mind. She sounded truly conflicted.

"Please, Ziya," Olivia whimpered as Jed screamed again.

Ziya was quiet for a beat, but her voice was back to normal when she spoke. "I'll alert Dr. Cordova and Mr. Murphy that they need to go to your room as soon as possible. And I'll make sure the guards outside your room do not harm Mr. Henley when your father and Dr. Cordova arrive."

"Thank you," Olivia answered, heaving a grateful sigh. She hung up the phone and padded back down the hall to her bedroom.

Jed was still gripping his head. He lay on his right side, his knees folded up toward his face.

"Can I get you some aspirin?" Olivia asked, but didn't elaborate on her phone call.

"Yes!" Jed yelled back.

Olivia retrieved the bottle from the kitchen, then sat down on the bed after handing him two pills and a glass of water. Jed closed his eyes and went completely still about fifteen minutes after Olivia gave him the aspirin. She touched his arm and said his name several times, her voice full of more and more anxiety each time. Olivia found his pulse and stared at his chest to see it rise and fall. She sat forward with her face in her hands.

About ten minutes later, there was a loud knock on her door. She hurried to answer it, trying to catch her breath. Dr. Cordova was standing on the other side, her father just behind, the guards lingering on each side of the doorway.

"He's in the bedroom! He's not moving now, but his heart is beating and he's breathing!" Olivia cried. "We need to get out of here! Please let us out!"

Dr. Cordova ignored her and said to the guards, "If we're not back in fifteen minutes, come in after us."

Both men nodded.

Edward made to follow the doctor as she walked down the hallway toward Olivia's room, where Jed still lay.

But Olivia, who had fallen behind them, picked up a chopping knife from the counter and pointed it toward her abdomen. "You have to let me out of here. He's going crazy! His brain is deteriorating. I think his implant is shutting down! I'm not going to stay in here with him!"

"You check him out. I'll stay out here with her," Edward called after the doctor. She continued down the hall without acknowledging him. Edward turned back to Olivia. "If this is some kind of trick, it won't work. Cordova is physically strong in a scary way, and the guards can be in here in a second's notice."

"What reason would I have to trick you? It's just me now. You need to let me out of here!" she yelled, the knife shaking in her unsteady hand.

"Olivia, everything will be fine," he said in what Olivia was sure was his typical gaslighting tone. "I know this is all very confusing, but it's all been done for your own good—for yours and the good of so many others. I can explain everything soon." One of his hands reached for her knife, but she saw the other twitch toward his coat pocket. He had his remote ready.

As she went to jump at him, scuffling sounds came down the hall from her bedroom. Olivia's heart felt like it would burst from her chest as she saw her father's expression change to one of annoyance.

"Get in here now!" he yelled toward the suite door, which wasn't fully closed, but nothing happened—no guards. Gratitude overpowered Olivia's fear. If she got through the next several minutes, she'd have to thank Ziya.

"What the fuck?" Edward snarled and charged over to the door, throwing it open, confirming the hallway outside Olivia's suite was empty. She heard him call for reinforcements on a walkie talkie.

Olivia still held the knife as she turned and ran toward her bedroom. Would she be brave enough to stab the doctor if it meant saving Jed? *I'll have to at least try.*

She arrived in the doorway in time to see Jed, his face already bloodied, twisting the doctor's arm behind her back. Dr. Cordova performed some elaborate spin, freeing herself and punching Jed right across the jaw. He staggered back.

The doctor was heaving as she reached toward her suit jacket, where her own remote must be. Olivia started forward. Jed was recovering from the punch, but as Dr. Cordova pulled the device from her pocket, he flung himself toward her and jabbed the sedative needle, which Olivia had slipped him that morning, into the doctor's arm. She stared at it for a few seconds, a shocked expression on her face, then she crumpled to the floor. Jed grabbed the remote from Dr. Cordova's fingers.

At that moment, Olivia's father flew into the room, his remote already in hand. Without hesitation, Olivia smacked his upright fist with the side of the knife. The device fell to the floor as he growled in surprise. Olivia dove for it.

Jed was swiping on Dr. Cordova's remote. A flash of triumph lit his eyes as he pointed it at the doctor and pushed the screen, attempting to pause the implant in her brain. The physician's body became so limp it appeared she was melting into the floor. Jed let out a cry and raised the device to point it at Edward, who pushed Olivia aside to try to retrieve his own remote. Edward froze when he saw Jed, then got slowly to his feet, his hands raised to shoulder level. Olivia snatched her father's remote from the ground and pointed it at him as she stood.

She noticed the simplicity of the screen. Toward the top, it showed a picture of each of the three conscious people in the room. Below those three pictures was one of the doctor. An orange symbol indicated that her implant was paused.

"Hang on," Edward said.

Olivia had no desire to hear more of his lies. She tapped on her father's picture, swiped the bar marked *pause* just underneath it, then tapped a button to confirm her choice. She watched Edward's eyes go wide.

But nothing happened.

Edward still stood before them, the fake fear gone from his face.

Panic coursed through Olivia's body, turning into pure adrenaline. "What the hell?" She turned her head to look at Jed, who swiped the screen on Cordova's remote. Nothing changed.

A slow grin made its way onto her father's lips. He laughed, and Olivia felt like she truly understood the concept of evil.

CHAPTER 24

YOU THOUGHT YOU could control my implant? That I'd be so stupid as to allow that to happen? I'm the creator of all of this." Edward motioned around the room. "Even your friends outside the institute haven't been able to shut me down."

"You were stupid enough to allow it for all of your staff members," Jed spat. "Such a messed-up job requirement, to require computer chips be implanted in their brains."

Olivia felt a moment of pride at Jed's comment, but then she heard running footsteps coming from the front of her suite. Her father's reinforcements were here.

"Give me the remote, Olivia. You have no need for it now." Edward reached his hand toward her.

Four more men came into the room behind him, all dressed like members of a SWAT team. From the side of her eye, Olivia saw Jed's hand move. One of the men fell to the ground. Her father lunged for Jed, who'd already paused a second guard's implant. "See? Stupid," Jed said. Edward shoved him into the wall, grabbing for the remote.

One of the remaining guards grabbed Olivia's arm. His fingers felt strong enough to snap it in half.

"Don't hurt her!" Edward screamed.

Olivia kicked her knee into the guard's crotch and shoved her palm up the other one's nose. She swiped on her device's screen two more times. The men fell to the ground.

"*Those* are the people you hired to keep you safe?" Jed laughed, but grunted when Edward punched him in the face. Jed dropped his remote to the ground as Edward kneed him in the stomach. Olivia cried out and dove for the device, but her father reached it first and pointed it at Jed, swiping the screen before Olivia could stop him. Jed crumpled.

Olivia saw figurative and literal red as she threw herself at Edward's back. For the first time in her life since she was four years old, she had something to lose. She wasn't going to let that happen without a fight. She began beating on him with her fists, then scratching at his face when he whirled around to shake her off. Random memories filled her brain of times when she'd wondered where her father was. Now she understood that he'd hidden away because he was a coward, using his covert control of others to further an inhumane experiment.

"Olivia!" her father yelled as she continued her assault and he put his hands up to try to block her. But he didn't strike back. A wild scream escaped her as she continued to hit, punch, and scratch wherever her fists and nails landed. The struggle lasted for several minutes until he managed to grab one of her arms and flip her to her back on the ground. In the process, the remote she'd been trying to keep hold of in her right hand flew across the room, hitting the wall by her bedroom door. Her father made no move to get it. Instead, he held the remote he'd taken from Jed above her, his thumb hovering over the screen. She knew her picture was displayed there.

"Olivia, stop!" he ordered, his chest heaving.

Hot tears sprang to her eyes, but she willed them not to fall. Her field of vision was fully red now, but she didn't try to make it go back to normal. Her throat stung from her scream. She moved her hand toward Jed, but he was just out of reach. "Let us go! We haven't done anything to you! You stole parts of our lives! You couldn't just let us be people—real people who can face consequences, experience grief, experience joy!" She thought of Jillian and Mikayla. "You had no right to do this to any of us! Let us be real people again! I won't even tell anyone about the deaths you're responsible for. Ivy, Jed, and I will leave you alone. You'll never hear from any of us again. Just let us go!"

Edward took a deep breath, still holding the device above her. "Olivia." His voice had already calmed. "Haven't you ever looked at the world and felt terrified and depressed by all of the division? The sadness? The anger? The pain and stupidity? Haven't you ever wished you could push a button and make it all go away? Just calm everyone down—make them focus on the things that really matter? Haven't you wished people could just be good—just do their jobs and live their lives as they should—not try to push their dark, sinister, money-driven, uneducated ideas derived from trauma and pain on others? That's what The Survivor Institute is all about! And I knew for it to work, the technology had to repair people at the most basic level—to take away the trauma in their lives that would one day manifest into actions that would hurt and disappoint others and themselves."

Olivia concentrated on the feeling of the carpet beneath her, the light coming in her bedroom windows to keep from passing out. Her anxiety was like an avalanche threatening to bury her alive. *He truly believes all of this, thinks all of this is okay.*

"Take a politician, for example," Edward continued. "He begins as a young, lonely boy who is bullied, who doesn't feel love or support from his parents. He doesn't feel connected to others. As he gets older, he also doesn't feel like he's getting the love he needs from romantic relationships. He yearns for control, for power, because he thinks it will fill the empty spots in his heart. He believes it will grant him acceptance from a group of followers. He thinks it will put him in a position too high for others to knock him down. Then, when he's secured his seat in our government and still feels all the anger and loneliness he did as a child, he uses his newfound power to take vengeance on those he disagrees with.

"The Survivor Institute could wipe out his trauma before it even becomes a problem. Our technology could erase those painful parts of his life—perhaps erase his unsupportive family and those bullies from his mind all together. In the future, we could have social workers go from school to school across the country, across the world, searching for traumatized children, as well as children like your friend Akiko, who have experienced brain injuries.

"The social workers could meet with the children's families to suggest the surgery as a solution. Grants could be offered to families that couldn't afford the cost. The social workers could also arrange better families and housing situations for certain children if needed. At that time, the institute's work would be mostly proactive, but we could still take cases like Jed's or Jillian's when necessary, to snuff out trauma or biological mistakes when they surface later than young childhood. Can you understand the importance of ridding these people of their trauma and the overall positive impact it would have on the world?"

Olivia was stunned. *He's delusional—insane even!* "But it doesn't work! Even if we ignore all the problems with everything you just said, your technology doesn't work! The implants are shutting down. People are remembering their trauma and having debilitating side effects in the process. Doesn't that mean the implants have caused their own trauma?"

"Technology is never perfect in the beginning, Olivia. It always takes some trial and error," he responded, his tone steady.

"And you chose to conduct that trial by putting your technology right into people's brains! Children's brains! Do you not see the moral issues with that?"

"Trials have to be performed somehow," Edward responded. "We spent many years designing and testing the implants in a laboratory, but that was never going to be enough. We found a population of willing parents whose children had experienced a wide range of trauma. They wanted us to help their children—to bring them some peace."

After pushing herself up into a sitting position, Olivia leaned back against her bed. She shook her head and took several deep breaths. The red in her vision finally drifted away. "But that takes away a basic aspect of our humanness. Humans are supposed to have the chance to work through their trauma and pain. We should have the opportunity to grow and move forward with consequences, coping mechanisms, therapy, things that help us heal. That's what makes us people—the right to navigate the messiness of life, to learn and adapt, no matter what we've been through.

"And in terms of willing parents, what about me? I don't think Mom was all that willing, especially after you killed her uncle. But you intimidated and gaslighted her into agreement. Aunt Ivy wasn't willing, and I know she counted herself as one of my guardians. So, unsurprisingly, it was just *you* who was willing," she said in a confrontational tone, as if her father didn't have the remote still pointed at her face.

Edward sighed like she just didn't get it. "Jack's death would have cast an unending darkness on your life—cultivated a sadness and fear you could never have moved on from."

"My grief wasn't yours to erase!" she yelled. "Uncle Jack wasn't yours to erase from my mind! What you actually cared about was erasing my knowledge that you killed him! And I know the truth; Ivy told me. You were going to give me the implant *before* you killed Uncle Jack. That's what he was so pissed about. That's what he tried to fight you over!"

Several silent moments went by as he watched her. His expression didn't change. Olivia's rage grew, until another thought surfaced in her mind. "You suggested Jillian had a biological mistake. Were you referring to the fact that she's gay? Jillian and Mikayla weren't suffering from any kind of trauma or mistake—they were just in love. They wouldn't have hurt anyone with love, but you were clearly using your personal biases against them. What other prejudices influenced your implant placements?"

Her father nodded with a sigh. "In hindsight, Jillian and Mikayla were two cases I should have given more consideration to. It wasn't me who cared that they were gay, but one of the sets of parents, I don't remember which, believed it *was* a biological mistake. And in the end, because both women were no longer children, but young adults, and their brains were close to being fully developed, the implants didn't seem to take like they did in minor patients."

Edward motioned toward Jed. "Jed's implant was more successful than either of theirs, even though he was only a handful of years younger. I believe that's why Jillian and Mikayla reignited their romantic relationship at the institute, albeit without realizing it was a reunion. The implant couldn't completely erase their feelings for each other."

"So, the parents were homophobic, and you supported that. You let that darkness win. You're no better than they were."

"Their parents were paying clients, Olivia. I was offering a solution. I wanted to be inclusive of all those who were interested."

"Inclusive of hatred. Those words don't go together," Olivia growled back. "How did you even get them here to perform their operations? They must have been anesthetized against their wills."

He waved her words away. "Those details are irrelevant now. And as I said, I should have thought more about their cases, but this was all a learning process at the time."

"Mikayla is dead!" she said in a ragged cry. "You experimented on us, Jillian spoke up against the institute, and Mikayla was murdered as a result! If you hadn't okayed her implant, she would still be alive! She and Jillian could be living normal, loving lives."

"She wasn't murdered. Her symptoms merely sped up a medical condition that would have happened anyway. Dr. Cordova tried to save her, but, unfortunately, it didn't work." His voice reflected some sympathy, but his shoulders shrugged as he spoke, making it clear he thought that tragedy was better left in the past.

"Bullshit! Why do you keep lying? We know what really happened! You and Cordova were pissed that Jillian spoke out. You wanted to punish her, but it would have been too obvious to kill her after you'd already killed Sam Murillo for the same thing. So, you killed Mikayla instead. Jillian will be grieving for the rest of her life, so I'm sure Mikayla's death has had the effect you desired. And now Jillian is in that hospital bed because you can't deal with the fact that your experiment is failing and we're remembering. You have to shut us up. Will you just keep adding to those beds? Or will you keep killing people instead? Do you think any of their loved ones will ever wonder? Do you think any of the families that sent them here are already wondering what happened to their children?"

When her father spoke again, it was in the same lecturing tone. "Our world needs progress and change, Olivia. And sometimes we lose people in that process because those people don't know enough to get out of the way. We'll lose the residents here, but they will always be remembered for advancing this technology. Based on their experiences, we'll be able to fix the malfunctions. We've been working on it for months. We'll be able to make everything right. Those who receive implants in the future will be all the better for it."

Yep, Akiko had been right. Edward would kill the residents because he'd never cared about the people, just the advancement of his technology—his method of controlling bits and pieces of the world. Olivia calmed her voice as she said, "So where do I fit in with this? Why did you give me less sedative when I was in the clinic? Why did you tell the guards not to hurt me? Why did you let Jed stay here with me?" She let her eyes travel to Jed's prone body on the floor and saw he was still breathing. "Why am I getting special treatment?"

"Because you're my daughter. Whether or not you believe it, I love you. I want you to be safe. And even though I know I can't trust you because of this little trick, I still don't want you to be harmed."

Olivia wanted to laugh in his face, but she was also starting to spiral. They'd managed to distract Edward, like Akiko had asked, so hopefully the resistance group was getting the residents out. But Akiko had also wanted Olivia to get information from her father, something that would help shut down his implant. It was doubtful Edward would tell her anything now.

I have to keep trying anyway, she told herself, and then said, "And what about you? You have one of those things in your head too. You've clearly modified it somehow to keep yourself safe, but won't it eventually shut down like the rest of ours?"

A smile spread across his lips. "No, I don't have to worry about that. I'm sure your friends would like to know all about my implant, wouldn't they? Tell me, Olivia, where are Akiko and Dr. Garside?"

"I have no idea," Olivia answered in a flat tone, glad Akiko had never told her the resistance group's location.

"He wants to steal the technology for himself," Edward said. "He may play at having these *awakened morals*, but I guarantee you won't approve of whatever Garside is going to do with the implant technology any more than you approve of what I'm doing."

Olivia stayed quiet, hoping he would keep talking.

"They're liars and cowards." Edward frowned at her silence. "They gave up when things got hard. Now they're trying to make me look like the monster. Garside knew what he was doing as much as I did. You know nothing about him and neither does Akiko. She's blindly following a man who could be called an expert at brainwashing."

"Of course you would say that about someone who is now working against you," Olivia couldn't help but mutter.

"You have no idea what's happening," Edward said.

"Then please enlighten me. You haven't paused me again. And forgive me for not believing that you hold affection for me. I think you need me for something. What is it?"

"Not now," he said.

Olivia rolled her eyes. This was ridiculous. She wanted to help Akiko, but how would she get past his barriers? *Maybe I should just let it rest for now. At least I've given the group a good amount of time.*

"Will he wake up on his own?" she asked, her eyes going back to Jed.

"No. It's better for him to stay this way for the time being. I'd have to shut him down if he continued to challenge me." Edward's gaze appeared to lose focus as they stared at Jed. "His case was a particularly dramatic one. His mother was ashamed of him, and his dead girlfriend's parents wanted *him* dead. He served two years in prison for involuntary manslaughter. When he got out, his girlfriend's parents continued to harass him. He was trying to start college and they weren't okay with him moving on.

"Jed's mother found out about the institute when she did an internet deep dive on dealing with traumatic experiences. She pleaded with the girlfriend's parents to leave him alone if he got the implant. They agreed because they wanted to remove their daughter from Jed's mind, just like he'd removed her from their lives. Unfortunately, Jed refused to have the procedure. At nineteen, he was an adult who could make that choice. So, I had to sedate him one night while he slept and bring him here. Like I said, although he was one of our older candidates, his implant worked exceptionally well for many years."

As he must have done with Jillian and Mikayla. They all deserved so much better. Olivia kept her eyes focused on the carpet, sure she would break down if she let herself look at Jed.

"Well, I guess it's time to go," Edward said suddenly, reaching for her left arm.

She tried to scramble away from him, but he grasped her wrist and pulled her to her feet, the remote still in his other hand. He dragged her to her bedroom doorway, stopping only to retrieve the second remote from the floor, shoving it in his pocket.

"You can't leave him here!" Olivia said as her vision blurred with tears.

"He'll be fine."

What if someone wakes Cordova or the guards up while they're still in here with Jed? He won't stand a chance. "And Cordova? You're just going to leave her here? Don't you need her?"

"Not really," Edward answered. He was now leading Olivia through the living area toward the door. "She's not essential when I'm here."

"Wow," Olivia murmured.

Edward opened the suite door and pulled her into the hallway, heading in the direction of the elevators. She thought about trying to fight him again, but his grip was fierce and he still had a remote in his other hand. Jed would be safe; he had to be. When Olivia got away from her father, she would come back to her room.

Edward punched the down button when they reached the elevators. His hold on her arm was becoming painful. Olivia looked up at the ceiling, trying to think of the ocean, Uncle Jack, and Aunt Ivy. Edward tapped his foot, glaring at the closed doors. The bell dinged for the elevator on the right. The doors opened.

"What are you doing here?" Her father asked, his voice low.

Olivia looked up to find Ziya standing in the elevator.

CHAPTER 25

ZIYA'S FACE HELD its typical professionalism. She moved to the side to let Olivia and Edward onto the elevator. "I tried to call Dr. Cordova, but I couldn't reach her, so I came to find her. I need to tell her—"

"You should be at your desk," Edward interrupted.

"I made sure the doors were locked, just as you said, but I considered this to be an emergency. I was attempting to call some of the medical staff in the clinic, where all the," she took a breath, her eyes flicking toward Olivia for the briefest moment, "recently injured residents are being housed, but no one answered. When I went to check on the staff, the clinic doors were all locked. I unlocked its main entrance, but it must also be barricaded, because I wasn't able to get in. I called up to the engineering lab. No one answered. Then I tried calling Dr. Cordova, but again, no answer. I need to find her."

Edward sighed. "Don't worry about reaching her right now. Escort us to the clinic. Call all the remaining residents to the large conference room. Have some of the guards make sure everyone gets there. Then return to your desk."

Ziya's eyes once again moved to Olivia's face and then to Edward's as she pushed the button for the fourth floor. Putting her phone to her ear after pushing several times on the screen, she said, "All residents please immediately report to the main conference room for an important meeting. Thank you." The message must have been broadcast throughout the building, as Olivia heard it echo in their elevator.

"Won't they notice that so many of their fellow residents are missing? Or are they already aware of the comatose group in the clinic?" Olivia asked, enjoying the subtle snark in her voice.

Both Edward and Ziya looked straight ahead, ignoring her.

When the elevator doors opened, the hallway was empty and silent. Ziya lead them to the clinic as if Edward didn't know how to get there, as if he hadn't created every sinister detail of this place.

Ziya stopped when she reached the entrance, pushing the door handle. The door moved forward a couple inches, but as she had said, there seemed to be something blocking it from the other side. Edward was no longer holding Olivia's arm and had taken the second remote out of his pocket. He held one device in each hand, ready to fight whatever foe burst out at them. Did Olivia also see a gun sticking out of his back pocket, partially hidden by his jacket? No, she must have been imagining that. If he had the power to shut everyone down, why would he need a weapon?

"You can go back to your desk now," Edward ordered Ziya. "Make sure the guards are assisting the residents to the conference room."

Ziya hesitated for a moment. Olivia wondered if the woman might break her cover. Edward didn't seem to know that Ziya was a spy, although he was clearly suspicious of everything right now. But all Ziya said was, "Are you sure? Would you like some of the guards to assist you?"

"No, I want them patrolling the building and watching the residents in the conference room. We'll be fine here."

"And should I try Dr. Cordova again?" The smallest note of concern danced through Ziya's voice.

"No, she'll be occupied for a while," Edward responded, his tone sharp.

Ziya nodded and turned to walk back down the hall just as Edward added, "Ziya, if anyone tries to get into the building, let me know right away."

"Of course," Ziya said, then continued walking.

Please don't go, Olivia said silently to the woman's back, although she knew that wasn't an option.

Edward turned his attention back to the clinic's door, trying to push it open. It budged the smallest bit more, but Olivia could tell he wasn't getting inside on his own. He pulled his phone out of his pocket and brought up what looked to be a security app. Olivia saw cameras from all over the institute displayed on the screen, but when Edward typed in "clinic," the images that came up were blacked out. He frowned and put his phone away. She watched as he held one of the remotes just inside the cracked door. A long list of faces populated the screen. Edward scrolled through them, his annoyed expression morphing into one of rage.

"They have all the members of the medical team who are on shift right now," he growled.

"Who has them? The residents? When I was in here, the residents were all unconscious," Olivia said. "Maybe your medical team is turning against you?"

"They've all been paused, Olivia. Someone paused them. Whereas all the residents appear to be awake," he said, still scrolling the screen. He moved quickly, pointing the remote at her, shoving it in her face. "How did those bastards get in here?"

"I—" Olivia stumbled backward, scared by how red his face was getting.

"They resumed the residents and paused my medical team! How did they get in here?!" he screamed.

"How should I know?" she found her voice and yelled back. "You had me locked in my room!"

"Cordova told me Jed was awake when she came to get you from the clinic. I kept you both sedated after I resumed your implants, but I wanted you to wake up, so you had a light dosage. Jed did not. I kept him sedated rather than paused to try to appease you, so he shouldn't have been awake when she came in. Cordova also said your restraints had been cut. How did that happen? Was it Akiko?"

Olivia said nothing, but by this time she was up against the hallway wall, her vision once again turning red. She tried to dispel the color but found she couldn't this time; her anxiety was too strong. *How can I possibly get away without him using that remote on me?*

Edward whirled back to the clinic door, stuck the remote back through the opening, and scrolled through the list of residents' pictures. Olivia noticed he wasn't trying to pause any of their implants—he was trying to shut them down. Her hands flew to her mouth to cover a sob, but the expected sounds of bodies hitting the ground as Edward scrolled and tapped the screen, never came.

A noise of strangled surprise ripped from her father's throat. It wasn't working. The residents were still awake according to his remote—awake and alive. Next, he tried to resume the implants of the medical team members, but their statuses didn't change.

"What the fuck!" he screamed.

He pulled out his phone, punching in a number. "Ziya, are all other residents in the conference room?"

The sound of 'yes' was easy enough to hear, but Olivia couldn't make out the words that followed.

"Are you seeing anything on the cameras?" Edward asked after listening for a moment. "Something's going on. We need—" He pulled the phone away from his ear and stared at the screen.

He turned his whole body to scan the hallway, as if someone might be hiding in plain sight. He jabbed his phone screen with his finger, but pulled it away as soon as he put it to his ear. "I lost reception," he said numbly. Edward trained his eyes on Olivia. "What's going on?" His words were quiet and garbled, like he was talking through a storm.

"Why are you asking me?"

"What the fuck is going on?" he screamed now. "Is Garside's group in this building, Olivia? Where are they?!"

"I don't know!" she screamed back, rage exploding from her.

At that moment, one of the clinic's side doors down the hallway to their left, rattled as if someone was trying to get out. Edward swung the remote toward the door, but before he could do anything else, the sound stopped.

"When did Akiko contact you?" He stood still as a statue, still pointing the remote at the door. His other hand gripped the second remote so hard, it looked like he might snap it in half.

When Olivia said nothing, Edward's eyes flickered to hers, but left a moment later. He was too distracted by the clinic door. "Do you know of anyone working in this facility who is trying to undermine the institute's mission?"

"All of them," she said with a snarl, just to see if the words would have any impact.

"Stop trying to be someone you're not, Olivia. You were never brave, never spoke for yourself growing up. What you're trying to do, this new person you're trying to be, it isn't you. I'd have no problem shutting you down if I wanted to."

"There you go with your love of gaslighting," Olivia laughed back, proud at how well she was hiding her fear. "Everything that comes out of your mouth is a lie! If it'd be so easy to shut me down, then do it!"

Edward didn't move either remote her way. She wondered if she could just run for it. He needed her for whatever reason. He wasn't going to shut her down, but—

A sudden bang from inside the clinic made them both jump. Edward rammed his shoulder against the cracked door, but it only opened a couple more inches. He shouted through the opening, "You're not getting out of this! No one will leave this building unless I say they can. You're all serving a bigger purpose and it will not fail."

Several more banging sounds erupted from inside the clinic. Her father slipped one remote in his jacket and pulled a handgun from his back pocket. Olivia felt her face go pale, and the world seemed to spin around them. Then an elevator dinged from down the hall. The doors slid open.

Olivia yelped in surprise as Edward shoved her to the floor. He brought his gun up and fired two quick shots at the elevator. No one was there. The doors closed again, and the hall returned to silence. Her father turned the gun on her. "I don't want to hurt you, Olivia. I need you alive. You will experience the difference the institute will make; the difference you are helping to make."

"I'd rather live with this thing in my brain for the rest of my life than help you in any way," she said from the ground.

"You're already helping. You've been helping all these years," he said with a neurotic smile.

"What do you mean?" she demanded.

Edward ignored her, once again putting his face near the opening in the door. "I'm going to the large conference room now. I expect all residents to report there immediately, or I will begin killing everyone who *is* in the conference room. No one will be leaving here today." He waited for a moment, but no sound or response followed his words.

Pulling Olivia from the floor with a yank of her hand, Edward made to grab for her arm, but she twisted away. He waved both a remote and the gun in her face and ushered her to walk ahead of him, in the opposite direction of the elevators. He banged open the stairwell door and pushed her toward the first step. Olivia's hand was sweaty as she tried to grip the staircase's railing during their descent.

A crackling walkie talkie lay on the stairwell's third-floor landing. It was partially covered in a substance that looked like blood. Olivia focused on the hard metal of the banister beneath her fingers to ward off an immediate bought of nausea. Edward eyed the device as they went by, then pulled out his own walkie talkie. He attempted to contact Ziya, then other names Olivia didn't recognize. No response. When her father threw open the door for the second floor, she hoped someone would jump at him, but the hallway was abandoned. She wished she knew if Jed was still unconscious in her suite.

Edward pushed Olivia down the hall to the large conference room. After cautiously slipping through one of its frosted doors, he pulled her in behind him. She breathed a shaky sigh of relief. No one was there.

"What the hell?" he fumed. "Where are they?"

"I don't know," she mumbled. How many more times would she say this to him? Did he believe her? Did it even matter? Maybe he would just kill her after all.

Instead, he silently motioned for her to back out of the room. They returned to the stairwell and moved down to the first floor.

As they walked through the door into the lobby, Olivia's eyes flew to a table by the windows—one she, Jed, and Akiko had shared many times. She'd give anything to be with them now. Olivia imagined Akiko sending her a warm smile and beckoning her to join them. And she could almost see Jed looking up from his computer, ready to charm her with a tender smile after making an awkward joke.

Her father shoved her forward to Ziya's desk, which stood empty for the first time in Olivia's memory. The lobby was completely vacant. Even the café, typically buzzing with machines and chatting customers, was dead silent.

"They can't have gotten out of the building; the exits are all secured." Edward pocketed the gun and pulled out his phone again, bringing up the institute's camera feed. "A trick. They're all still here somewhere."

"Or not," Olivia said. "I think they're all gone. I think your great experiment has reached its end."

He didn't respond, but yanked on her arm with a grunt as he hauled her back to the pool. They passed the spot where Akiko had told Olivia her story, then the spot where Jed had knelt to make sure Olivia was okay under the water. Their past selves seemed to be hovering there like ghosts.

Edward opened the door to the women's locker room. He held up a remote, but only his and Olivia's faces registered on the screen. Like the lobby and café, the room was bereft of its usual noise. Edward pushed her down onto one of the benches between the lockers and searched each shower stall, keeping the remote aimed her way. Olivia took inventory of his other weapons: the second remote was still in his jacket, the gun replaced in the back pocket of his jeans.

Burying her face in her hands, Olivia pictured herself standing on a beach, staring out at the ocean. Gulls flew in lazy shapes above her. The water reached for her toes. She could see the sun breaking through the clouds. She had to stay strong for Uncle Jack, who'd been without his beloved sea for so much of his life.

As her father pulled back the last shower curtain, Olivia's ears picked up a sound to her left. She turned her face a few inches in its direction, keeping her hands in place. The door to the locker room was cracked open. Olivia's heart skipped as it opened more. Was she imagining the half of Jed's face she saw there? The figure she hoped was Jed put a finger to his lips and held up a remote. She widened her eyes, giving the smallest shake of her head. Jed already knew the remotes didn't work on her father. He nodded as he studied the device's screen.

Edward grunted and strolled back to her. She clocked the moment he saw the gap in the door. Olivia let out a cry of warning. The locker room door closed at the same time her father snatched out his gun, bringing it up and firing four shots in quick succession.

Olivia screamed. "Are you insane?!"

Her ears were still ringing as Edward pulled her out of the room and swerved left. He barreled through the door to the men's locker room, and Olivia gasped at the sight that greeted them. At least ten of her father's guards were on the floor, some of them collapsed on top of each other. She could see the rise and fall of their chests, and none of them showed signs of injury.

They must have been dragged here after they were already paused, she thought, before saying, "I'll never understand the thinking behind giving all your staff implants. It makes for a pretty fragile army."

"Shut up! God dammit!" He raised his gun to the door.

"Can't you just be done?" Olivia said. "They've got you beat. You'll be the one not walking out of here."

"In the end, none of this matters," Edward replied. "They can dismantle those defective implants if they want. You're all I need to stay safe and on the path to a real breakthrough in this technology. We just have to get out of here and go somewhere new." He reached for her, but she jumped away and crossed the room. Olivia saw his fingers twitch around the gun, but he kept it pointed at the door.

"No! I have no intention of going anywhere with you. And I won't stay here either. I'll be walking out of the institute today. I'm all done being a pawn in your sick experiment!" she said with as much confidence as her thumping heart would allow.

He stared at her for a few quiet seconds, then, to her surprise, he laughed.

CHAPTER 26

❙❙ YOU **MUST HAVE** forgotten you still have a failing implant in your brain, Olivia. It will eventually kill you. And if someone kills me first, you die as well," Edward said, an unsettling smirk on his face.

"What are you talking about? Why would killing you also kill me? Stop your games and tell me the truth!"

"I don't need you passing information onto your friends, so I think I'll keep you in the dark on that. But just know, your life ends when mine does. Remember that when you're trying to help them shut me down."

He was lying; she wouldn't let him get to her. "Whoever is out there is not going to let you get away, because they don't want you wreaking havoc on any other vulnerable people. Whether they kill you or not, they will win."

"Let's just see, shall we?" Edward laughed again as he sprinted toward her. He shoved her through the locker room doors.

As Olivia tripped and fell to the ground near the pool, the space around them went black. Her eyes slowly adjusted with the help of the muted light coming through the frosted windows across the room. Still, anxiety rose in her chest.

No! she commanded, taking several deep breaths to calm her nervous system. They were doing this to her father, not her. She thought of Uncle Jack and Aunt Ivy, and it gave her strength.

"Speaking of being in the dark," she murmured.

Edward gave an annoyed sigh, but she could hear his breathing quicken. She wasn't the only one experiencing anxiety.

He marched her away from the pool and into the lobby—this time with the gun at her back. Afternoon sunlight filtered in through the windows, but the lobby lights were all off. Edward made his way to a light switch behind Ziya's desk, which he flipped several times before giving up.

Doing the same thing over and over and expecting a different result. Isn't that the definition of insanity? Olivia thought to herself.

Her father pushed her toward the main entrance, but a sudden crash from the direction of the café had him spinning around. His voice was ragged as he yelled, "Just come out here! Stop being fucking cowards hiding in the shadows! Garside is just as guilty as me, but you're following him like a bunch of cult members!"

"The difference between you and me is that I understand what we did was unethical. Now I'm trying to make it right—as much as I can," said a calm voice tinged with guilt.

Olivia turned her head from side to side in an attempt to find the man connected to the voice, but he seemed to be hidden somewhere on the other side of the room.

Edward twisted his body toward the sound, his eyes wide and crazed. "Garside, you bastard, how did you get in here?"

Dr. Garside didn't answer the question but said, "It's over. You need to let Olivia go. I know you poured your life into this project. We both did. And now it's failed and caused too much suffering along the way. We need to end it."

"She's my daughter and her implant will continue my legacy," Edward said. "She stays with me. You can do what you want with the others."

In the quiet that followed, Olivia thought about what her father had said before. If he died, she died too. She wondered if Garside could explain that. "He told me there's some kind of connection between us," Olivia said toward the shadows. "He said if he dies, I die too. Do you know what he means?"

Silence again, and then Dr. Garside spoke, "Ed, you didn't—Did you somehow connect her implant to yours? Is her implant the thing keeping yours from being paused or shut down? You're using your daughter as a fail safe?"

"W-what?" Olivia said, surprised she could still feel such a strong sense of shock after all these weeks. "You made it so our implants rely on each other? So, if they shut yours down and you die, I will too. And vice versa. That's why you need to keep me alive?"

"You have it partially right." Her father shook his head. "If my implant shuts down, yours will too, and you will die. When Garside and I started creating the implants, there were pieces of information regarding their design that I didn't want him to have access to. I didn't want him to be able to replicate them on his own. I buried that information in some nondescript coding in your implant, so he would have access to it only if he had your chip and knew where to look. Those design specifics would have much it much easier for him to figure out how to neutralize the implants, hence why it's taken him so long to do so. And he will never be able to perfectly replicate the implants, because he'll never get to the information that's hidden in your brain.

"I couldn't allow that data to be available if I died, so I had to program your implant to shut down if mine did. The connection from your implant to mine is a little different. If yours shuts down first, it simply wipes out one of my fail safes, making it slightly more possible to shut my implant down. However, I still have extensive— firewalls I guess is the best word, coded into my implant. Someone would have to get past those firewalls to shut it down. It would be impossible for most."

As it had done many times since Olivia arrived at the institute, her world was imploding around her. Countless thoughts sped through her mind. She plucked one out and voiced it, "But all those years when I was growing up, you weren't there to keep me alive. What if something had happened to me that destroyed my implant?"

"I may not have physically been around, Olivia, but I was always monitoring you through your implant. Until your implant started shutting down, I was always able to do that. I was aware of every- thing you ever did. I made sure you never did anything so idiotic that you'd get yourself killed."

Just like Aunt Ivy said. Olivia walked toward one of the lobby tables, but only made it halfway before sinking to the ground. Maybe she should feel grateful she'd had so much of her life without her father in it.

"And now you know, Garside!" Edward yelled toward the other side of the lobby. "Little good it will do you, even if you manage to shut her down, which I know Akiko and Jed wouldn't allow. I'll repair Olivia's implant and use it to advance my technology in the future."

Garside made no response.

"And now it's time to go," Edward said, walking to the front doors as if he hadn't just been speaking to the vocal apparition of his friend-turned-rival. He tried the first handle. It wouldn't budge. He tried the other with the same result. Then, removing a key ring from an interior pocket of his jacket, Edward attempted to use one of the keys. It didn't fit. "That's impossible!" he screamed, standing motionless in front of the exit.

Olivia made to stand up, but something like a zap of electricity from inside her brain caused her to double over. *What's happening!* she cried.

Akiko appeared, not as a physical being in Olivia's field of vision, but as a projection inside her mind. "I'm sorry to hack in so abruptly; I know that wasn't comfortable. I don't think there'll be another chance to communicate with you while you're sleeping, so it had to be done now. First thing, Jed is here and he's fine. Jillian is too. Thank you for giving us the time we needed to get the rest of the residents out. Dr. Garside is starting to neutralize everyone's implants. We did it, Olivia; it's finally ending. But the last part of this isn't going to be easy. Your father is ready to do anything to get you out of the building. We're fighting to keep him there. We think—We think we know what needs to be done to get you away from him, now that we know the truth of what he did to you. Garside had a hypothesis that Edward connected your two implants somehow, but he'd hoped it wasn't true."

"Your voice is shaking," Olivia tried to say, but she didn't hear the words come out.

Akiko nodded. "I know. And Jed wants you to know he's not okay with this idea. But Dr. Garside and his team don't see any other way to stop your father and separate your implant from his."

"So, you get to be the bearer of bad news," Olivia mumbled, hoping her friend understood the humor. Somewhere in the distance, she heard Edward talking to her.

"Yes." A small smile played at Akiko's lips. "We're running out of time. Olivia, we—we need you to shut yourself down."

Olivia flinched. "Is that even possible?"

"Dr. Garside says yes. You just have to get one of the remotes from Edward. If you bring yourself up on the screen, you should be able to swipe to shut yourself down. When you do, Garside believes he can at least pause Edward. And if we start your implant again right away, you will survive. Dr. Garside believes there will be minimal," her voice cracked, "minimal damage to your brain, as long as we can get to you right away."

"And do you believe Dr. Garside?" Olivia asked.

"I have to, and he hasn't given me a reason not to." Akiko nodded, but there was a small waiver in her voice. "I don't know how else to get you out of there."

"But there's something about him making you uncertain," Olivia whispered in her mind. She heard her father getting closer to her, calling her name.

Akiko didn't elaborate, but Olivia could read her friend as if she'd known her for years. "It's the option we have. Are you willing to try?"

Olivia nodded.

"Okay, we'll be monitoring your implant. We'll know when you have the remote and we'll be ready." Akiko's tone was determined again. "See you soon."

Akiko disappeared and Olivia came back to reality with her father standing over her, shaking her by one shoulder. He didn't seem aware of her conversation. His voice was unsympathetic and flat as he said, "Let's go."

CHAPTER 27

THEY MADE THEIR way into the café and through a door behind the grill. The door, including the handle, was painted white like the wall. Olivia had never noticed it before. On the other side of it was a long corridor lit by dim fluorescent ceiling lights—nothing like the grand look of the rest of the institute.

Her father's grip on her arm was not quite as tight as before, but she didn't feel any urge to get away. She knew her purpose now—how she would end this. But how could she get one of those remotes? Edward still held one in his hand, the other in his jacket pocket. The gun was in the opposite jacket pocket. Olivia was confident now that he wouldn't shoot her. With information on secret implant components hidden in her brain, she was even more important than she'd realized.

Edward made a right turn and then a left. Olivia wondered if the stark, cold back hallways were haunted by the lives the institute had taken. The more her mind wandered as they traveled the maze, the crazier she felt. *Can't lose focus.*

As she zeroed in on the path ahead of them, she saw they were fast approaching the end of a corridor. A simple door with a long, metallic handle waited there. There were two locks on the left side of the door, one on the top and one on the bottom.

"Where does that go?" she asked.

"Out of here. Only Garside and I knew about this part of the building, but I'm the only one with the current keys."

"Probably not. How do you think Garside's group got in here?" Olivia muttered, realizing too late that maybe she should just keep her mouth shut.

Edward glared at her but kept walking. She bit the inside of her cheek, trying to think. If he got them outside, would it be harder or easier for him to get away? If she didn't have the remote by then, it would be more difficult to get it.

When they reached the door, he let go of her arm after motioning for her to stand in the corner to his right. A small, triumphant noise escaped her father when he pushed the handle and found it was still locked. He pulled the gun from his pocket with the same hand that held the remote, then found his wallet with the other hand, almost dropping the remote in the process. He flipped the remote in the air, trying to cover up his clumsiness, but Olivia noticed. He was slipping, feeling less confident about escaping than he was letting on.

Flinging open the tri-fold leather, he reached into the cash pocket of his wallet, holding it against his chest for stability. He mumbled to himself as he searched, Olivia once again clocking his fragility. He might have a dark soul, but he was still human and much older than when he'd started the institute all those decades ago.

Edward produced two keys connected by a small ring. He situated the gun to sit between his upper left arm and ribs, barely clutching the remote as he removed one of the keys.

He reached the first key up to the top of the door. It fit easily in the lock. He turned it to the left but didn't remove it. Then he squatted down to put the second key in the bottom lock.

This is it. He'll open the door, and I have no idea what'll happen on the other side.

Olivia slammed her body into his, pushing her weight against him. He was still squatting and hadn't expected her to fight back. She'd been emotional and not ready to overpower him in her suite, but not now. She channeled the rage, fear, and sadness she'd felt since that October day when red covered her world for the first time.

"Olivia, get—" Edward managed to stand halfway up, but she continued repeatedly shoving him into the door. The gun clattered to the ground, and she managed to kick it a small distance away. Olivia reached around his chest to find the hand holding the remote. She squeezed, twisted, and dug her nails into his flesh. He yelled in pain, and the remote fell to the floor. Edward turned his body, taking advantage of her momentary distraction, and shoved Olivia with both hands. She fell backward and landed hard on the floor. Refusing to register the immediate pain, she twisted to retrieve the gun, flinging her body over to the wall where the remote had landed.

Stumbling to her feet as her father lunged at her, Olivia bent at the waist and rammed her shoulder into him, knocking him back just enough to give her time to regain her full balance, with both the gun and remote in her hands.

Edward chuckled like she was a child, putting his hands halfway up. "What's your plan here, Olivia? You can't shut me down and you wouldn't shoot your own father. You've never even used a gun before."

"You're right and doesn't that scare the shit out of you?" She waved the gun in his face after successfully turning off the safety, mimicking what she'd seen him do earlier in the locker room. "Give me the other remote."

He flinched, his levity gone as he slowly pulled the second remote from his jacket pocket and handed it to her. Olivia tucked it in her back pocket.

What do I do now? Several minutes went by, but her stance didn't change.

"You're not going to shoot me. Go if you want, but you'll die when they kill me!" he said. "Your friends are cowards! They don't care about you. They only care about stopping me—killing me. And when they do, they won't be able to save you!"

Akiko said they would know when I had the remote, but how? What if I shut myself down and they can't get to the back of the building in time? I didn't come all this way to die, not when I'm so close to getting out of here. It'll be easier for them to reach me in the lobby.

"Back to the lobby," Olivia said, motioning with her head for him to walk back the way they'd come.

"Do you understand how ridiculous you look right now?" Edward sneered. "What are you doing? Don't want to stay but can't bear to leave?"

"You still have a gun in your face, don't you?" she screamed, jamming the barrel almost into his nose.

He flinched again and started back down the hall, his frustration clear in the way he clenched and unclenched his fists. *He'll have a new plan soon. I can't let him get to me.*

They pushed through the door into the café and trudged back to a table in the lobby. Edward sat down, but Olivia continued to stand. She held the gun and remote aloft. He kept his gaze on her, but every now and then it would flicker around the room. After about ten minutes, her father relaxed back into his chair, his face taking on a bored expression. Olivia gripped the remote so hard her fingers ached.

Should I just do it now? She wished for some kind of sign from Akiko.

"You know," Edward cleared his throat, "Jack murdered someone too, back in Northern Ireland, not long before his father kicked him out. But, unlike Jed, he got away with it. Never served any time. His father helped him cover it up. Did Ivy mention that?"

Keep your face blank. Don't let him get under your skin.

"How much did Ivy underplay his violent nature? In that situation, he got drunk one night and killed a man outside a bar—strangled him to death in the alley. He was never charged, but there was a lot of gossip. It wasn't long before his father heard it. He knew his son was trouble and didn't want anyone finding out he'd helped Jack come up with a believable alibi. Jack's father was ashamed of him—couldn't wait to get rid of him."

Her father wanted a reaction. He wanted Olivia to doubt. To call him a liar. To yell. If she got emotional again, he'd take advantage. She didn't know everything about Jack's past, so she didn't know if her father was in fact lying. But none of it mattered now. There was no way in hell she would let her guard down.

"So, what are we doing here?" He asked with a flick of his wrist. "Wasting time for the fun of it? They won't be able to hack my implant, because of the defenses I mentioned before. So, if you're trying to give them time…"

She stared back at him, not uttering a single word. They stayed that way for another seventeen minutes. Olivia knew, because she'd counted the sets of sixty seconds, feeling like she might be frozen in this moment for the rest of her life. Edward had leaned so far back in his chair, his head was resting on the top of it. His eyes had closed just over six minutes ago, but she knew he was very much awake.

Then a blinding pain filled Olivia's head. Her stance wobbled, but kept her eyes on her father.

Akiko appeared in her mind again, standing in front of her, but not. Jed was next to her—his face grim, his emotions easy for Olivia to read. He was scared—scared and pissed.

"I'm sorry to keep doing that to you," Akiko murmured, her eyes sad. "We're ready now, Olivia. We're right outside and we'll get you out right away. Garside says your implant can be restarted as soon as you're in the car. He believes he can break the firewalls in your father's implant as well. So—you can go ahead." She pointed to the remote in Olivia's hand and nodded. The frown on Jed's face deepened. Olivia tried to give him a comforting smile, although she'd never been so terrified, and his face softened. The truth of the matter was they weren't sure this would work, but they had to try, or Edward would find a way to set himself loose on the world again.

Olivia nodded back at Akiko and hoped they both understood how much she loved them.

"Olivia?" She heard Edward ask. What must her face look like as she stood in this trance, staring at the two best people she'd ever known? Then Akiko and Jed were gone and Olivia's vision refocused.

"What's going on?" her father asked. "What did you just do?"

The decision had to happen within seconds. A feeling of calm blanketed her. Time slowed, her mind cleared. Olivia saw the whole of her life in brief snippets, including her memories of Uncle Jack and Aunt Ivy. They had been, and always would be, part of her soul.

Edward shoved himself up from his chair. Olivia brought the remote up, found her picture, saw where she needed to swipe on the screen. She turned the remote to her own face. Swiped. Her father yelled. Then she was floating. No pain. Blackness enveloped her like the waves of an ocean at midnight.

CHAPTER 28

SHE WAS AWARE of certain things: lights shining through her closed eyelids, many voices, Jed's murmurs, beeping machines, Dr. Garside's confident tone, Akiko's soothing one, whispers near her ears, a sense of loss so profound it made her ache.

"He's gone now, Olivia, and you're safe in Dr. Garside's lab with all of us," Akiko said. Although Olivia could feel her friend holding her hand, her eyes were too heavy to open. She tried to squeeze Akiko's fingers. "It took a while, but Garside was able to hack Edward's implant and—and shut him down. I'm sorry. He was a not a good person, but he was still your father, so it's okay if you have mixed feelings."

They murdered him, Olivia thought, because she physically couldn't make her mouth say the words. It's what she knew would happen, and yes, he was overall a sociopath and had to be stopped, but she'd played a part in the murder of her own father. It was something she'd carry with her for the rest of her life, most likely second guessing the situation a million times.

"They can't remove our implants," Akiko continued, "but they're neutralizing them one by one, except in people like me, the ones who had legitimate medical conditions before the implants. Garside had to leave my implant on to keep me alive, but it's no longer controlling my mind. It's amazing. And everyone is surviving their procedures! Garside found a way to release people's memories slowly so it's not as overwhelming, but there are a team of therapists and psychiatrists here for when any of us need to talk.

"You did an amazing job, Olivia. Just what you needed to do. Garside had some—some trouble restarting your implant, but it worked. He's going to neutralize it when you're a little more stable. The shutdown and restart took a toll on your brain and your body, but you're strong. Keep fighting. It will take a little time, but Jed and I won't leave you. You saved us, Olivia. Not only us, but anyone Edward might have experimented on in the future."

Because I helped murder him. The words trickled through her exhausted mind as Akiko's presence drifted away.

At some point later, Jed was next to Olivia. He kissed her forehead and told her how much he loved her. He sounded less worried. It brought her own panic down. Her body still wouldn't obey any of her commands, and she wanted nothing more than to touch him—to keep him there with her, to ask him an endless number of questions.

Is Ivy okay? Olivia shouted inside her head. *Does she know I'm alive? Is this loss I'm feeling because my connection to my father's implant has been severed? Or is it because of something else?*

An indeterminable amount of time after Jed spoke to her, he was there again, holding her hand and brushing her hair from her face. "Akiko had to go. It was for something important, but we'll see her again soon. I didn't want you to wonder why she hasn't been around. Everything's fine."

But was it? Akiko had said they wouldn't leave her. Why would she go? Olivia's anxiety rose, but Jed kissed her hand, as if sensing it, and she tried to release her fear.

What felt like days after that, but could have been just hours, Jed was back. "I have to leave for a while, Liv, but I promise I'll be back really soon. You're doing great. Dr. Garside is very happy with your increased brain activity. He seems sure you can hear us talking to you. I wish you could say something back to me." He paused, as if trying to work through a difficult emotion, then continued, "I know you will when you can. Garside thinks you'll regain your normal motor skills soon. While I'm gone, just think about when you're all better and we can start our future. I love you."

His words indicated that he was done talking, but he'd put a hand on her right arm and it was still there. The pressure from his fingers was keeping her anxiety spiral at bay.

Start moving! she screamed at her body, but nothing happened. She heard Jed give a heavy sigh, felt his hand slip away. *Don't leave me here! I love you too!* she cried inside her head, but no sound came out.

The next thing she heard was Dr. Garside's voice. Olivia assumed he was talking to a nurse, because he didn't seem to be addressing her. His tone was kind and sure. A little bit of calm returned as she drifted off to sleep.

When Olivia's eyes opened for the first time, a different sight awaited her. Dr. Garside was by himself, looking confused. His movements were erratic. Since the doctor didn't seem to have noticed her, Olivia closed her eyes to slits and kept watching him. The beeping from the machine next to her sounded normal, but he threw it a glare as he strode to the end of her bed. Then he turned that glare on her. Olivia tried to even out her breathing, closing her eyes again, willing herself to stay calm. She must be half awake and not seeing things properly. Dr. Garside would have no reason to be upset with her. Maybe he was frustrated by her lack of progress?

But I just opened my eyes. That has to mean I'm getting better.

"What are you doing?" Olivia heard a curious, or possibly suspicious, female voice ask later, but now her eyes wouldn't open to see who it was. Why couldn't she open them anymore? Whose voice was that? She remembered hearing it once over the humming noise of the institute's lobby.

"You can't give her that!" the voice continued, sounding angry now. "Have you been giving her that this whole time? That's why she hasn't been able to wake up! What the hell do you think you're doing?"

"Get the fuck out of here!" Dr. Garside shouted.

"No! You can't do that!" the voice screamed back. There were sounds of a struggle, of flesh and bone hitting flesh and bone, but Olivia still couldn't open her eyes. Her body felt so heavy. She fought to stay awake, but something forced her back to sleep.

Aware again, Olivia thought she heard more voices shouting from farther away. Her bed felt like it was moving, and the shouting became more distant as she picked up speed. Whoever was pushing her was breathing hard—running. There were more yells—commands—getting closer, but her bed didn't stop. It was like she existed under the sea, but she could still breathe. The ocean washed over her, pushing her down. Olivia yearned to see Uncle Jack, like she used to in her dreams and visions, but he wasn't there. Her mind was full of fear and questions, but she was so tired. Suddenly, she stopped moving. There was a sharp, pained cry from somewhere nearby. Then Olivia once again succumbed to sleep.

1 0 1 0 1 1 0 1 0

The sounds of seagulls and waves inched into her mind. Olivia couldn't process the noises at first, but they made their way into her ears, and brain, and then into her soul. Uncle Jack's face floated behind her closed eyelids, and peace settled around her. Moving her fingers against whatever rests they lay upon, she was surprised to feel sanded wood. Olivia scrunched up her toes. This was met with the undeniable texture of sand. Her eyes flashed wide open as she sucked in a breath, realizing the air tasted and smelled like the sea.

Olivia scanned her immediate area by shifting her eyes from side to side, then up and down, not yet daring to move her head. She was sitting in an Adirondack chair on a beach. The legs of the chair, made of a medium-hued wood, seemed to be firmly planted in the sand. Her arms gripped the armrests, feeling how solid they were—how real. Olivia recognized that she wasn't wearing shoes and didn't know if there were shoes nearby. That was fine; she could run better without them.

This place looked like heaven, but it couldn't be actual heaven, because she was alive. She could feel herself breathing, the sea breeze filling her lungs and touching her face. Gulls called to each other as they drifted through the sky. The sun was comfortably warm. Olivia recognized that her hair was in a low ponytail, but several tendrils had come loose and were dancing around her cheeks with the gentle push of the wind.

Her eyes closed again for a moment, Olivia felt as if her body was moving in and out with the rush of the waves. Then she heard a child's laughter—the kind of laughter that was the result of authentic joy. Olivia's eyes flickered open, her head turning toward the sound, which was coming from down the beach. She felt safe. There was no pain. She pushed the bottoms of her feet into the sand, her hands down onto the chair's arms, and moved upright, coming to a slow stand. The breeze was still soft on her face. The child's happy squeals circled in the air around her. There were no scary, dramatic changes.

Olivia took several slow steps toward the water, following the sound. Squinting her eyes against the sun, she became aware of a pair of sunglasses resting on the top of her head, but left them where they were. The sunshine was bright, but Olivia could handle it for now. She wanted to experience everything around her in its truest form.

There were two figures at the shoreline: an adult and the child Olivia had heard. Their hands were clasped as they spun and danced together, chasing the waves when they came in—the little girl giggling when the water lapped around her feet. The woman's hair was in a knot at her neck, but as she spun, it came loose and flowed around her shoulders and toward her waist. It was the color of midnight.

Olivia sucked in another breath. Akiko. Akiko looking the happiest Olivia had ever seen her—had ever imagined that her friend could look. Olivia wanted to run to her, to grab her into a hug, but she stopped herself.

What if she's not really there—just another figment of my implant?

At that moment, Akiko looked up and found Olivia. She waved with abandon, throwing her hand back and forth through the air, and flashed a grin. She said something to the little girl, who also waved. The movement seemed shy, her free hand still holding Akiko's. The girl was wearing a yellow sundress and no shoes. Her brown hair was wild around her face. Olivia raised her hand and returned their waves with a slow one of her own, feeling her smile grow. Tears gathered in her eyes.

Akiko didn't act as if it were strange to see Olivia standing there on the beach—or that it was strange for any of them to be on a beach. She moved freely, like this was something she and the little girl had done hundreds of times—dancing and running near the water. Akiko and the girl continued their journey down the sand, moving farther away. Olivia felt content instead of afraid. She didn't have the sense that she was losing Akiko, as she had when she'd been unable to move in Garside's lab. Akiko wasn't leaving; Olivia would see her again soon.

Olivia turned around, the heat of the sand becoming a bit much on her feet, which had to be another sign that she was alive. She made her way back to the chair and found a pair of flip flops pushed underneath it. They were cool from being in the shade of the chair's shadow.

Pushing them onto her feet, she wondered what she was supposed to do. Based on the sun's location in the sky, it was afternoon. Olivia turned in a circle to take in her full surroundings, her loose T-shirt soft on her arms as she moved. She noticed she was wearing a pair of linen shorts that were the color of the ocean.

At the peak of the beach's incline, a rocky cliff rose up from the sand. At the top, Olivia spotted different-colored picket fences bordering what must be backyards. She shuffled backward toward the water until she could see the tops of the beach houses attached to those yards. The strange thing was that, although she didn't know how she ended up here, this place felt familiar—like the place she had always dreamed of living.

Her heart quickened as her gaze landed on the cliffside property directly in front of her. A man was standing there, leaning forward, his forearms resting on the fence. Before she could do anything to acknowledge his presence, he turned and disappeared out of sight. Olivia's heart dropped.

Olivia's feet caught up with her brain, and she ran. When running in flip flops did indeed prove to be inefficient, she tossed them aside. At the top of the sandy incline, she came to a set of wooden stairs built into the rocks and took them two at a time. If there was even the slightest chance he was up there, she was going to find him.

She reached the top of the stairs and let herself in through the small gate. There, Olivia was met with a yard full of coastal plants, arranged to look like a seaside secret garden. Primroses, poppies, and lupines greeted her as they shifted in the breeze. A winding path of pavers made its way through the garden and ended at a set of French doors. The doors were attached to the most beautiful two-story house Olivia could have imagined. Despite its location, it didn't feel ritzy. Some of the siding looked like it should be replaced, and it needed a new coat of paint. But it had the cozy aura of a home that had withstood many decades of sand, sun, and fog and was all the better for the history its walls contained.

She looked to the right and noticed another set of stairs leading to the deck off the second story. Olivia didn't see him anywhere, so she took a moment to turn back to the sea. The view was something out of her dreams: the nearly empty beach below turned into glittering ocean that stretched on forever. Since she couldn't live in the sea itself, this was where she wanted to be.

At the sound of a door closing and feet crunching on gravel, Olivia whirled around to confirm what she'd been hoping for: Jed. As he approached her in a stroll, she couldn't see any of the thinly veiled strain he'd held in his expression during their last days at the institute. His guard was down, his smile confident. Olivia's shock must have been written all over her face. Jed stopped abruptly, then reached out a hand to take one of hers.

"Are you okay?" he asked.

"I—I don't know," she answered. With her free hand, she pushed the nail of her pointer finger into her palm. Just like the hot sand, it was uncomfortable. Another reminder that whatever this place was, it wasn't perfect. That thought made her feel better. Perfect wasn't true, so this place must be real.

"What happened, Liv?" Jed asked as he took a step closer.

She took a gulp of air. "Are we—dead?"

His eyes scrunched together in concern and confusion, then relaxed. "You're not remembering any of this?"

Olivia shook her head, wondering why he wasn't having the same reaction she was. "I don't remember how I got here, or even where here is. Do you?"

He nodded. "I do. This happened to you once before. Dr. Chambers said it might happen every now and then."

"*What* might happen?" Olivia was obviously missing something big.

"You might lose your short-term memory," Jed answered in a soothing voice. "Liv, your brain suffered severe trauma after your implant shut down and the connection with your father's implant was lost. Restarting your implant was a lot more difficult than Dr. Garside anticipated, probably because of how your father designed it.

"At first, we thought it was just that trauma that was keeping you from fully coming back to us, but now we know Dr. Garside was also giving you some sort of paralytic medication through your IV. Garside said he was going to neutralize your implant when you got better, but because you weren't getting better, he never did. After Akiko and I left, and I promise you we didn't suspect Garside at that point, you got worse. He might have upped your dose or given you something else on top of it, we're not sure. Jillian was checking on you in secret, because she had a feeling something wasn't right. We don't know what Garside's ultimate goal was, but presumably it had to do with the information your father hid in your implant.

"Jillian thought Garside intended to move you somewhere after Akiko and I left. Her intuition kept her from leaving his lab, although she was healthy and could have done so. And remember Karlene? The medical assistant working undercover in the institute? She was about to leave for another job, but Jillian approached her with the concerns about you. By that time, Garside was a little hard to pin down. He seemed to be avoiding almost everyone, which makes sense now.

"Ziya was still there too, helping integrate the residents back into their previous lives or setting them up with new ones. Garside trusted her the most, but Ziya was also starting to doubt him. She was suspicious of why he couldn't seem to wake you up and was still refusing to neutralize your implant, so she kept an eye on him. Ziya let Karlene know when Garside was coming in to examine you, and Karlene was the one who discovered he was drugging you. She walked in on him when he was administering the medication."

"I think I have a memory of that." Olivia shivered as she recalled hearing the argument, but being unable to do anything about it. "It sounded like they were physically fighting. Is she okay?"

Jed nodded. "She is now. He hurt her pretty badly, then wheeled your bed out of the room while she was on the floor. But she managed to get to a phone and call 911 before he could leave the building. But it was close, Liv. The FBI opened an investigation on everything: Garside's lab and The Survivor Institute. They discovered all the documentation we were hoping to find. The records helped fill in any remaining blanks about the residents' previous lives.

"Turns out Cordova's office was hidden on the twelfth floor. Its door was concealed behind a built-in shelving unit. Very nefarious, TV-crime-drama kind of shit. Garside is awaiting trial now, as are most of your father's staff, including Cordova. Karlene got a job at a hospital in Maine, but she'll be back out for the trials. Jillian moved down to San Diego with some friends. She'll be back up to visit next month. She's been checking in every week to make sure you're okay. Ziya also stayed in California. She started a foundation to assist all of us as we transition back to the real world."

"I'll have to thank them all," Olivia said, her voice a whisper.

"You have, many times," Jed said with a small smile. Then his expression turned to one of guilt. "I'm so sorry we left you. By that time, Garside had neutralized everyone else's implants. He seemed to have nothing but good intentions, but I guess your implant was too much of a temptation. Or maybe it was all he ever cared about. I never would have left you if—"

"Why did you leave?" Olivia's voice broke. "I heard you every time you spoke to me. Akiko said you would both stay."

Jed closed his eyes before answering. When he opened them again, they held a great sadness. "I know. We've both tortured ourselves about that. We never expected to leave, but I'd been looking at beach houses. I knew this one would be perfect for you if it looked to be in okay shape: still in California, in a small community with very few tourists. A house right off the beach, where you can put your feet in the sand and ocean any time you want. So, I had to drive down to see it. And Akiko—"

"I saw her on the beach. She was with a little girl. She looked—so happy," Olivia sighed, remembering the bliss on her friend's face.

Jed's face burst into a smile. "That's her foster daughter, Tania. She's why Akiko had to leave. They live in a house in town, but they're down here all the time. Tania loves the beach. Akiko is going through the process to adopt her."

"Adopt her? That's amazing!" But then a thought stopped Olivia's excitement. "How did that get arranged so quickly?"

Jed hesitated before answering, "Liv, you were in Dr. Garside's facility for close to a year."

"A y-year?" Olivia grabbed the picket fence with her free hand. "And how long have we lived here?"

"Almost four months. You've had one memory loss incident before—about three weeks after we moved in. It lasted a couple days. Then, like a switch was flipped, you remembered everything. Dr. Chambers said it could get better over time, but you'll have regular visits with him—so will Akiko and I. He lives and works about an hour from here."

"Wait, who is Dr. Chambers? I don't recognize that name," Olivia said

"He's a neurologist and was part of Garside's team. He left for a new job a few months after we brought you to Garside's lab. Dr. Chambers understands the implant technology and the things it's done to our brains. He rebuilt diagnostic machines that can detect and display our implants, because they still won't show up on scans we get anywhere else. He reserves special appointments for us on his schedule. You've been seeing him a little more often than the rest of us have."

"And you trust him?" Olivia wasn't sure how she was going to trust any doctor who had been associated with this part of her life.

"Yes," Jed answered firmly. "He helped neutralize many of our implants. He knew nothing about what Garside was doing to you, because Garside was the only doctor assigned to your case."

Olivia was quiet, trying to process everything he'd just told her. There was another Adirondack chair behind her—this one a pleasant robin's egg blue. She sat down, closing her eyes and lifting her face to the sky. "This all feels so strange. To have just skipped a chunk of time..."

She heard Jed crouch down next to her, once again taking her hand in his. "I know none of this makes any sense right now, but you have all the time you need to sit with it. Your memory should come back soon. I can also promise you one thing: I'll never leave you again."

Taking a deep breath, she nodded, trying to focus on the feeling of his hand and the sound of the waves crashing on the beach below. Nothing about her life since discovering her implant made sense, so everything he'd told her could very well be true. And he was here with her. Akiko was here too—here in this imperfectly perfect place. It had to be real.

But as she exhaled, just for a few beats of her heart, the waves became too loud. The feeling of Jed's touch disappeared. Her mind struggled to comprehend this, but then she heard someone call her name—a voice full of joy.

This is just like those dreams I used to have. Or were they visions? I was at the ocean, feeling like I was finally home, hearing someone call my name. Didn't Jed mention a dream like that once too, a long time ago? He was at the ocean, saw Akiko. Is this—

"Liv, open your eyes," Jed murmured. Olivia once again became aware of his hand in hers, his other smoothing itself over her hair as he said, "You're still here with me."

Her eyes snapped open. Aunt Ivy was making her way toward Olivia from across the yard, grinning and holding out her arms.

Olivia jolted up from her chair and Jed chuckled. "She got here yesterday. She still owns the orchard, but Ron will continue to run things. We can go there whenever you'd like, but Ivy didn't want to be away from you again, so she'll be living here with us."

Just then, Ivy enveloped Olivia in a hug. "Livie, are you okay?"

Olivia was bursting apart at the seams. Her aunt's signature scent surrounded her, and Olivia wanted to both laugh and cry. When she didn't answer her aunt's question, Ivy pulled away to study her face.

"She's having a little memory trouble, but we're here with her," Jed murmured. "I told her the memories should return like last time."

"He's right, Liv," Ivy said in a soothing voice. "You're safe here. That awful experience is finally done."

Olivia nodded and continued to tell herself they must be right. It was okay to stop being suspicious and just be happy. She *deserved* to be happy.

"Just give it some time," Jed said as they all turned to look back out toward the ocean. "And just to be safe, we'll make an appointment with Dr. Chambers."

Ivy, who still had her arm around Olivia's shoulders, gave her a little squeeze. "We'll be here for you, for whatever you need." She took a deep breath of the salty air. "Look at this view. Can you imagine how happy Jack would be to know you're living here?"

Tears filled Olivia's eyes and the sea became blurry. "I wish he could've seen it."

Then, just as it had happened before, the sound of the ocean grew too loud. The gulls that were floating above the water now seemed to be screaming in her ear. She grasped Jed's hand as hard as she could, but it didn't feel like it was there.

Olivia squeezed her eyes shut, and the sounds returned to their normal volume. She felt Jed's hand in hers, felt Ivy's arm around her shoulders.

"Liv?" Jed asked.

Ivy hadn't seemed to notice the change. She let go of her niece to wave down the steps, and Olivia heard Tania's laughter drifting toward them, Akiko's voice just behind.

"I felt like I went away for a second," Olivia explained to Jed. "Like I wasn't here. Like everything was gone. I couldn't feel your hand."

"I'm here and you're here. This is all very real. Everything is going to be okay," Jed reassured, pulling her close.

Then Akiko and Tania were up the steps. Akiko, after following the little girl through the gate, clocked Olivia's face and the confusion that must still be sitting there. Akiko pulled her into an embrace. Her arms felt just as real, caring, and strong as they always had. Olivia looked down to see Tania's shy face gifting her with a smile. Olivia felt a rush of joy, followed by the spark of a thought that she really did know this place. Akiko pulled away, rubbing Olivia's arms.

"Okay, my friend?" Akiko asked.

Olivia could feel their love for her. She understood the happiness this place brought them. Taking a deep breath and allowing herself a smile, she said, "I will be."

EPILOGUE

AS THE DAYS meandered by, Olivia remembered certain things about moving to their beach house, including the nerves and excitement that went along with the relocation. The rest of the memories, she kept telling herself, would return in time. Every now and then, Olivia's world would glitch. She would feel as if she wasn't where she was supposed to be—like Jed's hand wasn't in hers, or she wasn't carrying five-year-old Tania along the beach to avoid the hot sand when the little girl had left her sandals at Jed and Olivia's house.

On two separate occasions, Olivia had a vision of Dr. Garside's face floating above her own as she woke from dreams in the early morning light. The sight startled her, but then the apparition disappeared.

The worst glitch happened one morning when Olivia waved down to Ivy from the second-floor deck. Ivy was reading in one of the backyard's blue Adirondack chairs. Then she wasn't; she was gone and the chair was empty. Olivia jammed her eyes closed as her heart plummeted. After two deep breaths, when Olivia dared to take another look, Ivy was there, pouring over her book.

When the glitches happened, Olivia always closed her eyes, always reminded herself that she was happy and in the place she was meant to be. After a few seconds, things always returned to normal. Olivia didn't always tell her little family about these moments of—vacancy, because she didn't want to see the worry in their eyes. She had an appointment with Dr. Chambers every month, and each time he confirmed that her scans looked normal—as normal as they could look with a neutralized computer chip nestled in the tissue of her brain. He said the glitches were just a result of the significant trauma her brain had endured.

She was inclined to believe him, because the alternative was too terrifying to consider.

One day, Olivia received a hand-written letter from her mother. It said simply, *I'm sorry.*

Olivia kept the folded piece of paper in her nightstand. She wasn't sure if anything would ever come of it, but it was nice to have Beth's acknowledgment.

Jed eventually reached out to his high school girlfriend's parents. He'd finally been able to remember her name—Nicole—and then he remembered her parents' address. He wrote them a letter and received a response from Nicole's mother several weeks later. Time had softened her heart, and she seemed open to talking. Jed sobbed as he read her words, Olivia at his side for support. As a result of their reconnection, Jed was finally able to release some of the guilt he'd now had to process two different times.

Olivia's world felt real. It felt right. Life was not without its challenges, but it was also peaceful and full of love. So, she got up every morning and chose it. She chose Jed's body curled against hers and the lazy grin he would give her when he was just waking up. She chose the ocean air and the sounds of the gulls in the breeze. She chose the weekly emails she had with Jillian, Ziya, and Karlene, who had all become her close friends. She chose Ivy's radiant face, resilient heart, and animated stories. She chose Akiko's newfound joy and laughter. And she chose Tania's sweet smile and abiding love of the ocean waves.

Olivia thought of Uncle Jack every day, knowing he would be so proud that she was sharing her life with the sea.

This family, this place, this life, this light—it was hers now. And she was never letting go.

The End

ACKNOWLEDGMENTS

I **WANT TO FIRST** thank my readers. You make all my author dreams come true every time you read, review, and spread the word about my books. I am eternally grateful.

The Man from the Ocean was written to the music of many of my favorite artists, but specifically David Gray's album *Mutineers*. And although I know he will never read this, I am forever grateful to him for the inspiration this group of songs provided me. The song *Gulls* is number one on the soundtrack for this novel.

I wrote this book in three of the best coffee shops/cafes in my area. Thank you to Tree House Cafe in West Sacramento, Maestro Coffee in Sacramento, and The Fig Tree in Roseville. You supplied me with the coffee and treats I needed to create The Survivor Institute and tell the story of Akiko, Olivia, and Jed's revolution! You will always have my heart.

But even with all the delicious coffee and avocado toast in the world, I would be incredibly lonely without my writing tribe. A huge thank-you to MP Smith, Ida Jones, and Annie Rosendale. I feel the most productive and fulfilled as a writer when we write together. Your kindness, support, and guidance have made such a positive impact on my life. I love commiserating with you and laughing with you. Here's to many, many more years of making our love of writing a priority!

To Allison Albright, thank you for being the very best beta reader a girl could ask for (and also an amazing friend)! Your insight and endless support keep me going and help me look at my stories (and my marketing plan) with fresh eyes. I appreciate you more than I could ever say!

To Susan Chase, the character Ivy is a gift for you. Her warmth, intelligence, and determination are directly inspired by you. And although Ivy didn't get the chance to tell many light-hearted stories in this book, I know they would have been just as fun to listen to as your stories are! Our boys are so lucky to have had you as a teacher. Your support of my writing has meant the world, and I will forever be grateful for you.

And to the many other teachers who've had an impact on my life and my children's lives, endless thank-yous! I am in awe of the work you do. You are the true heroes of every story. A special note of gratitude to Mr. Stanley Kevin Chambers. I'll always remember your joyful love of teaching, as well as your hilarious stories. Thank you for letting us high-schoolers know we could take on the world, and for introducing me to The Beatles and Simon & Garfunkel. I wish I could tell you one more time just how much you've changed my life.

An amazing team of people helped me make this book what it is. Thank you to MP Smith for the fantastic editing and for always telling me to keep writing when I feel overwhelmed. Your friendship over these last several years has meant so much to me. Julia Park, thank you for the gorgeous cover. From the beginning, you understood my vision, and it was so much fun to work with you! I'm so glad our sons being friends brought us together as friends too! Thank you to Caerus Kourt for the interior formatting! It was so nice to work with you again on this one, and I hope there will be more collaborations in the future!

A huge thank-you to the book community on Instagram. There are some fantastically creative people making amazing book content on that app. A big shout-out to Katie Holcomb (@married.bookworms). Your bravery and strength are remarkable, and your love for reading and Taylor Swift is the perfect combination. I'm so happy to call you a friend! Plus, you and Cory make some of the funniest and most relatable reels in the Bookstagram space!

To my friends and family who support me through this writing journey, thank you. Life is crazy sometimes, but I'm so thankful for the solid foundation you all provide!

To Greg and our boys, thank you for being there for me while I pursue this dream. It's not an easy road, and it often feels like there's still such a long way to go, but I'm so lucky to have you by my side on the journey.

And finally, a note of gratitude to the Pacific Ocean. As a Californian who can get to the coast in two to three hours (depending on that traffic), I'm so spoiled to have this vast, overwhelming, fantastical, beautiful body of water as a staple in my life. It inspired so much of this story. May I never take it for granted.

ABOUT THE AUTHOR

Bridget Sheppard has been deeply in love with writing stories for as long as she can remember. Born and raised in Northern California, her life is fueled by reading, coffee, music (Fleetwood Mac, David Gray, and Taylor Swift forever), the beach, TV shows from the 1970s and 80s (M.A.S.H is on her mind at least once a day), and anything having to do with Ireland! *The Man from the Ocean* is her third novel. Bridget lives in the Sacramento, California area with her husband, three sons, and two dogs.